倍斯特出版事業有限公司
Best Publishing Ltd.

哈英文學文法

Hot English- English Grammar So Easy

Resa Sui ◎著

第一本文法故事書

- 讀完**勵志故事**，領悟了人生的道理，還不小心地學會了英文文法
- 讀完**幽默笑話**，笑得眼淚狂飆之際，還不經意地熟悉了英文句型
- 讀完**生活情境對話**，品嚐了各式人生，還靜悄悄地讓英文詞彙大增、默默地讓口語能力變強…

本書不是「無痛」學習，
而是**『無形』學習**，
讓您在不小心、不經意之間就靜悄悄地、
默默地學會英文文法

作者序
PREFACE

想要有效率地學會第二外語，文法與句型絕對是不可忽略的重點！

如果只在生活中枝微末節地學習第二外語，雖然現學現賣感覺不錯，但是片段式地內容與經驗讓語言進步有限；但如果學習第二外語只偏重學理上的文法句型，那麼我們好像又回到中學時期把英文當成數學在學的考試生涯。

語言是活的，有其骨架與血肉；而文法句型就像是英文的骨架，不同的文章情境內容就是語言的血肉。要學活生生的語言，就要兩樣兼顧，不可偏廢。所以本書精選 40 篇笑話與勵志故事以及常用生活會話，在飽含情意的文章與生活情境之中引導文法與句型，滋潤您的英文學習時光，並讓您的英文是活生生的語言。

再次感謝各位讀者的支持，不管是工作、學習，還是純粹把這本書當成輕鬆的讀物來看，都希望本書能對您有所幫助。如果有不同的意見，也請不吝指教。

Resa Sui

編者序
WORDS FROM THE EDITOR

透過大量的閱讀來加強英文能力是許多專家學者所建議的方式之一，從閱讀英文文章中，眼睛所接收到的影像再轉換成大腦中的記憶，藉以學得文法及獲得大量的字彙。

本書裡有 40 個勵志、有趣的故事，再加上該篇故事的文法重點解說，讓讀者在影像記憶的同時，能再讀到更進一步的文法重點整理，輕鬆的學習文法。同時也能從活潑有趣的故事當中學到單字及一些寫作的技巧，可說是一舉數得。

還有書中的心情小語，與讀者分享故事的讀後感，也示範了許多在英文寫作上可以利用的小技巧－原來寫出一篇文情並茂的英文文章是這麼的簡單！另外還有生活中常用的情境對話，讓讀者不只知道要怎麼寫，還知道要怎麼說！

想學英文嗎？想加強英文嗎？

“JUST READ IT!!”

『讀就對了！』

倍斯特編輯群

貼心小說明

句型結構是按照一定的文法規律組成的，用以表達一個完整的意義。以下為英文基本的五大句型，以及在本書句型解析中所用到字詞縮寫表。

英文基本五大句型

句型1：S+V（主詞+不及物動詞）

句型2：S+V+SC（主詞+動詞+主詞補語）

句型3：S+V+O（主詞+及物動詞+受詞）

句型4：S+V+I.O.+D.O.（主詞+授與動詞+間接受詞+直接受詞）

句型5：S+V+O+OC（主詞+及物動詞+受詞+受詞補語）

字詞縮寫表

縮寫	英文全稱	中文意思
S	Subject	主詞
N	Noun	名詞
Pron.	Pronoun	代名詞
Adj.	Adjective	形容詞
Adv.	Adverb	副詞
Prep.	Preposition	介系詞
Conj.	Conjuction	連接詞
Aux.	Auxiliary	助動詞
O	Object	受詞
D.O.	Direct Object	直接受詞
I.O.	Indirect Object	間接受詞
V	Verb	動詞
Be V	Be Verb	Be動詞
Vpt	Verb of past	動詞過去式
Vpp	Verb of past participle	動詞過去分詞

V Progressive	Verb Progressive	進行式動詞
V Passive	Verb Passive	被動式動詞
V Perfect	Verb Perfect	完成式動詞
C	Complement	補語
SC	Subject Complement	主詞補語
OC	Object Complement	受詞補語
Cl.	Clause	子句
N. Cl.	Noun Clause	名詞子句
Adj. Cl.	Adjective Clause	形容詞子句
Adv. Cl.	Adverb Clause	副詞子句
Phrase	Phr.	片語
Infinitive Phr.	Infinitive Phrase	不定詞片語
Adv. Phr.	Adjective Phrase	形容詞片語
Adj. Phr.	Adverb Phrase	副詞片語
V. Phr.	Verb Phrase	動詞片語
Appositive Phr.	Appositive Phrase	同位語片語
	Participial Construction	分詞構句

目 次

CONTENTS

Unit 01 名詞

勵志篇 故事

Marshal hopped into a taxi one day and took off to the airport. When the taxi was driving fast on the road, a black car jumped out of a parking space right In front of them. The taxi driver slammed the brakes and missed the black car by just inches.

The driver of the black car whipped his head around and started yelling at them. The taxi driver just smiled and waved at the guy. Marshal was really surprised, because he was expecting the taxi driver did the same thing.

“Why did you do that? The guy almost hit us and you didn’t get angry about it?” asked Marshal.

“Well, this is what I call the law of the garbage truck.” said the taxi driver, “You see, many people are like garbage trucks. They run around full of garbage like anger, frustration and disappointment. As their garbage pile up, they’ll need a place to dump it and sometimes they’ll dump it on you. When that happens, don’t take it personally, just smile, wave and wish them well. Don’t take their garbage and spread it to other people at work, at home or at streets.”

馬歇爾跳上一輛計程車，並朝著機場開去。當計程車在路上快速奔馳的時候，一輛黑色的車子突然從路旁的停車格衝出來到他們面前。計程車司機用力的踩下煞車，然後在千鈞一髮之際，以很微小的差距從黑色車子旁閃過。

黑色車子的車主探出頭，對著他們大叫。計程車司機卻只是微笑，然後對他揮了揮手。馬歐爾覺得非常驚訝，因為他本來預期計程車司機也會用同樣的方式回敬對方。

「你為什麼要這麼做？那傢伙差點撞到我們而你卻一點都不生氣？」馬歐爾問道。

「這就是我所謂的『垃圾車定律』，」計程車司機說道：「你看喔，其實很多人都像垃圾車一樣。他們帶著一堆垃圾，像是憤怒、挫折和失望，在路上走來走去。隨著垃圾越積越多，他們就會需要找的地方傾倒，而有些時候就會倒到你身上。當這樣的事發生時，不要太在意，只要微笑、揮手，並祝他們一切順心就好了。千萬不要繼續帶著他們的垃圾，然後散佈給你工作中、家裡或者在路上遇到的其他人。」

文法重點

名詞 (Nouns)

> As their garbage pile up, they'll need a place to dump it and sometimes they'll dump it on you.
> （隨著垃圾越積越多，他們就會需要找的地方傾倒，而有些時候就會倒到你身上。）

名詞指一般人、地、事物或者是概念的名稱。在英文文法中，名詞分成兩種：可數名詞與不可數名詞。

- 可數名詞(countable nouns)：指可以計數的名詞，如 person（人）、book（書）、place（地方）等，因為可數，所以有單、複數之分。

  a. 單數可數名詞：之前一定要有冠詞(a/an/the)、限定詞(this/that/his/her...)，或是量詞(one)。

b.複數可數名詞：字尾變化通常是加 s 或是 es，前面通常不加冠詞，但可加限定詞(these/those/his/her...)，或是量詞(two/ three/ some...)。

可數名詞 — “apple”		
單數	複數	限定詞
an apple	apples	a （冠詞）
the apple	the apples	the（冠詞）
one apple	two apples	one, two（數詞），some（量詞）

例句：My mother gave me <u>an apple</u>.（我媽給我一顆蘋果。）

I like to eat <u>apples</u>.（我喜歡吃蘋果。）

- 不可數名詞(uncountable nouns)：指無法計數的名詞，如 time（時間）、water （水）、garbage（垃圾）、courage（勇氣），既然不可數，也就無單、複數之分。抽象名詞和專有名詞也屬於不可數名詞的範疇。

  例如：money（金錢），furniture（傢俱），homework（作業），luggage（行李），milk（牛奶），meat（肉），electricity（電），love（愛），compassion（同情心），Yellow River（黃河），National Palace Museum（故宮博物院）……。

- 既可以當可數名詞又可以為不可數名詞的名詞。有些字既是可數名詞，又是不可數名詞，但須注意意義上有不同的詮釋。

  例句：Parents should not let their kids watch too much TV.

  （家長不該讓小孩看太多<u>電視</u>。）→<u>抽象名詞，指的是電視節目</u>

  There is a doll on the TV.

  （<u>電視</u>上有一個洋娃娃。）→<u>具體名詞，指的就是一台電視</u>

句型解析

The taxi driver slammed the brakes and missed the black car by just inches.

1. The taxi driver (S) slammed (V1) the brakes (O1) and (Conj.) missed (V2) the black car (O2) by just inches. (Adv. Phr.)
2. slam *(v.)* 猛甩；砰然關上。這裡 slam the brake 的意思是「猛踩煞車」。
3. 英文中用來表示「差距差多少」用介系詞 by。以這句為例，missed the black car by just inches 的意思是「以很微小的差距從黑色車子旁閃過」。

   例句：Kate is older than Tim by two years.
   Kate 大 Tim 兩歲。

Well, this is what I call the law of the garbage truck.

1. Well, this (S) is (BeV) [what I call the law of the garbage truck] (N. Cl.→SC)
2. 本句的 what I call the law of the garbage truck 是名詞子句補語用。
3. law *(n.)* 法律；規則。這裡的 the law of the garbage truck「垃圾車定律」是司機用來戲稱人們的行為。

As their garbage pile up, they'll need a place to dump it and sometimes they'll dump it on you.

1. [As their garbage pile up], they' ll need a place to dump it

[As their garbage pile up],	they'	ll	need	a place	to dump it
Adv. Cl.	S1	Aux.	V1	O1	Infinitive Phr.

and	sometimes	they'	ll	dump	it	on you.
Conj.	Adv.	S2	Aux.	V2	O2	Adv. Phr.

2. 本句的 as 是連接詞，意為「隨著…」(=while)。

心情小語

Emotions are infectious. One Christmas Eve when I transferred through Frankfurt to Taiwan, I just could not find my transfer counter since Frankfurt am Main Airport was quite huge. I thus went asking a staff member for direction. However, the staff member had poor manners and left me alone after telling me "Who knows". I had no choice but to try hard on my own to find out where the right transfer counter was. After I found the transfer counter, the clerk did not seem happy. She looked indifferent when she interacted with people queuing in front of me. I was not happy about this scenario at first, but not until I found it was Christmas Eve did I realize why the staff seemed so unhappy at that night. It was an unpleasant thing for the Westerners to go to work on Christmas Eve. Therefore, after the check-in, I said "Merry Christmas, and thank you" to the unhappy clerk when getting my boarding pass. She smiled back to me and said thank you as well. It seems that my "Merry Christmas" to her really made her day. Obviously, negative thinking only bring about negative thoughts. To stop this vicious circle and melt down negative emotions, positive thoughts are always the cure.

人的情緒是會互相感染的。有一年聖誕夜，我正好要從法蘭克福轉機回台灣。由於德國機場很大，我一時之間不知道要去哪找轉機櫃台。剛好旁邊有個工作人員，便過去問了一下，不過那位工作人員的態度並不太好，撂下一句「我哪知道！」，就不理人了。後來是瞎跑了一陣之後，才終於讓我找到轉機櫃台。但一到轉機櫃台，櫃台前的小姐臉色也不是太好看，看她和排我前面的幾個人應對，都沒什麼表情。一開始我的確覺得不是很高興，後來我才注意到，這天是聖誕夜！對他們來說，聖誕夜還要在這裡工作，一定不會是件太愉快的事吧？於是在我登機手續辦完之後，我接過登機證，便對小姐說了一聲「聖誕快樂，辛苦妳了」。小姐露出燦爛的微笑，並對我說了聲「謝謝」。從她的笑容看來，我的那句「聖誕快樂」，似乎真的讓她的心情也變好了。所以要記得用正面的情緒去化解別人加諸在我們身上的負面情緒，否則當我們以負面情緒去回報別人的時候，就會陷入負面情緒交互感染的無窮迴圈裡，再也走不出來。

幽默篇 故事

Two guys were sitting at a bar on the 60th floor of a skyscraper and were pretty wasted.

The first guy said, “Hey, I’ll bet you a hundred bucks that I can jump out of this window, fly around the building, and land right next to you.”

Being so hammered, plus hearing this completely impossible bet, the second guy replied, “Sure, you’re on!”

So the first guy jumped out of the window, flew around the building and came right back to the same spot.

“WOW!” the second guy shouted, “That’s incredible! Do it again!”

So the first guy jumped out of the window, flew around the building and came back again.

“That’s just amazing! “, the second guy said.

“Now,” The first guy said, “I double my bet that you couldn’t do the same thing.”

“If you can do it, there’s no reason I can’t!” The second guy took the bet, stepped up to the window, took a deep breath, and jumped.

He fell straight to the ground and died instantly.

“Wow, you can be so mean when you’re drunk, Superman.” The bartender remarked.

兩個男子在一個位於摩天樓中的 60 樓酒吧裡喝得爛醉如泥。

第一個男子説道：「我跟你賭一百塊，我可以從窗戶跳出去，繞著這棟建築物飛一圈，然後回到你旁邊。」

因為已經醉到一個不行，再加上聽到這根本不可能實現的賭局，第二個男子説道：「沒問題，跟你賭了！」

於是第一個男子就從窗戶跳出去，繞著建築物飛了一圈，又回到原位。

「哇塞！這太不可思議了！再做一次！」第二個男子叫道。

於是第一個男子便再次從窗戶跳出去，繞著建築物飛一圈，回到原位。

「這真是太驚人了！」第二個男子説道。

「現在呢，」第一個男子説道：「我賭你不敢跟我做一樣的事。」

「如果你都做得到，沒理由我不行。」第二個男子説著便站在窗戶旁，做個深呼吸，然後縱身一躍。

他直直的往下掉到地面，當場死亡。

「噢，你喝醉的時候還真的蠻賤的啊，超人。」酒保在一旁説道。

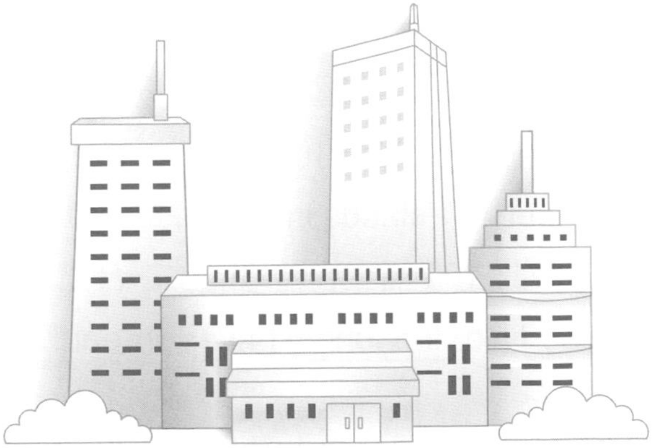

文法重點

名詞 (Nouns)

Two guys were sitting at a bar on the 60th floor of a skyscraper and were pretty wasted.
（兩個男子在一個位於摩天樓中的 60 樓酒吧裡喝得爛醉如泥。）

名詞指一般人、地、事物或者是概念的名稱。在英文文法中，名詞在句子裡可以作為主詞、受詞、補語或同位語。

- 名詞在句子作為主詞(subject)

  Durians are my favorite fruits.（榴槤是我最喜歡的水果。）

  Vases are on the desk.（花瓶在書桌上。）

- 名詞在句子作為受詞(object)

  Kathy had much homework yesterday.

  （Kathy 昨天有很多功課。）

  Please bring some flowers tomorrow.

  （明天請帶一些花過來。）

- 名詞在句子作為補語(complement)

  Olivia is a famous writer.

  （Olivia 是一位有名的作家。）

  Danny made himself the victim of this fight.

  （Danny 把他自己搞成了這場打鬥中的受害者。）

- 名詞在句子作為同位語(appositive)

  Taipei 101 stands in Taipei, the capital of Taiwan.

  （台北 101 矗立在台灣的首都台北市。）

  The Nile, the longest river on earth, runs through northern part of Africa.

  （尼羅河，是世界上最長的河流，橫跨過非洲的北部。）

除了名詞之外，動名詞、不定詞、名詞子句也可以當作是名詞相等語，在句中扮演主詞、受詞、補語、同位語。
例如：

- 動名詞(Ving) 在句子作為名詞用

  Mandy are fond of dancing.

  （Mandy 喜歡跳舞。）

- 不定詞(to V)在句子作為名詞用

  To master a foreign language takes time.

  （要能駕馭外語需要時間。）

- 名詞子句在句子作為名詞用

  Graham suggested that you should revise your article.

  （Graham 建議你應該要修正一下你的文章。）

句型解析

Hey, I'll bet you a hundred bucks that I can jump out of this window, fly around the building, and land right next to you.

1. Hey, I' ll bet you a hundred bucks [that I can jump out of this

   S Aux. V I.O. D.O. N. Cl. → O

   window, fly around the building, and land right next to you.]

2. bet 可以當動詞，意為「打賭」，或當名詞，意為「賭注」。在本句的 bet 是動詞「打賭」。

3. 本句的“I can jump out of this window, fly around the building, and land right next to you”意為「我可以從窗戶跳出去，繞著這棟建築物飛一圈，然後回到你旁邊。」 這句 S +V1，V2，and V3 句構，強調先做 V1，再做 V2，然後再做 V3，三個順序的動作。

Being so hammered, plus hearing this completely impossible bet, the second guy replied, "Sure, you're on!"

1. Being so hammered, plus hearing this completely

   Participial Construction

   impossible bet, the second guy replied, ["Sure, you're on!"]

   S V N. Cl. → O

2. 這裡的"Being so hammered, plus hearing this completely impossible bet"是分詞構句，可以還原成副詞子句 Because the second guy was so hammered, plus heard this completely impossible bet, ...。
3. hammer *(v.)* 錘打。
4. plus *(conj.)* 加上(=and)。

If you can do it, there's no reason I can't!

1. "[If you can do it], there 's no reason [(why) I can't]!"

   Adv. Cl. Adv. BeV S ↶ Adj. Cl.

2. 這裡的 if 是連接詞，引導副詞子句 If you can do it 表示條件。
3. 本句的 (why) I can't 是形容詞子句，修飾先行詞 reason。

心情小語

The famous character "Superman" has been revised and refined many times since its creation in 1938. He has become younger and younger and more human-like. At first, Superman was flawless and invulnerable except for the Kryptonite. He was even God-like. In the past, the God-like version offered people an ideal of a savior, helping people to get rid of the harsh reality while reading comic books. However, as time goes by, people in the modern times do not believe in an almighty version anymore. What people need now is a super hero whom they can identify with and project their feelings to. That is the reason why the superman has his negative dark side in recent "Superman" movie series. He is no longer a scout with a red cape. Whether a movie featuring a super hero with his dark side will be well accepted takes time to prove. However, it is clear that heroes in the future will become more and more human-like.

超人這個角色從 1938 年被創作出來到現在，整個角色經過無數次的改進。除了外表越變越年輕外，個性也一直在朝著「人性化」演變。主要就是因為當初超人被設定得太過完美，除了氪星石以外他幾乎沒弱點，個性也是好到沒話說，根本和神一樣！早期大家生活困苦時，這樣的超人的確可以提供給大家一個很美好的「救世主」形象，幫助大家在看漫畫時找到暫時脫離現實的力量。隨著時代的演進，現代人已經不再相信這套；現代人要的是一個我們可以認同、將自己的情感投射到他身上的超級英雄。這也就是為什麼新版的超人電影，要將超人演得那麼地沈重、黑暗，就是不希望這個角色被當成穿著披風的童子軍。這樣顛覆的手法到底能不能成功可能還需要時間的考驗，但可以想見的是，未來的超級英雄們，可能會越來越「超級」不起來了。

生活篇 對話 1

Situation: Paul and Joe are colleagues working at the same department of an international venture. Now they are just going into their office, chatting about the party last night.

情境：Paul and Joe 是在某國際公司的同部門同事。現在他們剛進辦公室，聊著昨晚的聚會。

Paul	How was the party last night?	昨晚的聚會如何？
Joe	It was really fantastic! Fine food, drinks, a lot of nice people…We really had a lot of fun. You should have joined the party last night.	很棒！美食，飲料，許多不錯的人……我們真的玩得很開心。你昨晚應該去的。
Paul	It sounds cool! I think I will join the party next time. By the way, did Jean show up in the party last night?	聽起來很酷喔！我想我下次會參加聚會。對了，Jean 有出席昨晚的聚會嗎？
Joe	Yes, and she looked gorgeous!	有啊，她看起來不錯。
Paul	Really! What has Jean been up to lately?	真的嗎？她最近在忙什麼呢？
Joe	She was busy for a project our boss had assigned her last month. It went well. Our boss was happy for the result. I think she will be promoted next year.	她之前在忙一個老闆上個月派給她的專案。做得不錯。我們老闆對結果很滿意。我想她明年應該可以獲得晉升。

生活篇 對話 2

Situation: Paul and Jean are colleagues in an international venture but they work for different departments. Now they just finish their work and were ready to go home in the evening.

情境：Paul 和 Jean 是同間國際公司但不同部門的同事。現在剛好是傍晚而他們剛結束工作正準備回家。

Paul	How is everything going? You look a little bit tired.	最近好嗎？妳看起來有點累。
Jean	I just caught a cold. I think that's because the changing weather these days.	我感冒了。我想是因為最近天氣多變化。
Paul	Take care.	保重。
Jean	Thank you! Oh, shoot! Look, it was sunny in the morning but raining now.	謝謝！天哪！今天早上還是晴天，但現在卻下雨了。
Paul	You know. The weather is very unpredictable in spring.	妳知道的。春天的天氣總是難以捉摸。
Jean	I know. But it is raining so badly and I forgot to bring an umbrella with me when I left home this morning.	我知道。可是雨下得這麼大，而我今天出門卻忘記帶傘。
Paul	I get one. We can go together.	我有一把（傘）。我們可以一起走。
Jean	It is so nice of you! Thank you so much!	你真好！謝謝你！

單字與實用例句

- colleague *(n.)* 同事

  Kate and Lisa are colleagues in the same office.
  Kate 跟 Lisa 是同辦公室的同事。

- department *(n.)* 部門（在公司指的是個工作部門，而在大學指的是系所）

  Mike works as the manager of the marketing department.
  Mike 是行銷部的經理。
  Parry is a student in the department of Education.
  Parry 是教育系的學生。

- office *(n.)* 辦公室

  Oliver takes MRT to his office in Beitou every day.
  Oliver 每天搭捷運去北投的辦公室。

- party *(n.)* 宴會，聚會

  Vivian dresses herself up to attend the party.
  Vivian 打扮好要去參加宴會。

- sound *(v.)* 聽起來

  The project sounds workable.
  這個項目聽起來是可行的。

- look *(v.)* 看起來

  Mother looked happy when I sent her a gift.
  當我送媽媽禮物時，她看起來很高興。

- gorgeous *(adj.)* 很棒的，非凡的

  The scenery in Mt. Jade is gorgeous.
  玉山的風景很漂亮。

- tired *(adj.)* 疲累的

  After jogging for 10 miles, I am really tired.
  跑了 10 哩後，我十分疲累。

好用主題用語，用法解說

It sounded cool!
You looked tired!

連綴動詞：在本單元句子裡 sound, look, taste, smell, feel 的文法功能與 be 動詞相似，是一種沒有動作(action)的不及物動詞，主要是跟用來連接主詞與描述主詞狀態的的名詞、代名詞或形容詞（即主詞補語）來修飾主詞。

- 連綴動詞 (1)：be（是）

  He was sad.

  （他很難過。）

- 連綴動詞 (2)：become（變成）、get（變成）、grow （變成）、turn（變成）

  The tree grows taller.

  （樹長高了。）

  The leaves turn yellow.

  （樹葉變黃了。）

- 連綴動詞 (3)：feel（感覺起來）、look（看起來）、taste（嚐起來）、smell（聞起來）、sound（聽起來）

  The plan sounds nice.

  （這計畫聽起來不錯。）

  The cake taste good.

  （這蛋糕嚐起來不錯。）

Unit 02 代名詞

勵志篇 故事

One day, a teacher brought 30 balloons to the class. He gave each of the students a balloon, and asked them to write their name on it. Then he collected all the balloons, and put them in another room.

Now the game began! The teacher asked his students to go to that room, and found the balloon which had their name on it within 3 minutes. Everyone was frantically searching for their name, pushing and colliding with each other. It was a chaos!

After 3 minutes, no one could find their own balloon.

The teacher then asked each student to randomly take a balloon, and give it to the person whose name was written on it.

Within minutes, everyone had their own balloon.

The teacher said “This is what happened in our lives. Everyone is frantically looking for happiness, but never realizes that our happiness lies in the happiness of other people. Give them their happiness and you’ll get your own happiness.”

有天，一位老師帶了 30 顆氣球到班上。他將氣球交給班上的每一位同學，並要求他們在上頭寫下自己的名字。然後他就把氣球都收集起來，放到另一個房間。

現在遊戲開始！老師要求他的學生們到那個房間裡，並且在三分鐘之內，找到上面寫有自己名字的那顆氣球。每個人都瘋狂地開始找他們的名字，互相地推擠和碰撞，場面一團混亂。

三分鐘之後，沒有半個人找到他們自己的氣球。

接著老師便要每個同學隨便拿一顆，然後將氣球交給名字被寫在上頭的那個人。

不到幾分鐘，每個人都拿到自己的氣球了。

老師說道：「這就是發生在我們生命中的事。每個人都瘋狂地在尋找幸福，卻從沒發現我們的幸福其實就在別人的幸福裡頭。讓別人幸福，你才會得到屬於你自己的幸福。」

文法重點

代名詞 (Pronouns)

He gave each of the students a balloon, and asked them to write their name on it. Then he collected all the balloons, and put them in another room.
（他將氣球交給班上的每一位同學，
並要求他們在上頭寫下自己的名字。）

在英文文法中，代名詞的主要作用是代替句子中先前提及的名詞，以避免重複。

例句：The little boy ran home happily because he knew his mother would have the dinner ready.
（小男孩快樂地跑回家，因為他知道他的媽媽可能已經準備好晚餐了。）

- 代名詞的單複數需與所代替的名詞一致

代名詞必須與它所代替的名詞的「數」一致，像例句中 the little boy 是單數名詞，則須用到 he, his, him 這組代名詞。

例句：The students are complaining about their heavy workload.

（學生抱怨著他們的功課太多。）

- 代名詞的性別需與代替的名詞一致代名詞必須與它所代替的名詞的「性」一致，像例句中 the little boy 是陽性名詞，則須用到 he(他), his, him 這組代名詞，而不用 she(她), her, her。

例句：The old lady forgot to bring her cane with her when she got off the bus.

（老太太在下公車的時候忘記帶她的枴杖。）

- 不定代名詞不需要代替句子中先前提及的名詞

例如 everyone, someone, anyone, everything, something, anything, nothing 等不定代名詞可單獨出現，不需要代替句子中先前提及的名詞。

例句：Everyone is created equal.

（每個人都生而平等。）

Are you looking for something special in this shop?

（你在這間店裡要找什麼特別的嗎？）

句型解析

The teacher asked his students to go to that room, and found the balloon which had their name on it within 3 minutes.

1\. The teacher asked his students to go to that room, and found the balloon [which had their name on it within 3 minutes].

The teacher	asked	his students	to go to that room,	and	found
S	V1	O1	Infinitive Phr.	Conj.	V2

the balloon	[which had their name on it within 3 minutes].
O2 ↶	Adj. Cl.

2. ask *(v.)* 問。其用法為 ask sb. to V。

3. 本句的"which had their name on it within 3 minutes"是形容詞子句，修飾先行詞 the ballon。

Everyone was frantically searching for their name, pushing and colliding with each other.

1. Everyone was frantically searching for their name,

   S BeV Adj. V. Phr.→V O

   pushing each other.

   Participial Construction

2. search *(v.)* 搜尋。search for *(v. phr.)* 尋找 (= look for=seek)。

   例句：The police officer is searching the suspect.
   這位警官正在搜那位嫌疑犯的身。

3. 本句的"pushing and colliding with each other"是分詞構句；本句可還原成：Everyone was frantically searching for their name, and they were pushing and colliding with each other.

Everyone is frantically looking for happiness, but never realizes that our happiness lies in the happiness of other people.

1. Everyone is frantically looking for happiness, but never

   S BeV Adv. V. Phr.→V O Conj. Adv.

   realizes [that our happiness lies in the happiness of other people].

   V N. Cl.→O

2. look for *(v. phr.)* 尋找 (= search for=seek)。

All of us are looking for keys to happiness in our life journey. However, many of us become more selfish and meaner and even jealous of others when we only fix our eyes on our small gains and forget that we can gain more happiness through sharing. In fact, only when we are willing to share our happiness to others will we find that happiness is within our reach. For example, I saw a mother with her baby and a lot of bags on the MRT this morning and I yielded my seat to her immediately. She felt happy because she had a seat to sit down and could take a short rest on the train. Meanwhile, I was joyful because I gave her a hand. If I had not yielded my seat to her, I would have had a comfortable MRT trip. However, I would have felt guilty after I got off the train. Was the small gain real happiness in this case? Actually, it is more worthless than we think. Like the students who tried hard to find the balloon with their names on in the story, the harder we chase happiness, the farther it will become from us. Yet, when we think for others and try to help others to get their happiness, happiness will come to us.

每個人的一生，都一直在尋找如何讓自己幸福的方法；但往往在這過程中，我們會不知不覺變得越來越自私、越來越小氣，尤其有些人還會看到別人幸福而眼紅，甚至嫉妒。這都是因為我們總是只顧著追尋眼前那小小的幸福，卻沒注意到如果我們願意和別人分享的話，身邊的幸福其實隨手可得。今天早上在捷運上，看到一個媽媽大包小包，還一邊抱著一個小孩，這時我們如果趕緊起來把位子讓給這位媽媽，她會因為暫時可以坐下來休息一下而感到快樂，而我們也會因為幫了別人覺得自己做了件好事而內心充滿喜悅；反之，如果我們沒有讓位，的確我們可以一路坐到下車不用站著跟人家人擠人，這樣真的蠻爽的，但一下車之後，內心一定會備受煎熬，覺得自己當時應該要讓位才對。所以，這樣真的就會得到幸福？幸福並不是一件我們理首追求就追求得到的東西，反而你越是追求、越是在意，幸福就會離我們越來越遠；就像故事中那些要找到寫著自己名字氣球的人；但是當我們開始在為別人著想，試著讓別人得到幸福時，幸福才會真正的降臨到我們身上。

幽默篇 故事

Ted was driving home one evening, when suddenly realized that it was his daughter's birthday!

"Oh no! I forgot to buy her a present completely!" said Ted, turning the steering wheel and drove to the mall.

He ran to the toyshop and asked the sales lady "I'm in a hurry. Can you tell me how much the Barbie in the window is? "

"Barbie? Which Barbie?" the sales lady replied, "We have Work-out Barbie for $19.95, Prom Queen Barbie for $19.95, Nightclub Barbie for $19.95, Shopping Barbie for $19.95, Bathing Suit Barbie for $19.95, Wedding Gown Barbie for $19.95, of course, there's the Divorced Barbie for $265.00"

"Huh? Why is the Divorced Barbie $265.00 while the others are only $19.95?" asked Ted.

"That's quite obvious you see," the sales lady replied, "Divorced Barbie comes with Kenny's house, Kenny's car, Kenny's boat, Kenny's furniture..."

有天傍晚泰德正開車回家，突然想起今天是女兒的生日！

「糟了！我完全忘了要幫她買禮物了！」泰德說道，一邊轉動方向盤，往購物中心的方向開去。

他跑到玩具店，並且問了售貨小姐：「我在趕時間，妳可以告訴我櫥窗裡的那個芭比要多少錢嗎？」

「芭比？哪個芭比？」售貨小姐回到：「我們有售價 19.95 的健身芭比、售價 19.95 的舞會皇后芭比、售價 19.95 的夜店芭比、售價 19.95 的購物芭比、售價 19.95 的泳裝芭比、售價 19.95 的婚禮禮服芭比，當然，還有售價 265.00 的離婚芭比。」

「啊？為什麼離婚芭比要賣 265，而其他的都只要 19.95？」泰德問道。

「這很明顯啊，你看喔，」售貨小姐回道：「離婚芭比還包括了肯尼的房子、肯尼的車子、肯尼的船、肯尼的家具……」。

文法重點

代名詞 (Pronouns)

Ted was driving home one evening, when suddenly realized that it was his daughter's birthday!
（有天傍晚泰德正開車回家，突然想起今天是女兒的生日！）

在英文文法中，代名詞的主要作用是代替句子中先前提及的名詞，以避免重複。

在上一篇已經討論過英文中代名詞具有「單複數」、「陰陽性」的特性，現在我們要來看看代名詞的「格」。代名詞的「格」是指代名詞作主詞時用主格，作受詞時用受格，另外還有一種代名詞所有格。

例句：I am a student. (主格)
（我是一個學生。）
My name is Mary. (所有格)
（我的名字是Mary。）
Please feel free to contact me. (受格)
（隨時都可以聯絡我。）

代名詞的格					
人稱	單複數	陰陽性	主格	受格	所有格
第一人稱	單數		I	me	my
	複數		we	us	our
第二人稱	單數		you	you	your
	複數		you	you	your
第三人稱	單數	陽性	he	him	his
		陰性	she	her	her
		中性／無性	it	it	its
	複數	陽性／陰性／中性／無性	they	them	their

句型解析

"Oh no! I forgot to buy her a present completely!" said Ted, turning the steering wheel and drove to the mall.

1. ["Oh no! I forgot to buy her a present completely!"] said Ted,

   N. Cl.→ O　　　V　S

   turning the steering wheel and drove to the mall.

   Participial Construction

2. buy 是授與動詞，其後會接直接動詞與間接受詞。以本句"I forgot to buy her a present completely"為例，直接受詞是 a present，而間接受詞是 her。本句亦可改寫成：I forgot to buy a present to her completely。

3. 本句的"turning the steering wheel..."是分詞構句，可還原成"..., and he turned the turning the steering wheel and drove to the mall"。

Can you tell me how much the Barbie in the window is?

1. Can you tell me [how much the Barbie in the window is]?

   Aux. S V I.O. N. Cl.→ D.O.

2. tell 是授與動詞，其後會接直接動詞與間接受詞。以本句“Can you tell me how much the Barbie in the window is?”為例，直接受詞是名詞子句 how much the Barbie in the window is，而間接受詞是 me。

Why is the Divorced Barbie $265.00 while the others are only $19.95?

1. Why is the Divorced Barbie $265.00 [while the others are only

   Adv. BeV S N→SC Adv. Cl.

   $19.95]?

2. divorce *(v.)* 離婚。這裡 the Divorced Barbie 的 divorced 是過去分詞當形容詞用，表示「被動」或是「已經」。

3. 本句的 while 是連接詞，意為「但是」、「然而」。

4. the others= the other Barbies= the rest (其餘的)。這裡的 the others 是代名詞，代替 the other Barbies。

心情小語

Nearly 50,000 couples got divorced in Taiwan last year, which makes the divorce rate in Taiwan ranked top 3 (the first is Russia and the second is the U.S.A.) in the world. Even so, many people are still eager to get married. To me, it is quite a strange phenomenon. For example, if I tell you, "the crash rate of our airline is ranked top 3 in the world, and welcome you to take our flights", will you be desperate to take the dangerous flight? However, few people think they may get divorced someday when they get married; most people think that they will live happily ever after. Owing to this attitude, people tend to get panicked whenever they have problems in their marriages. Therefore, I think the best solution should be that, like the safety instructions on the plane, we have to think about solutions to possible problems in the marriage before we get married. Thinking about these issues is far from pessimistic. Say, will you take it as a curse when flight attendants are giving you the safety instructions demos on the planes? Sure you won't! Moreover, it is a good thing for a couple to have a discussion about those possible problems and then find out they are not meant for each other before getting married. It will save them a lot of worries.

台灣去年一年內就有將近 5 萬對夫妻離婚，離婚率高居全球第三（第一、二名分別是俄羅斯和美國）。即使這樣，還是很多人趕著要結婚，這真的是蠻奇怪的一件事；因為如果今天我告訴你說，「本航空公司的飛機失事率是全球第三高喔～歡迎搭乘」，你會搶著說「我我我，讓我上飛機」嗎？不過當然沒有人會在結婚時就認為自己可能會離婚，每個人都覺得自己可以跟另一半白頭偕老，但就是因為這樣，當婚姻發生問題的時候，大家往往都慌了手腳，不知道該怎麼處理。因此我們就應該像搭飛機時都會教你逃生步驟這樣，在結婚之前先想好，要是有一天婚姻出問題了我們該怎麼辦。這並不是悲觀，難道空服員在飛機上教你逃生步驟，就是在詛咒說等等飛機會掉下去嗎？當然不是！再說，當我們在婚前思考這些可能面臨的問題時，說不定還會突然發現其實對方和自己根本就不適合，或許可以直接避免掉一場災難呢！

生活篇 對話 1

Joan and Mia are colleagues. They are chatting while heading to their elevator .

Joan 與 Mia 是同事。他們邊走邊聊天進電梯。

Joan	Oh, it feels so cold this morning.	喔，今天早上真的好冷。
Mia	It sure is. The temperature was 9 degrees Celsius when I woke up this morning. I was freezing as soon as I got out of bed. The cold weather just hit me by surprise.	對啊。我今天早上起床的氣溫大約攝氏九度。我離開床上時真是冷得半死。這麼冷的天氣真是嚇了我一跳。
Joan	I watched the weather forecast this morning and it said that there would be rain this afternoon.	我看了今天早上的天氣預報，它說今天下午會下雨。
Mia	Is it going to rain this afternoon?	今天下午會下雨？
Joan	Not only this afternoon, but also the rest of the week.	不只是今天下午，整週都會下雨。
Mia	Cold and wet, Yuck! No hope for better weather this week?	又濕又冷，煩耶！這週沒有可能天氣變好嗎？
Joan	There is a slim chance of sunshine by Saturday. However, it will be foggy, windy, and rainy before the sun comes out this weekend.	到週六為止，要看到陽光是不太可能的。在週末太陽露臉之前，天氣都是有霧、多風又陰雨綿綿。
Mia	Oh, it is going to be miserable.	啊，這聽起來真糟糕。

生活篇 對話 2

Joan and Lisa are colleagues. They were chatting during their coffee break in the kitchen.

Joan 和 Lisa 是同事。他們正在茶水間裡聊天休息。

Joan	Well, the rain does not seem to stop!	嘿，這雨好像都下不停。
Lisa	Sure does it. It seems that it will rain forever!	是啊，這場雨似乎就會這樣無止盡地下下去。
Joan	Well, as long as there is no thunder or lightning, I can bear the rain.	唉，只要沒有打雷閃電，我還可以忍受下雨這件事。
Lisa	So do I. To be frank, I am glad that it rains even though I do not like rainy weather. We have a very dry season so far this year. I can hardly remember when it rained last time.	我也是耶。老實説，雖然我不喜歡雨天，但是今天下雨我還蠻高興的。今年到目前為止降雨量不足，我都不太記得上次下雨是什麼時候了。
Lisa	Is it going to rain hard or just drizzle?	那是會下大雨還是只是飄毛毛雨而已啊？
Joan	The news said that it would start to drizzle around noon, and then it would rain really hard by the night.	新聞説中午的時候開始下毛毛雨，然後到傍晚就會開始下大雨了。
Lisa	Well, I have to juggle my bags and my umbrella trying not to get wet on my way home.	啊，那回家時我得護著包包，撐著傘儘量別淋濕了。

單字與實用例句

- elevator *(n.)* 電梯

  Visitors tend to take the elevator to the top of the building and then visit the museum while going downstairs.

  參訪者往往都搭電梯到建築物頂樓，然後邊走下樓邊參觀這間博物館。

- temperature *(n.)* 溫度

  The temperature today is quite moderate. It's neither high nor low.

  今天溫度還蠻溫和的，不是很高也不是很低。

- freezing *(adj.)* 冷凍的，結冰的

  The water is freezing cold. You had better take care.

  這水超冰的，你最好要注意一點。

- miserable *(adj.)* 可悲的

  Caught in the sudden rain this morning, Gina looked miserable.

  今天早上的突然降雨，使得 Gina 看起來很悲慘。

- stop *(v.)* 停止

  The heavy smoker had better stop smoking.

  那個老煙槍最好停止抽菸。

- bear *(v.)* 忍受

  I cannot bear the smell of stinky tofu.

  我無法忍受臭豆腐的臭味。

- hardly *(adv.)* 幾乎不

  Dian is lazy; she hardly does her own laundry.

  Dian 很懶惰；她很少自己洗衣服。

- drizzle *(v.)* 下毛毛雨

  You don't have to bring an umbrella with you. It is just drizzling.
  你不必帶雨傘，外邊只是下毛毛雨。

好用主題用語，用法解說

Is it going to rain this afternoon?
By the way, is it going to rain hard or just drizzle?

未來式(be going to)：英文文法中，未來式是用來「未來即將發生的動作或狀態」，主要有兩種句型：will+ V 與 be going to + V。

- will + V：助動詞 will 表示「將要」，表示未來我們決定要做的動作或是未來的狀態，強調的是個人的決定和意願。

  I will go to New York for a business trip.

  （我將要去紐約出差。）

  Elsa won't give up her dream on painting.

  （Elsa 決不會放棄她繪畫的夢想。）

  Will you marry me?

  （你願意嫁給我嗎？）

- be going to + V：be going to 或是 be about to 用來表示未來式時，表示說話前就打算要作，或可預見馬上要發生的事。

  Yvonne is going to leave the office.

  （Yvonne 要下班了。）

  The Wangs is going to throw a party on Saturday.

  （王家人這星期六要辦派對。）

  Vincent is going to be a father.

  （Vincent 要當爸爸了。）

Unit 03

不定詞與動名詞

勵志篇 故事

There was a man who had worked all of his life and saved all of his money. He loved money more than anything else in the world.

Just before he died, he said to his wife, "Now listen, when I die, I want you to take all my money and place it in the coffin with me. I want to take my money to the afterlife."

His wife promised. Few days later the man died. After the ceremony, just before the undertaker was going to close the coffin, his wife said "Wait a minute!"

She came over with a shoe box and placed it in the coffin.

"I hope you weren't crazy enough to put all that money in the coffin.", the wife's closest friend said.

"Yes, I've made a promise, and I can't break that promise." the wife said.

"You mean to tell me you put every cent of his money in the coffin with him?"

"I sure did. I got all of his money, put it in my account and wrote him a check." said the woman, pointing at the shoe box with her chin.

有個男人認真的工作了一輩子，並且將所得的每一分錢都存了下來。他愛錢勝過於這個世界上的任何東西。

有一天，在他快死的時候，他跟他的妻子說：「聽著，當我死了之後，我要妳把我所有的錢都放在棺材裡，我要帶著它們到下輩子繼續用。」

他的妻子答應了。幾天之後，男人死了。在葬禮結束之後，送葬人正要來蓋上棺木之前，他的妻子說道：「等一下。」

她拿著一個鞋盒，並將它放到棺材裡。

「我希望妳沒有神經到把他所有的錢都放進棺材裡了。」妻子最要好的朋友說道。

「我已經答應他了，我不能破壞這個承諾。」

「妳是想告訴我妳真的把他的每一分錢都放進去了？！」

「沒錯，我把他的錢全部存到我的戶頭裡，然後寫了張支票給他。」妻子說著，用下巴指了指那個鞋盒。

文法重點

不定詞 (Infinitives)

Now listen, when I die, I want you to take all my money and place it in the coffin with me.
（聽著，當我死了之後，我要妳把我所有的錢都放在棺材裡，我要帶著它們到下輩子繼續用。）

在英文句子中，不定詞的形式是「to + V」。其用法可分為下述幾類：

- 句中有第二個動詞時，則須用「不定詞」的形式：

  例句：The little girl hopes to be an engineer when she grows up.
  （小女孩希望長大之後要當工程師。）
  The new comer wants to adapt himself to the environment as soon as possible.
  （新來的人想要愈早適應環境愈好。）
  The visitor plans to go to the amusement park by train.
  （訪客計畫要坐火車到遊樂場。）

- 定詞當主詞

  例句：To see is to believe.
  （眼見為憑。）
  To stay health takes time.
  （要維持健康需要時間。）

- 不定詞當受詞

  例句：例：The athlete tried to reach the finishing line.
  （跑者試著要跑到終點線。）
  Kelly loves to watch films.
  （Kelly 喜歡看電影。）

- 不定詞當補語

例句：例：My ambition is to become a lawyer.

（我的志願是要成為一名律師。）

Olivia needs a friend to talk to.

（Olivia 需要一個可以傾吐心聲的朋友。）

句型解析

There was a man who had worked all of his life and saved all of his money.

1. There was a man [who had worked all of his life and saved all of his money].

   Adv. BeV S Adj. Cl.

2. 本句的“who had worked all of his life and saved all of his money”是形容詞子句，修飾先行詞 a man。
3. 這個句子的主詞是 a man who had worked all of his life and saved all of his money，故動詞用 was。

Yes, I've made a promise, and I can't break that promise.

1. “Yes, I' ve made a promise, and I can 't break that promise.”

   S1 Aux. Vpp O Conj. S Aux. Adv. V O

2. promise *(n.)* 承諾。promise 常見的搭配詞為：make a promise「許下承諾」和 break a promise「毀壞承諾」。

"I sure did. I got all of his money, put it in my account and wrote him a check.", said the woman, pointing at the shoe box with her chin.

1. ["I sure did. I got all of his money, put it in my account and wrote him a

   N. Cl.→ O

   check."], said the woman, pointing at the shoe box with her chin.

   V S Participial Construction

2. 本句的"I got all of his money, put it in my account and wrote him a check."意為「我把他的錢全部存到我的戶頭裡，然後寫了張支票給他。」 這句 S +V1,V2, and V3 句構，強調先做 V1，再做 V2，然後再做 V3，為三個順序的動作。

3. 本句的"pointing at the shoe box with her chin"是分詞構句，可還原成"..., and she pointed at the shoe box with her chin."

4. 本句的"pointing at the shoe box with her chin"的 with 是介系詞，意為「用……」。這句話是說「用下巴示意鞋盒」。

心情小語

When it comes to money spending, going to the extremes-being extravagant or stingy-is never a good thing. Life is short. We work hard and pinch each penny, but what actually we can take away with us when we breathe our last breath? The point that I am trying to stress here is not that everyone should spend all his money and live from paycheck to paycheck, but that while money is something, it is not everything in our life! That is, all we have to do is save enough money which can help us lead a decent life. That is enough. Some people dream of having much money and even others will feel extremely happiness when they see the numbers in their account books. However, the fact is that more money brings about more worries. People living in Bhutan, the world's happiest country, are not necessarily the richest in the world. Sometimes, the incompleteness in the material life can help us learn and experience the great spiritual contentment. Compared with money in account books, the real spiritual happiness should be the goal we should pursue in life.

花錢這件事，過度節省或是過度奢侈，其實都不好。人的一生並不長，一輩子辛苦賺錢、省吃儉用，把賺的每一分每一毫全部存下來，然後呢？當要蒙主寵召的那天，這些錢又能帶得走嗎？當然這並不表示大家就通通放棄儲蓄，來當月光族算了；而是說對於錢，真的不需要看得太重，錢這種東西只要「夠用」，戶頭裡不要說整個空無一物就可以了。很多人夢想銀行戶頭裡可以有個幾億、幾千萬，光是看到存款數字就好爽！但仔細想想，當你銀行戶頭真的有那麼多錢的時候，是不是同時會衍生出更多的煩惱呢？反觀全世界最快樂的國家不丹，其國民平均所得僅有台灣的二十分之一，物質上的不滿足，反而造就了心靈上更大的滿足；比起戶頭裡有更多的錢，讓自己獲得心靈上真正的快樂才是人生更應該追求的目標。

幽默篇 故事

One day, Marcus was busy at home, trying to reply to some emails from work. Those emails were from a very difficult customer so he had to stay focused. However, his daughter wanted him to play with her, and kept distracting him.

Annoyed by his daughter, Marcus took a magazine, found a page with a world map on it, torn it into several pieces and said to his daughter.

“Now go back to your room and don’t come out until you put these pieces together. ”

Thinking this could take her a good several hours to complete, Marcus went back to his work. To his surprise, 10 minutes later, his daughter came out of her room with a perfect map in her hand.

“How did you do it so quickly?” Marcus asked.

“Well, there’s a man’s face one the other side of the paper. So I made the face perfect.” replied his daughter with a big smile on her face.

有一天，馬克斯在家裡忙著回覆一些工作上的電子郵件。這些信件是一個非常難搞的客戶寄來的，所以他必須要非常專注才行。然而，他的女兒希望他可以陪她玩，而不斷地在旁邊鬧。

被女兒搞到很煩，馬克斯拿出一本雜誌，找到上面一張印著世界地圖的一頁，將它撕成好幾個小塊，並且對他女兒說：

「現在回去房裡，在妳沒有把這地圖拼好之前不要出來。」

想說這樣應該可以耗她個好幾小時才拼完，馬克斯繼續回到他的工作上。但讓他驚訝的是，十分鐘後，女兒手上就拿著拼好的地圖走了出來。

「妳怎麼這麼快就拼好了？」馬克斯問道。

「啊就那張紙的另外一面有個人的臉啊，所以我就把那張臉拼好。」女兒帶著一個大大的微笑回道。

文法重點

動名詞 (Gerunds)

However, his daughter wanted him to play with her, and kept distracting him.
（然而，他的女兒希望他可以陪她玩，而不斷的在旁邊鬧）

在英文文法中，動名詞的形式是「Ving」。其用法可分為下述幾類：

- 有些特定動詞之後如需接動作，一定要接 Ving 的形式，如 enjoy, practice, avoid, deny, mind, finish, consider, keep

  例句：Would you mind my smoking here?
  （你介意我在這裡抽煙嗎？）
  Peter enjoyed listening to pop music.
  （Peter 喜歡聽流行音樂。）

- 動名詞當作主詞

  例句：Keeping early hours is not easy.
  （早睡早起並不簡單。）
  Reading enriches your life.
  （閱讀能豐富你的人生。）

- 放在介系詞之後的動詞需變化成動名詞

  例句：Olivia is interested in swimming.
  （Olivia 喜歡游泳。）
  Eric did not worry about speaking in front of the public.
  （Eric 不會擔心要在公眾面前談話。）

- 動名詞當作補語

例句：My favorite hobby is snorkeling.
（我最喜歡的興趣是浮潛。）
Teaching is learning.
（教學相長。）

句型解析

One day, Marcus was busy at home, trying to reply to some emails from work.

1. One day, Marcus was busy at home,

   Adv. S BeV Adj.→SC Adv. Phr.

   trying to reply to... from work.

   Participial Construction

3. busy *(adj.)* 忙碌。其用法為 S+ be busy Ving/ with N。

   例句：Before the Chinese New Year, my mother was busy preparing for the feast while my father was busy with household chores.
   在農曆新年前，我母親忙著準備年夜飯而父親則是忙著家務。

4. 本句的“trying to reply to some emails from work”是分詞構句，可還原為“..., and he was trying to reply to some emails from work.”

Those emails were from a very difficult customer so he had to stay focused.

1. Those emails were from a very difficult customer

   S BeV Adv. Phr.

   [so he had to stay focused].

   Adv. Cl.

2. 本句的 so 是連接詞，意為「所以」。

Annoyed by his daughter, Marcus took a magazine, found a page with a world map on it, torn it into several pieces and said to his daughter.

1. Annoyed by his daughter, Marcus took a magazine, found

   Participial Construction S V1 O1 V2

   a page with a world map on it, torn it into several pieces and

   O2 V3 O3 Adv. Phr. Conj.

   said to his daughter.

   V4 Adv. Phr.

2. 本句的“Annoyed by his daughter, ...”是分詞構句，可還原為“Because he was annoyed by his daughter, ...”。

3. 本句的“Marcus took a magazine, found a page with a world map on it, torn it into several pieces and said to his daughter”意為「馬克斯拿出一本雜誌，找到上面一張印著世界地圖的一頁，將它撕成好幾個小塊，並且對他女兒說」這句 S +V1,V2, V3, and V4 句構，強調先做 V1，再做 V2， 再來 V3，然後再做 V4，為四個順序的動作。

心情小語

The father in the story thought, based on his own experiences, that completing a jigsaw puzzle of a world map composed of small pieces was not an easy task since the world map was very complicated. To him, it took much time to identify which country a piece belonged to. On the other hand, although his daughter did not have as much knowledge as her father nor have as many experiences as he, she saw this difficult task from another aspect. She played with the pieces and unexpectedly found there was a human face in the back of the jigsaw puzzle. Compared with a jigsaw puzzle of a world map, it was easier to complete a jigsaw puzzle of a human face. Similarly, when we are confronted with a problem which could not be sorted out simply by our past experiences and knowledge, we can try to calm down and think about this problem from another way. We may start with the most impossible way. Perhaps, we can find the answer just lies in the most obvious place.

故事中的爸爸，他以他本身的經驗來判斷，要將一張被撕成許多小片的世界地圖拼好，並不容易；因為世界地圖很複雜，光是要找到這塊是屬於哪個國家，大概就要花上很長的時間了。只是女兒並不這麼想，她沒有像爸爸這樣懂很多，更不可能有跟他一樣多的經驗來當作判斷的依據，但她卻在拼不出來的時候，可能因為無聊，所以把紙片拿去玩，意外的發現原來紙片的背面這邊有張人臉！比起地圖，拼一張人臉是不是就簡單多了？所以同樣道理，如果我們遇到問題，發現照著我們過去的經驗和先入為主的想法都很難解決時，不妨先靜下心來，換個角度思考；首先就從那個我們認為「最不可能」的地方去想，說不定會瞬間豁然開朗，發現原來答案就在這麼明顯的地方。

生活篇 對話 1

Situation: Fanny and Daisy are college students and they are flatmates as well. Now, Fanny is baking cakes when her flatmate, Daisy, gets home from school.

情境：Fanny 跟 Daisy 是大學生而且她們也是室友。當 Daisy 從學校回來時，Fanny 正在烤蛋糕 。

Daisy	Hello, Fanny. It is nice to come back home.	嗨，Fanny。回到家真好。
Fanny	How was your day? How did you do on your midterm examination?	妳今天如何啊？妳期中考考得怎樣？
Daisy	Well, not too bad. I was so worried about this test at first, but now I feel great. What a relief!	嗯，還不算太糟。我之前還很擔心這場考試，但我現在覺得心情不錯。真是令人鬆了一口氣。
Fanny	I am glad to hear that. You have been studying so hard the past few weeks. Now, you can relax and enjoy life.	聽到妳這麼說我真高興。這幾週妳都很努力用功，現在妳終於可以放鬆享受生活了。
Daisy	What are you cooking? It smells so good.	妳在做什麼？聞起來真香。
Fanny	I am baking cakes. This is carrot cake, my favorite.	我正在烤蛋糕，是我最喜歡的胡蘿蔔蛋糕。
Daisy	It looks really yummy. And I see muffins over there too. You were busy, weren't you?	看起來真好吃。我看到那兒也有馬芬。妳剛剛就是在忙這些，是吧？

Fanny	Yes. But I do enjoy baking.	是的。但是我很喜歡烘焙。
Daisy	It looks inviting, and I bet it is delicious. Can I have a piece of carrot cake? I want to enjoy life right now.	這蛋糕看起來真是好吃啊，我猜它一定很可口。我可以來一片胡蘿蔔蛋糕嗎？我現在就想要享受人生。
Fanny	OK, go ahead.	好啊，妳自己拿。

生活篇 對話 2

Situation: Jeff and Daisy are college students and they are friends as well. Jeff comes to visit Daisy's flat while she is baking.

情境：Jeff 跟 Daisy 是大學學生而且他們彼此也是朋友。Daisy 正在烘焙時，Jeff 來 Daisy 的住處拜訪她。

Jeff	Wow, see those tempting muffins. You are surely good at baking.	哇，看看這些可口的馬芬。你真會烘焙啊！
Daisy	Thank you, but I think I am too flattered.	謝謝你，你太過獎了。
Jeff	Do you want to try the new recipe? I read a new recipe that was posted on Helen's Facebook wall? I believe it was Cherry Pie.	你想要試試新的食譜嗎？我剛讀到 Helen 臉書塗鴉牆上貼的一張新食譜。我想那是櫻桃派。

Daisy	I love pies and this is the cherry season. Let's make a cherry pie.	我喜歡派，而且現在正好是櫻桃的季節。我們就來做櫻桃派吧！
Jeff	That's great! Tomorrow, I will get some cherries at the supermarket, and we can start baking at my place in the evening when you finish your project from school.	太棒了！明天我會去超市買些櫻桃，然後等妳完成學校的計畫項目時，我們傍晚就可以在我家做派。
Daisy	You are going to wait for me?! I will not finish the project until 7 PM. Will it be too late to start baking? If it is, you can start without me.	你要等我？我要到晚上七點才完成計畫耶。等到七點再做派會不會太晚？如果太晚，你可以不用等我，自己先開始。
Jeff	Don't worry. I will have everything ready for the baking session before you get to my place.	別擔心。我會在妳到我這裡做派前先把所有東西準備好。
Daisy	It is really nice to have you. Thank you. See you tomorrow!	有你真好啊。謝謝你。明天見！

單字與實用例句

- flatmate *(n.)* 室友

  All of my flatmates are foreign students. It's amazing!
  我所有的室友都是外國學生。真是太令人驚訝了！

- bake *(v.)* 烘焙

  The maid is good at baking delicious muffins.
  那個女僕擅長烘焙好吃的馬芬蛋糕。

- midterm examination *(n.)* 期中考

  Few students like midterm examinations; however, they are necessary evil in school.
  學生幾乎不喜歡期中考；但是，期中考卻是學校裡的必要之惡。

- relax *(v.)* 使…放鬆

  The natural environment and slow pace of life in Maldives relaxes me.
  馬爾地夫的自然環境跟慢步調生活使我放鬆。

- tempting *(adj.)* 誘人的

  It is the high salary the company that is tempting to its applicants.
  吸引應徵者的部分就是這間公司所提供的高薪。

- recipe *(n.)* 食譜

  I'd like to have your recipe for chicken soup.
  我想要你做雞湯的食譜。

- wait *(v.)* 等待

  I am sorry for keeping you waiting for me for so long.
  抱歉我讓你等了那麼久。

好用主題用語，用法解說

Hello, Fanny. It is nice to come back home.
It is really nice to have you. Thank you. See you tomorrow!

虛主詞 it 代替不定詞片語 (to V) 作主詞：It is adj. + (for sb) + to V 是一種在英文會話中或是文章句子裡常見的句型。主要功能是在於使用虛主詞 it 代替不定詞片語 (to V) 作主詞，強調形容詞或是可避免主詞過長。

- 強調形容詞：

  It is important to have healthy diet.

  （健康飲食很重要。）

  It is good for you to keep regular hours.

  （規律作息對你來說很好。）

  It is dangerous to jaywalk.

  （隨意穿越馬路很危險。）

- To V is adj. + (for sb)的句子如以虛主詞 it 為句首，可避免主詞過長打斷句子連貫性。

  To finish the project in three days is impossible for Dickson.

  = It is impossible for Dickson to finish the project in three days.

  （Dickson 要三天完成這個計畫不太可能。）

  To seriously consider your attitude toward this matter is worthwhile for you.

  = It is worthwhile for you to seriously consider your attitude toward this matter.

  （認真思考你對於這件事情的態度是值得的。）

Unit 04 感官動詞與連綴動詞

勵志篇 故事

A man one day passed by an elephant. He suddenly stopped, and was surprised that the elephant was only being held by a thin rope tied to his neck. No chains, no cages to contain the elephant, the elephant could easily break the rope and run away, but instead, he just stood there quietly.

The man saw the trainer go by and asked him why the elephant wouldn't make any attempt to break free.

"Well," said the trainer "When he was very young, we used the same size rope to tie him. At that age, he was not able to break that rope. As he grows up, he still believes that the rope is something he cannot break away, and that's why he never tries to break free."

一個男子有天經過一頭大象，他突然停了下來。驚訝地發現大象竟然只是用條細繩子綁著，套在牠脖子上而已。沒有鐵鍊也沒有籠子將大象關住，這隻大象可以輕鬆的扯斷繩子並且逃走，但是牠卻只是靜靜地站在那邊。

男子看見訓練師過來，便問他為什麼這隻大象都不會想要試著逃跑？

「喔，」訓練師説道：「當牠還很小的時候，我們就用同樣的繩子來綁牠。在那個年紀，牠無法掙脫那條繩子。等到牠長大之後，牠還是相信這條繩子是牠所無法掙脫的，這就是為什麼牠從來都不會試著要逃走。」

文法重點

感官動詞(Sensory Verbs)

The man saw the trainer go by and asked him why the elephant wouldn't make any attempt to break free.
（男子看見訓練師過來，
便問他為什麼這隻大象都不會想要試著逃跑？）

感官動詞是指我們使用感覺器官的動詞，如 see（看見）、watch（觀賞）、hear（聽）、listen to（傾聽）、feel（感覺到）、smell（聞起來）、notice（注意到）等。感官動詞後面第二個動詞，可以是「原形動詞」，「現在分詞」(Ving)，或是「過去分詞」(Ven) 的形式。

- 感官動詞+受詞+原形動詞：強調事實

  例句：I heard the bell ring.（強調動作的真實性）
  （我有聽到鈴響。）

- 感官動詞+受詞+動名詞 V-ing：強調動作

  例句：I saw a dragonfly flying.（強調動作的連續或進行）
  （我看到蜻蜓在飛。）

- 感官動詞+受詞+動名詞 Ving：強調被動

  例句：I saw a butterfly caught in a spider's web. (強調動作的被動或已經完成)
  （我看到一隻蝴蝶被蜘蛛網補住。）

- feel（感覺）、smell（聞起來）的用法

  例句：The room smelled bad.
  （這房間聞起來很臭。）
  The dog smelled something burnt.
  （這隻狗聞到有東西燒焦。）

例句：The quilt feels comfortable.
（這一條被子感覺很舒服。）
The patient felt something dropping in his belly.
（這個病人感覺腹部有垂墜感。）

句型解析

He suddenly stopped, and was surprised that the elephant was only being held by a thin rope tied to their neck.

1. He (S) suddenly (Adv.) stopped, (V) and (Conj.) was (BeV) surprised (Adj.→ SC) [that the elephant was only being held by a thin rope tied to their neck.] (N.Cl.→ O)
2. 本句的"that the elephant was only being held by a thin rope tied to their neck"是名詞子句當 was surprised 的受詞用。
3. 本句的"the elephant was only being held"用到了進行被動式，強調「大象"一直"被綁著」。
4. a thin rope tied to their neck 可還原成 a thin rope which was tied to his neck，意為「被綁在脖子上的細繩」。

The man saw the trainer go by and asked him why the elephant wouldn't make any attempt to break free.

1. The man (S) saw (V1) the trainer (O2) go by (Infinitive V.) and (Conj.) asked (V2) him (IO2) [why the elephant wouldn't make any attempt to break free]. (N. Cl. →DO2)

2. 本句的"The man saw the trainer go by"用到了 see (看到；感官動詞)+ O + Vr/Ving 句型。

3. ask 是授與動詞，其後會有間接受詞或直接受詞。以本句"asked him why the elephant wouldn't make any attempt to break free"為例，him 是間接受詞，而 why the elephant wouldn't make any attempt to break free 是名詞子句當直接受詞用。

As he grows up, he still believes that the rope is something he cannot break away, and that's why he never tries to break free.

1. [As he grows up], he still believes

Adv. Cl. S1 Adv. V2

[that the rope is something he cannot break away],

N. Cl.→ O

and that' s [why he never tries to break free].

Conj. S2 BeV N. Cl.

2. 本句的 as 是連接詞，意為「隨著……」(=while)。

3. 本句 something he cannot break away 可還原為 something that he cannot break away，其中 that he cannot break away 是形容詞子句，修飾先行詞 something。

4. break free *(v. phr.)* 掙脫，衝出藩籬。

心情小語

Failure is an indispensable part of learning. To make progress, we have to learn to take defeat well and go beyond a sense of discouragement. When we know how to take defeat well, we can learn from our frustrations and gain valuable experiences to avoid making another possible mistake.

However, it is a pity that most people do not learn how to accept failures in their life. Most of the time when people are defeated, they are just whining, "Well, I failed so I am a loser. There is nothing I can do about it." By saying that, they are just giving up themselves and running away from the unwanted situations they have created rather than face the music. For example, when getting poor grades on English, many students may say, "I quit since I am not for studying English." When getting poor grades on math, they may say, "Well, I was not a born scholar. I quit!"

In this case, if they can stop making excuses and think about the real causes of their poor grades, say not reviewing what they learnt or playing online games in class, they can find possible solutions and make a difference.

Although progress may not be made one day, they can make themselves better and better.

失敗也是學習的一環，我們要學會面對失敗，但不要被失敗所困住。學會面對失敗，是因為我們要從每一次的失敗中學到東西，避免下一次的失敗。

不過大多數人「面對失敗」的方式，就是直接丟下一句「好啦，我失敗了，我沒用，不然你想怎樣？」；這並不是「面對」，這是在「擺爛」；擺爛其實說穿了也只是在逃避，只是這種逃避方式是在口頭上承認失敗，但心裡卻希望大家不要再提了，因為我不想面對這件事。

這就是為什麼很多人英文考不好，「啊，反正我就是讀不來，不念了」；數學考不好，「啊，反正我就不是這塊料，放棄了」。

如果我們能夠這樣想：今天我英文考很爛，是為什麼考很爛？因為我單字沒背、課文沒看、還是上課都在偷玩線上遊戲？那下一次我是不是改變個作法，例如多花點時間背單字，或者不要帶手機到學校以免自己分心。雖然不能保證下次就一定馬上成績突飛猛進，但保持這樣的「心態」，才能夠讓自己離成功越來越近。

幽默篇 故事

A drunk man got on a bus one day. He sat down next to a priest.

The drunk man smelled like a brewery and wore a stained shirt. His hair was messy, his face was full of all kinds of red lipsticks and he had a wine bottle sticking out of his pocket.

He opened his newspaper and started reading. A couple minutes later, he asked the priest, "Father, what causes arthritis?"

"It's caused by loose living, being with cheap, misbehaved women, too much alcohol and being a disgrace." The priest replied.

"Wow, imagine that" The drunk man looked at the priest and muttered and returned to reading his paper.

The priest thought about what he said, turned to the man and apologized:

"I'm sorry. I didn't mean to be so rude and straightforward. How long have you had arthritis?"

"I don't have arthritis, Father." The drunk man said, "but I just read in the paper that the Pope does."

一個醉漢上了一輛公車，坐在一個牧師身邊。

醉漢全身酒味重的像是個釀酒廠一樣，並且襯衫上還有污漬。他頭髮凌亂、臉上充滿各種的口紅印，然後口袋裡還有一瓶酒。

他打開報紙開始看了起來。幾分鐘之後，他開口問了身旁的牧師。

「牧師，我想請問一下，怎麼樣會導致關節炎？」

「它是由於生活的放縱、和便宜且行為不檢點的女人混在一起、喝太多酒精，並且被人們所鄙視。」牧師說道。

「哇，真是難以想像……」醉漢口齒不清的說道，並轉回去看自己的報紙。

牧師想了一會兒，覺得這樣講好像不太好，便轉過頭去要跟對方道歉。

「我很抱歉，我真的不是故意要講得這麼直接又無禮。你得到關節炎已經多久了？」

「我沒有關節炎啊。」醉漢說道：「我只是剛看報紙上寫說教宗有。」

文法重點

連綴動詞 (Linking Verbs)

The drunken man smelled like a brewery.
（醉漢全身酒味重的像是個釀酒廠一樣）

連綴動詞是一種沒有確切動作的不及物動詞，所以它後面不需要接受詞，但是需要名詞、代名詞或形容詞當作主詞補語補充說明主詞的狀態。

- Be 動詞

  例句：Jessica is a teacher.（Jessica 是位老師。）

  You were tired.（你累了。）

- 「變得」、「似乎」動詞：get（變得）、become（變成）、grow（變得）、turn（變得）、fall（變成）、remain（保持）、stay（保持）、appear（似乎）、seem（保持）

  Wearing that designer jacket, Joe got cool.

  （穿上設計師設計的夾克，Joe 變酷了。）

  Saving so many victims, the firefight became a hero.

  （在救了許多受害者之後，這一個消防員變成了英雄。）

Eat well, and you can stay health.（吃得好，你才能保持健康。）

You did not seem happy this morning.

（你今天早上看起來不高興。）

- 感官動詞：feel（感覺起來）、look（看起來）、taste（嚐起來）、smell（聞起來）、sound（聽起來）

Catherine looks beautiful in that dress.

（Catherine 穿那一件洋裝看起來很漂亮。）

The weather felt cold yesterday.（昨天的天氣感覺起來很冷。）

The cake did not taste good.（這塊蛋糕不好吃。）

- 需注意這一類的動詞如果接「介詞」like（像），其後須接名詞。

Frank looks like a frog.（Frank 看起來像隻青蛙。）

The idea sounds like a well-thought-out plan.

（這個主意聽起來像是個考慮周全的計畫。）

The dish smelled like crap.（這個盤子聞起來像大便。）

句型解析

His hair was messy, his face was full of all kinds of red lipsticks and he had a wine bottle sticking out of his pocket.

1. His hair was messy, his face was full of all... lipsticks

   S1 BeV Adj.→SC S2 BeV Adj. Phr. →SC

   and he had a wine bottle sticking out of his pocket.

   Conj. S3 V3 N.→ O

2. 句型 be full of N 意為「充滿著……」。以本句為例，his face was full of all kinds of red lipsticks 意為「他臉上充滿各種的口紅印」。

3. 本句 a wine bottle sticking out of his pocket 可還原為 a wine

bottle which stuck out of his pocket，其中 which stuck out of his pocket 是形容詞子句修飾先行詞 a wine bottle.

It's caused by loose living, being with cheap, misbehaved women, too much alcohol and being a disgrace.

1. It' s caused by loose living, being with cheap, ... and being a

   S V Passive Adv. Phr.

   disgrace.

2. 本句“, being with cheap, misbehaved women, too much alcohol and being a disgrace”可還原成“, which was with cheap, misbehaved women, too much alcohol and being a disgrace”，修飾先行詞 loose living。

3. misbehave *(v.)* 行為不良。這裡 misbehaved women 的 misbehaved 是過去分詞當形容詞用，意為「行為不檢點的」。

I'm sorry. I didn't mean to be so rude and straightforward.

1. I' m sorry. I did n't mean

   S BeV Adj.→SC S Aux. Adv. V

   to be so rude and straightforward.

   Infinitive Phr.

2. 句型 S mean to V，意為「有意（去做……）」。以本句 I didn't mean to be so rude 為例，意為「我不是有意那麼無理」。

3. straightforward *(adj.)* （個性）率直的，直言不諱的。

When we learn that a friend gets ill, many people may assume they must have some bad habits. Actually, it is a subjective bias that illness must result from poor habits. Once I went to see a doctor for a persistent cough. After several visits and physical examinations, the doctor finally asked me if I was a heavy smoker. When I told him I did not get into the habit of smoking, my doctor said, "How could you get a persistent cough for such a long time if you do not smoke?" I was totally upset and wondering if his diagnosis was correct. When we face a difficulty, we have to discard our stereotypes first. Stereotypes often do not help us find out the solution, but confine ourselves to our own experiences. For example, most people judge others by their appearances: a man with an ugly and ferocious look must be a psycho intruder while a man with a fair face and delicate features is a nice person. However, in real life, the fierce psycho intruders are often those with a beautiful face and delicate features. Therefore, it would be better for us to open up our minds so that we can see the truth behind the surface.

很多人聽到對方得到什麼病，就會立刻假設對方一定是生活習慣什麼的出了問題才會這樣；這其實也是一種主觀的偏見。之前曾經去看醫生時，也發生過類似的事；因為當時咳嗽咳了很久都不會好，所以去看了很多次，最後醫生終於問我有沒有在吸煙？當我說沒有的時候，醫生竟然說「沒有吸煙怎麼會咳那麼久？」問我？我還想問你為什麼你的藥都沒效咧！ 所以當我們遇到一個問題時，就必須先摒除掉「啊，那一定是這樣啦！」的成見。因為這樣的想法有時候不但幫不了我們解決問題，反而會讓我們一直在同樣的地方繞圈圈而找不到答案。對事情如此，對人更是如此；我們會很習慣的從外表去判斷這個人：長得一臉橫肉的就一定是壞人，眉清目秀的一定是好人，可是大家都沒注意到，那種手段兇殘的殺人魔，通常都長得乾乾淨淨的不是嗎？因此，我們一定得保持開闊的心胸，不要用有色的眼光去看事情；也唯有這樣，我們才能夠看清所有的真相。

生活篇 對話 1

Situation: Lucy is having some problems with her newly-bought bike, and now she is calling 123 Bike Store to have it repaired.

情境：Lucy 新買的腳踏車有些問題，她現在正打給 123 腳踏車店要維修她的腳踏車。

Staff	Thank you for calling 123 Bike Store. May I help you?	謝謝您撥打 123 腳踏車店。有什麼需要協助的地方嗎？
Lucy	I bought a bike from your store. I need to have it repaired.	我從你們那裡買了一輛腳踏車。我需要維修。
Staff	What seems to be the problem?	那是什麼問題呢？
Lucy	I think there is a problem with the bike's brake because it does not stop when I ride it.	我想腳踏車的剎車有問題。我騎腳踏車時，它停不太下來。
Staff	What is your bike model?	您的腳踏車型號是？
Lucy	It is a FLEETING 456 Bike.	FLEETING 456。
Staff	When did you purchase it?	確切購買的時間是？
Lucy	About five months ago.	大概五個月前。
Staff	Well, the standard warranty covers a year. I think you can take your bike to our store and we will be happy to have it repaired for you.	嗯，我們的一般保固期為一年。我想您可以把腳踏車帶到我們店來，我們很樂意為您維修。
Lucy	That's good.	太好了。

生活篇 對話 2

Situation: Lucy has her bike repaired and now she is calling Kate to invite her to go cycling with her.

情境：Lucy 修好了腳踏車，然後她現在正打電話給 Kate 邀她跟她一起去騎腳踏車。

Lucy	Hello, this is Lucy speaking. Is Kate home?	嗨，這是 Lucy。Kate 在家嗎？
Kate's mom	Well, no, I am afraid not. I do not see her around.	嗯，恐怕不在。我現在並沒有看到她。
Lucy	May I leave a message to her?	我可以留言給她嗎？
Kate's mom	OK, just a moment. I will take a pen and a piece of paper.OK, now you may speak.	好的，你等一下。我拿枝筆跟紙。好的，現在妳可以說了。
Lucy	I am Lucy and my phone number is 0956784128. Please let her know that I called her.	我是 Lucy，我的電話號碼是 0956784128。請讓她知道我打電話找她。
Kate's mom	Excuse me, your phone number again?	不好意思，能再說一遍妳的電話號碼嗎？
Lucy	0-9-5-6-7-8-4-1-2-8.	0-9-5-6-7-8-4-1-2-8。
Kate's mom	OK, I've took your message. I will let her know once she comes back home.	好的，我幫妳寫好留言了。她一回家我就會讓她知道。
Lucy	Thank you for your help. Bye.	謝謝妳的幫忙。再見。
Kate's mom	You are welcome. Have a nice day!	別客氣。祝妳一天愉快！

單字與實用例句

- problem *(n.)* 問題

  Lisa had problems with managing her time.
  Lisa 管理時間上有困難。

- bike *(n.)* 腳踏車

  Henry likes riding a bike in the mountains on weekends.
  Henry 喜歡週末在山間騎腳踏車。

- repair *(v.)* 修理，維修

  Would you help me repair my car?
  你可以幫我修一下車嗎？

- brake *(n.)* 煞車

  The faulty brake is the main cause of the car accident.
  煞車失靈是這場車禍的主因。

- invite *(v.)* 邀請

  Pete invited his classmates to his birthday party.
  Pete 邀請他同學參加他的生日宴會。

- afraid *(adj.)* 害怕的

  Little Johnny is afraid of darkness.
  小 Jonny 很怕黑。

- message *(n.)* 訊息

  Please leave your message after the beep sound.
  在嗶聲之後，請留言。

好用主題用語，用法解說

Thank you for calling 123 Bike Store.
Hello, this is Lucy speaking. Is Kate home?
May I leave a message to her?

電話英文：本篇主要介紹英文電話會話裡的常見用語。以下表格介紹電話英文中常用的句型與句子。

接電話	• Hello? / Hey!（哈囉？/嘿！） • Julie speaking./ Speaking.（我是 Julie。/請說。） • Thank you for calling ______.（謝謝您打電話到 ______。）
自我介紹	• Hello? / Hey!（哈囉？/嘿！） • It's Ken calling./ Hi, it's Peter from the dentist's office here.（我是 Ken。/嗨，我是牙醫診所的 Peter。）
找人	• Is Frank in? /Is Lisa there, please?/ Can I talk to your sister?（Frank 在嗎？/請問 Lisa 在嗎？/我可以跟你的姐姐說話嗎？） • May I speak with Mr. Smith, please?（我可以跟 Smith 先生說話嗎？）
請對方等一下	• Just a second./ Hang on one second./ Please hold. / One moment please.（請稍後。）
幫人留言	• I'm afraid he's not here at the moment. Would you like to leave a message?（他目前不在。你要留言嗎？）
請人留言	• Yes, can you tell him Ben called, please.（是的，請你告訴他 Ben 找他。） • No, that's okay, I'll call back later.（不，沒關係。我待會再打過來。） • Thanks. My number is 258-6957, extension 503.（謝謝。我的電話是 258-6957，分機 503。）
結束電話	• Talk to you soon. Bye.（之後再聊，再見。） • Thanks for calling. Bye for now.（謝謝您打來。再見。） • I have to let you go now.（我必須讓你離開了。） • I have another call coming through. I better run.（我有另一通電話進來。先掛囉。）

Unit 05

動詞：使役動詞與授與動詞

勵志篇 故事

Two angels traveled to a rich man's house one day. They disguised themselves into human form and asked to stay for the night.

The rich man's family was rude and refused to let the angels to stay in the guest room. Instead, they were given a small space in the basement.

As they made their bed on the cold floor, the older angel saw a hole on the wall and repaired it. The younger angel didn't understand and asked why. The older angel replied "Things aren't always what they seemed."

The next evening, they came to a poor man's house. Having nothing to offer, the family greeted the angels with great hospitality and shared everything with them. They even let the angels slept on their bed while the family slept on the floor. When they woke up next morning, the angles found that the family's only cow, whose milk was their sole income, was dead.

The younger angel was infuriated and asked the older angel "How could you let this happened? The first man had everything, you helped him. The second family had nothing but willing to share and you let their cow die?"

The older angel replied "The first man was greedy and selfish, so when I noticed there are gold hidden behind the walls, I sealed it so he'd never find it. The second man was kind and willing to share, so last night when the angel of death came for his wife, I asked him to take the cow instead."

兩個天使旅行到一個有錢人家裡。他們將自己偽裝成人類的樣子，並且要求借住一晚。

有錢人一家非常無禮而且拒絕讓天使們睡在客房，只願意讓他們睡地下室。

當他們在冰冷的地板上鋪床準備睡覺的時候，年長的天使看到牆上有個洞，便將它修好。年輕天使問他為什麼要這麼做？年長天使回道：「事情並不是像表面上看到的這樣。」

隔天晚上，他們來到一個窮人家裡。雖然沒什麼東西好招待，這家人還是以無比的熱情來招待兩位天使，並且和他們分享所有的東西。他們甚至還讓天使們睡在他們的床上，而一家人睡地板。當隔天早晨睡醒後，天使們發現這家人養的牛死掉了，而牠的牛奶是這家人收入的唯一來源。

年輕天使非常憤怒地問著年長天使：「你怎麼能夠讓這種事發生？第一個人家裡什麼都有，你幫了他們；第二家人什麼都沒有卻還願意分享，而你卻讓他們的牛死掉？」

年長天使回道：「第一個人非常貪心而且自私，所以當我注意到牆的另一邊埋藏著黃金的時候，我就把那它堵起來，讓他永遠沒辦法發現。第二個人非常和善而且願意分享，所以當昨晚死亡天使要來帶走他太太的時候，我請他帶走牛就好。」

文法重點

使役動詞 (Causative Verbs)

The rich man's family was rude and refused to let the angels to stay in the guest room.
（有錢人一家非常無禮而且拒絕讓天使們睡在客房，只願意讓他們睡地下室。）

英文中有三個特別的動詞 make、have、let 稱為使役動詞，have 跟 make 都是「叫/強迫…去做某件事」，而 let 是「讓…去做某件事」。要注意使役動詞的用法為其後的第二個動詞是用「原形動詞」，不可再加不定詞 to。

- make + O + Vr「使……」、「叫……」

  My mother made me run an errand for her.

  （我媽叫我去幫她跑腿。）

  Our boss made us clean up the office this morning.

  （我們的老闆今天早上叫我們打掃辦公室。）

- have + O + Vr「使……」、「叫……」

  The teacher had Tom get his microphone in the office.

  （這個老師叫 Tom 去辦公室拿他的麥克風。）

  Does your general manager have you work overtime every day?

  （你們總經理是不是每天都要你們加班？）

- let + O + Vr「使……」、「叫……」

  My parents let me make my own decisions.

  （我的父母讓我自己做決定。）

  The police did not let the suspect pass the road.

  （這個警察沒有讓那一個嫌疑犯通過那一條路。）

句型解析

They disguised themselves into human form and asked to stay for the night.

1. They disguised themselves into human form and aske
   S V1 O Adv. Phr. Conj. V2
   to stay for the night.
   Infinitive Phr.
2. 本句的“They disguised themselves into human form”用到了句型 disguise N1 into N2，意為「偽裝 N1 成 N2」。
   disguise *(v.)* 偽裝。
3. 本句的 asked to stay for the night 的 ask 意為「要求」(=require=request=demand)。

Things aren't always what they seemed.

1. Things are n't always [what they seemed].
   S BeV Adv. Adv. N. Cl.→ SC
2. 本句用到了部分否定 not always「並非總是」的用法。
3. 本句的 what they seemed 是名詞子句當主詞補語用。

Having nothing to offer, the family greeted the angels with great hospitality and shared everything with them.

1. Having nothing to offer, the family greeted the angels

   Participial Construction　S　V1　O

   with great hospitality and shared everything with them.

   Adv. Phr.　Conj.　V2　O　Adv. Phr.

2. 本句的“Having nothing to offer,…”是分詞構句，可還原成“Because the family had nothing to offer,…”。to offer 是不定詞片語，修飾 nothing。

3. 本句的“the family greeted the angels with great hospitality”可以改寫成“the family greeted the angels hospitably”。

心情小語

Wherever people confront difficulties, they tend to complain: Why did God not help me? Why did I not have good luck? However, the key to overcoming a difficult situation is to change our mindset instead of nagging and whining. Rather than be unhappy with our hardships, we may show our gratitude to the blessings in disguise to make a difference. For example, when we are stuck in the traffic, we can think that at least we have cars to drive. When we have trouble with our work, we can think that at least we have jobs. When our life seems aimless, we can think that some may not live as long as we do. Positive thinking is magical. Although we just change our attitudes, we might find the key to solve problem which we find it hard to be solved.

每當我們遭遇挫折的時候，總是很習慣開始怨天尤人；為什麼老天不幫我？為什麼我命這麼不好？但這種時候，與其在那裡怨歎自己的遭遇，不如換個角度想，或許自己該做的不是抱怨，而是感謝才對。當你塞車困在車陣之中，想想開車對有些人來說是多麼奢侈的事。當你的工作不順利的時候，想想有些人可能連工作都沒有。當你覺得人生失去目標，不知道繼續活下去是為了什麼的時候，想想有些人可能根本活不到你這個年紀去被這些問題困擾。正面的力量是很神奇的，雖然只是一念之差，但常常很多原本我們一直以為無法解決的問題，都會因為我們的念頭一轉而突然找到答案。

A man died and went to meet with the angel of judgment.

"Before you meet with the God, I should tell you this." The angel said, "we've looked over your life, and to be honest, you didn't do anything particularly good or bad. We're not really sure what to do with you. Can you tell us anything you have done that can help us make a decision?"

The man thought for a moment and said, "Yeah, once I was driving along and saw an old man being harassed by a group of thugs. So I pulled over, got out of the car, and went up to the leader of the thugs. He was big and muscular, with a ring pierced through his nose. I tore the ring out of his nose, and told him and his gang to stop bothering the old man or they have to deal with me first!"

"Wow! That's very impressive!" the angel nodded with astonishment," When did this happen?"

"About five minutes ago." the man replied.

一個男人死了之後遇到了審判天使。

「在你能夠去見上帝之前，我必須告訴你，」天使說道：「我們已經看過你的一生了，但老實說，你並沒有作過特別好或壞的事情。我們不知道該把你歸到哪邊才好，你有沒有什麼要補充的，好幫助我們作個決定。」

男人想了一下便說道：「有的，有一次我正在開車的時候，看到一個老人被一群混混騷擾。所以我就把車停下來，下車，然後走到那群混混的頭頭那邊。他是個高大、全身都是肌肉的男人，鼻子上還穿了個鼻環。所以我就將他的鼻環從鼻子上扯下來，然後跟他和他那幫混混說，不准再去煩這位老先生，否則就得先經過我這一關！」

「哇！這真的非常讓人印象深刻！」天使驚訝的點著頭：「這是什麼時候發生的事？」

「差不多五分鐘之前。」男人回答道。

文法重點

授與動詞(Dative Verbs)

Can you tell us anything you have done that can help us make a decision?
（你有沒有什麼要補充的，好幫助我們作個決定。）

英文中 give、bring、lend、send、show、bring、buy、write 與 ask 等其後須接兩個受詞的動詞，稱為授與動詞。其後的受詞有間接受詞（多為人）與直接受詞（多為物）。

- 使用介系詞 to 的授與動詞：give, offer, sell, hand, show, lend, send, take, tell, write, teach 等。

例句：Jo showed me the project.= Jo showed the project to me.

（Jo 向我展示這個項目。）

Please lend me a pen.= Please lend a pen to me.

（請借我一隻筆。）

- 使用介系詞 for 的授與動詞：bring, buy, get, sing 等。

例句：Katy bought her mother a birthday cake.= Katy bought a birthday cake for her mother.

（Katy 買一個生日蛋糕給她媽媽。）

Do you get me a cup of tea?= Do you get a cup of tea for me?

（你可以幫我拿一杯茶嗎？）

- 使用介系詞 of 的授與動詞：ask。

例句：David asked his tutor a question.= David asked a question of his tutor.

（David 問他的助教一個問題。）

句型解析

We've looked over your life, and to be honest, you didn't do anything particularly good or bad.

1.

We	've	looked over	your life,	and	to be honest,
S1	Aux.	V Phr.→V1	O1	Conj.	Adv. Phr.

you	did	n't	do	anything	particularly	good or bad.
S2	Aux.	Adv.	V2	O2	Adv.	Adj.

2. 本句的副詞片語“to be honest”意為「誠實說」(=to be frank = frankly speaking = to tell the truth)。
3. someone, anyone, nobody, anybody 等不定代名詞，須將形容詞放於其後修飾。

Yeah, once I was driving along and saw an old man being harassed by a group of thugs.

1.

Yeah,	once	I	was driving	along	and	saw	an old man
	Adv.	S	V Progressive	Adv.	Conj.	V	O

being harassed by a group of thugs.
Ving → OC

2. 本句的 once 是副詞，意為「曾經」。

3. 本句的“saw an old man being harassed by a group of thugs”用到了 see (看到；感官動詞) + O + Vr/Ving 的句型。

He was big and muscular, with a ring pierced through his nose.

1. He was big and muscular, with a ring pierced through his nose.

He	was	big and muscular,	with a ring pierced through his nose.
S	BeV	Adj.→SC	Adv. Phr.

2. 本句的“with a ring pierced through his nose”用到了句型“with (有……) + O + OC”，受詞是 a ring，而補語是 pierced through his nose。

- pierce *(v.)* 穿刺。本句的 pierced through his nose 用到過去分詞 pierced，表示「被穿刺」。

心情小語

Willing to help people is a good thing for us, but remember, do not bite off more than we can chew. That is, we have to be rational when giving others a hand; otherwise, we may not help those in need and even hurt ourselves in the end. In our daily life, we often see that many people lend a great sum of money to their friends in need even though they cannot live within their means. In every summer vacation, we can also read a lot of sad news that people were drowned because they, even though unable to swim, tried to help their drowning friends. In this dog-eat-dog world, it is indeed a heart-warming act to reach out to those in need. Yet, without careful evaluation of the situations and our abilities, our help will become mere aimless sacrifices. Be rational and smart, and our help will be truly worthy.

有心要幫助別人是好事，但也要量力而為，不要弄到最後忙沒幫到，還賠上了自己，付出慘痛的代價。例如有些人明明自己經濟能力不夠，卻常常因為朋友的一句話，或是為了「義氣」兩個字，就這樣把大筆的錢借給別人。又例如每年暑假的時候，一定會看到那種，因為同學溺水，自己其實也不諳水性，但仍然奮不顧身跳下水去救人，結果雙雙溺斃的新聞。這些都是沒有先衡量過自己的能力就貿然助人的例子。在現在這種冷漠的社會裡，有心要幫助別人當然是件好事，但如果沒有衡量過自己的力量就去做，結果要是真能夠幫到別人那也就算了，但往往結局都是自己白白犧牲了而已。助人之心的確值得鼓勵，可是不自量力地助人，那就不算是在幫忙，只是無腦的衝動而已。

生活篇 對話 1

Situation: Every year, July Day, a music band, holds a small concert at Forest Park. As its die-hard fan, Allen is inviting his two friends to attend the concert.

情境：每年七月天樂團都會在森林公園舉辦一個小型演唱會。身為他們的死忠歌迷，Allen 邀請兩位朋友參加這場演唱會。

Allen	Hey Lisa, Sam, July Day is holding a musical concert in the park. You want to go see the band play with me?	嘿，Lisa，Sam，七月天正在公園裡舉辦演唱會耶。你們要跟我一起去看看嗎？
Lisa	I have just completed my homework; I can go.	我作業剛寫完了，我可以去。
Sam	Me too. Let's go.	我也是，那我們走吧！
Lisa	Hey, look at that sports car. Isn't it neat?	嘿，看看那跑車。真是漂亮，不是嗎？
	They are heading toward the park.	他們正朝公園走去。
Allen	That is exactly the kind of car that I want once I get a good job. I bet it is very fast. I want mine to be red though.	那正是我一有工作我就要入手的車款吶！這輛車一定跑得很快。我的車要紅色的。
Lisa	Keep on dreaming, Allen. That car costs a fortune.	你繼續作夢吧，Allen。那款車很貴耶。

Allen	It does not hurt to set high expectations. Maybe one day I will make a lot of money, and I may surprise you.	設高標準沒關係啦。或許有一天我會賺很多錢，然後真的讓你刮目相看。
Sam	Well, wish you make it!	嗯，那就祝你成功囉！

生活篇 對話 2

Situation: Allen and his two friends are chatting while enjoying the concert in the park.

情境：Allen 跟兩位朋友正在公園聽音樂聊天。

Allen	They are fantastic! The band does play pretty good music. For the last three years, I have never missed the concert. I have always arranged my schedule so that I could attend the event once the band was in town.	他們真的好棒！這樂團演奏真的很棒！我這三年都沒有錯過他們任何一場演唱會。我總是事先安排好我的行程，這樣他們來，我才能參加他們的演唱會。
Lisa	Wow, you are really their loyal fan.	哇，你真的是他們死忠的歌迷。
Allen	You will enjoy this evening, Sam. There will be good country music and definitely a lot of stomping around.	你會喜歡今晚的，Sam。今晚會有超讚的鄉村音樂還有絕對會有很多人會跟著打節拍的。

Sam	It sounds like fun.	那聽起來真有趣。
Lisa	My favorite is Rock and Roll music; however, I have to say that country melodies can be quite enticing. I can listen to them all day long.	我最喜歡的音樂是搖滾樂。但是我必須説鄉村音樂也是動人心弦的。我可以一整天都聽著鄉村音樂。
Allen	Sam, what kind of music do you like?	Sam，你喜歡什麼音樂？
Sam	Oh, I like all kinds of music as long as it is not Hard Rock.	喔，除了重搖滾之外，我都喜歡。
Lisa	Wow, look at the number of people who have already shown up for the concert. Good thing that we are here already.	哇，看看這裡已經出席演唱會的人。好險我們已經在這裡了。

單字與實用例句

- concert *(n.)* 音樂會，演唱會

  The concert tonight is sponsored by BCC Company.
  今晚的音樂會是 BCC 公司贊助的。

- head *(v.)* 前往

  Nina is heading for Kyoto tomorrow.
  Nina 明天將前往京都。

- exactly *(adv.)* 精準地，恰好，剛好

  The gift is exactly what I want.
  這個禮物正好是我想要的。

- fantastic *(adj.)* 極佳的

  The magic show is fantastic. It really takes my breath away.
  這個魔術秀真的很棒，真是令我驚豔。

- arrange *(v.)* 安排

  Mother arranged the flowers in the vase well.
  母親把花瓶裡的花朵插得很好。

- definitely *(adv.)* 絕對地，必然地

  What our customers demand is definitely right.
  我們顧客要求的絕對都是正確的。

- enticing *(adj.)* 動人心弦的，誘人的

  The offer that company offered is really enticing. I am now considering jumping ship.
  那間公司開出的條件太誘人了。我現在考慮要跳槽了。

好用主題用語，用法解說

I have just completed my homework; I can go.
For the last three years, I have never missed the concert.
I have always arranged my schedule.

現在完成式：在英文對話中，當我們要表達某個動作從過去到現在已經完成，不久前才剛剛完成，或是從過去到現在的經驗，我們會用現在完成式：have/ has + Vpp。

- 某個動作從過去到現在已經完成：

  Patrick have seen the new manager this morning.

  （今天早上 Patrick 已經見過新經理了。）

  I haven't given the box to Miranda.

  （我還沒有把箱子給 Miranda。）

- 某個動作不久前才剛剛完成：

  William has just bought a new bicycle.

  （William 已經買了一輛新的腳踏車了。）

  Have you finished your homework yet?

  （你已經完成作業了嗎？）

- 從過去到現在的經驗：

  I haven't heard from Jane lately.

  （我最近沒聽說 Jane 的消息。）

  Cindy has been to Spain for five times.

  （Cindy 去過西班牙五次。）

Unit 06 現在式

勵志篇 故事

An unemployed man applied for the position of "office boy" at a big company. After the interview, the employer was very impressed by his enthusiasm and wanted to hire him.

"Very well, give me your email address and I'll send you the applications to fill. As soon as you fill them, you can start working."

The man replied, "But I don' t have a computer or email."

"Then I'm very sorry. We can't hire someone who doesn't even have an email."

The man left with no hope and only 10 dollars in the pocket. He didn't know what to do. He went to a supermarket and saw some tomatoes. Suddenly, he had an idea!

He bought some tomatoes with his 10 dollars, and sold them door to door. In less than two hours, he had earned 20 dollars!

He repeated this 3 times and returned home with 60 dollars. Realizing he could make a living with this, the man went on selling tomatoes every day. Soon, his money doubled, tripled... Five years later, he became the owner of the biggest food retailer company in town.

One day, a journalist came to interview him for his story to success. When the interview was concluded, the journalist asked him his email. The man replied "I don't have an email."

The journalist said curiously, “You don’t have an email and yet you’re so successful. Can you imagine what you could have done if you had one?”

The man smiled and said “Yes, an office boy.”

一個失業的男子去應徵一份「辦公室雜役」的工作。在面試之後，雇主對他的熱誠非常滿意，想要僱用他。

「非常好，給我你的電子郵件信箱，我會把一些表格寄給你，只要你一填好就可以隨時開始工作。」

男子回道：「可是我沒有電腦，也沒有電子郵件信箱。」

「這樣的話，我非常抱歉，我們無法僱用一個連電子郵件信箱都沒有的人。」

男子絕望的離開公司，口袋裡只剩十塊錢，他真的不知道該怎麼辦才好。他來到一個超市，看到一些蕃茄，突然，他有個主意！

他用十塊錢買了一些蕃茄，然後挨家挨戶的去推銷。不到兩個小時，他就賺了二十塊！他重複這樣的過程三次之後，賺了六十塊。發現自己可以靠這個過活，於是他每天都開始賣起蕃茄。很快的，他的錢增加了兩倍、三倍……五年之後，他就成了城裡最大的食物零售商的老闆。

有一天，一個記者來採訪他成功的故事。當訪問結束時，記者詢問他的電子郵件信箱。男子説道：「我沒有電子郵件信箱。」

記者好奇的説：「你連個電子郵件信箱都沒有就這麼成功了，你有想過要是你有的話會，你會有多大的成就嗎？」

男子笑了笑：「有的，我會變成辦公室雜役。」

文法重點

現在簡單式 (Present Simple)

But I don't have a computer or email.
（可是我沒有電腦，也沒有電子郵件信箱。）

英文句子裡的時態主要分成：現在式、過去式與未來式。其中，現在簡單式主要是用於表示現在一般的動作或是說明一件事實。

- 現在式簡單式可說明長期持續不變的情況，如「真理」或普遍認知的「事實」

  The sun rises in the east.（太陽在東邊升起。）

- 說明現在仍存在的事實或是正確無誤的事

  Jason graduates this year.（Jason 今年畢業。）

- 可用來表示習慣或是重複發生的行為

  Typhoons come every year.（颱風每年都會來。）

  經常會和頻率副詞搭配，如 always, never, usually 等用以形容規律發生的事，並指出其頻率

  I play tennis every Saturday.（我每個星期六都會打網球。）

- 表示按照著時刻表或計畫，在未來將會發生的事，或是安排好的事

  The plane to Hong Kong departs at 7 a.m.
  （這個往香港班機在早上 7 點起飛。）

  補充：動詞如 depart, come, go, leave, arrive, meet, start 等所組成的句子，可用現在簡單式來替代未來式。

- 連接詞如 when, before, after, if, until 等所組成的副詞子句通常用現在簡單式替代未來式。

  If it rains tomorrow, the sports meet will be called off.
  （如果明天下雨的話，運動會就會被取消。）

- 表示感受的動詞如 love, like, hate, dislike, want, wish 只能用現在

簡單式，不可以用現在進行式。

Lisa wants to have a rest.（Lisa 想要休息。）

句型解析

After the interview, the employer was very impressed by his enthusiasm and wanted to hire him.

1. After the interview, the employer was very impressed by his enthusiasm and wanted to hire him.

After the interview,	the employer	was very impressed	by
Adv. Phr.	S	V Passive	Prep.

his enthusiasm	and	wanted	to hire him.
N	Conj.	V	Infinitive Phr.

2. employer *(n.)* 雇主。

   補充：employee *(n.)* 員工。

   employment *(n.)* 就業。

3. impress *(v.)* 使…印象深刻。impression *(n.)* 印象。本句“the employer was very impressed by his enthusiasm”亦可寫成 “his enthusiasm gave the employer great impression”。

4. enthusiasm *(n.)* 熱忱，熱情

   例句：John has great enthusiasm for basketball. He practices basketball every day.
   John 對籃球有熱情。天天打籃球。

Realizing he could make a living with this, the man went on selling tomatoes every day.

1. Realizing he could make a living with this, the man went on

Realizing he could make a living with this,	the man	went on
Participial Construction	S	V.Phr.→V

selling tomatoes every day.

Ving→ O　　Adv. Phr.

2. make a living (*v. phr.*) 謀生。

例句：Mary makes a living by writing.
Mary 以寫作維生。

3. go on (*v. phr.*) 繼續(做…)。

例句：After taking a short break, Peter went on his reading.
短暫休息了一下，Peter 繼續他的閱讀。

4. every day (*adv. phr.*) 每一天。

Can you imagine what you could have done if you had one?

1. Can you imagine [what you could have done if you had one]?

Aux.　S　V　　N. Cl. →O

2. imagine (*v.*) 想像。其後須接名詞，動名詞或名詞子句。

例句：Can you imagine living in the world without water?
你能想像活在沒有水的世界嗎？

3. 本句的名詞子句裡使用了與過去事實相反的假設語氣"If S had Vpp, S would/could/should have Vpp."。

例句：If I had had money last week, I would have bought that purse for you.
如果我上週有錢，我就買那個包包給你。

心情小語

No one is perfect; however, most of us usually pay too much attention to our defects while overlooking our possible potentials. Though told to be disqualified for a position since he did not have the computer and any email accounts, the unemployed man in this story was not dejected at all. Instead, he found his own way in life despite all his defeats. Finally, he made it as an owner of the biggest food retailer company in the town. Well goes the saying, "Heaven never closes its roads against a man." Therefore, no matter what difficulties lie ahead in our life, we have to have faith in ourselves. We are surely to go beyond our limits and find a new life path in a difficult situation as long as we are confident of ourselves.

每個人都會有某部份的缺陷，而我們卻常常太過注意這些缺陷，忽略了我們其實有其他的潛力。故事中的主角因為沒有電腦，沒有電子郵件信箱，因此被認為無法擔任工作，但他並沒有因此而喪失鬥志，覺得自己完了，大概從此找不到工作；相反地，他遭逢逆境的時候，卻還能為自己找到一條出路，發現自己其實並不是一無是處，進而開創出一條成功的大道。這就是大家常講的，天無絕人之路。所以我們不管遭遇怎樣的逆境，都不應該過度鑽牛角尖，因為有時逆境反而可以幫助我們跳出既有框架，找到一條完全不同的道路。

Dear Mom,

I'm writing you this letter to confess that I haven't been honest to you lately.

I have a boyfriend, whose name is Daryl, and he lives in a trailer in the woods. He also wears biker clothes and deals drugs.

I'm moving in with him and I'm four month pregnant.

We will make a living out of growing marijuana and selling them to the neighborhood kids. We will live a life of drugs and alcohols, lots of alcohols.

Wish us luck.

Daisy

P.S. Well, actually all of the above is a lie. I just want to let you know there are worse things in life than my report card, which lies in the top drawer.

親愛的媽媽

我寫這封信是想要告訴妳，我最近並沒有對妳說實話。

我交了一個男朋友，他的名字叫戴洛，他住在樹林的拖車裡，穿著飛車黨衣服並且在販毒。

我將要搬去跟他一起住，而我也懷了四個月的身孕。

我們會靠著種植及販售大麻給附近小孩維生，我們將會過著一個充滿著毒品和酒精的生活，大量的酒精。

祝我們好運吧！

黛西

P.S. 好吧，以上說的都是騙妳的。我只是想讓妳知道，一生中還有很多比我放在最上面抽屜裡的那個成績單還要糟糕的事可能會發生。

文法重點

現在進行式 (Present Progressive)

I'm writing you this letter...
（我寫這封信是……）

除了粗分過去式、現在式與未來式，英文文法裡的時態還可以細分為：一般事實（簡單式）、正在或持續發生（進行式）以及已經發生（完成式）。其中，現在進行式主要是用來指說話當時正在進行的動作。

- 現在進行式用來說明某個動作現在正在進行或發生

  I'm cooking.
  （我正在做飯。）

- 現在進行式用來説明目前這一段期間所發生的事，或是某人的狀態正在改變或進展的事物

He's working very hard these days.

（他最近幾天非常努力工作。）

- 現在進行式用來代替未來式

It's getting cold at night.

（晚上天氣轉冷了。）

- 現在進行式+ always 表示總是及經常在做的事

She's always making promises that cannot be fulfilled.

（她總是承諾做不到的事。）

句型解析

I'm writing you this letter to confess that I haven't been honest to you lately.

1. I' m writing you this letter to confess that I haven't been...

   S V Progressive I.O. D.O. Infinitive Phr.

   lately.

2. 本句的"that I haven't been honest to you lately"是名詞子句，作為 confess 的受詞。

3. lately *(adv.)* 最近(=recently)。需與完成式連用。

   例句：Kate has been fond of swimming lately.

   Kate 最近喜歡上游泳。

4. confess *(v.)* 告解。confession *(n.)* 告解，懺悔。

He lives in a trailer in the woods.

1. He lives in a trailer in the woods.

   S V Adv. Phr. Adv. Phr.

2. trailer *(n.)* 拖車。
3. wood 本來是不可數名詞，意為「木頭」；但是片語 in the woods 意思則是「在森林中」(= in the forest)。

We will make a living out of growing marijuana and selling them to the neighborhood kids.

1. We will make a living

   S Aux. V Phr.

   out of growing marijuana... to the neighborhood kids.

   Adv. Phr.

2. make a living *(v. phr.)* 謀生。本句的 make a living out of growing marijuana and selling 亦可寫成 make a living by growing marijuana and selling。
3. marijuana *(n.)* 大麻。
4. neighborhood *(n.)* 鄰近地區，鄰里。neighbor *(n.)* 鄰居。

   例句：You can see a park in the neighborhood of the city hall.

   你在市政廳附近可以看到一座公園。

心情小語

Students have numerous ways to prevent their parents from reading their report cards. Some students write wrong addresses on the envelopes while others will rush home to receive their report cards from postmen before their parents do. Well, instead of spending time and energy on these trivial things, they can choose to study hard to have good grades on exams. Although most students know that it is the key solution to the problem, "to say is one thing; to do is another".
In reality, only top students seem to recognize the reality and take real actions to achieve their goals. Similarly, we can see that many people in our life, like students in schools, do not recognize the most important things in their certain phases of life until the time passes by. However, what is done cannot be undone. One's success depends on when he or she recognizes and realizes what his or her most important thing is in a certain phase of life. Realizing this earlier and then prioritizing things in life, he or she will leave no regrets in life.

學生總是有一堆花招想辦法不讓成績單寄到家裡；有些同學會故意把家裡地址寫錯、有些同學則是會抓放學回到家和家長下班回家之間的時間差，衝回去攔截。不過與其把時間和心力花在這些上面，不如當初就用功一點把成績考好，不就不用這麼麻煩了？不過這種話誰都會說，在當時真的能做到的，大概就只有名列前茅的幾位好學生吧！很多事情都是要到一定的年紀之後才會領悟，之前這麼做好像不太好、如果可以再重來一次，我一定不會再這麼做…但當你會這麼想的時候，通常都已經來不及也沒機會回頭去修改了。一個人的成功與否，就在於你能夠多早領悟現階段最重要的事情是什麼，然後依照優先順序去完成。能夠越早領悟這點，將來需要後悔的東西就越少。

生活篇 對話 1

Situation: Peggy, Fairy, and Sally are making plans for the coming weekend.

情境：Peggy，Fairy，跟 Sally 正在計畫接下來週末要做些什麼。

Peggy	So, what are your plans for this weekend?	所以，你們這週末有什麼計畫嗎？
Fairy	I don't know. Do you want to get together or something?	我不知道耶。你們有想要聚聚嗎？
Sally	How about going to see a movie? Cinema Max on Walnut Boulevard is showing "Maggie".	那我們去看電影好嗎？胡桃大道的 Max 影院正在播映「Maggie」。
Peggy	That sounds like a good idea. Maybe we should go out to grab a bite beforehand.	這個主意不錯。或許我們要先去吃些東西。
Sally	It is fine with me. Where do you want to meet?	我都可以啊。你們會想要在哪裡碰面？
Fairy	Let's meet at Happy Pizza House. I have not gone there for a long time.	我們在歡樂比薩屋碰面好了。我已經好久沒去那了。
Peggy	Good idea again. I heard they just came up with a new pizza. It should be good because Happy Pizza House always has the best pizza in town.	又是一個不錯的主意。我才聽說他們出了新的比薩。那應該很好吃，因為歡樂比薩屋的比薩是鎮上最好吃的。
Sally	When should we meet?	那我們什麼時候碰面？

Fairy	Why don't we go to the 2:00PM show? We can meet at Happy Pizza House at noon. That will give us plenty of time to enjoy our pizza.	我們去看兩點的電影好了。這樣我們中午就可以先在歡樂比薩屋聚聚，有足夠的時間吃東西。
Peggy	That's great!	這真是太棒了！

生活篇 對話 2

Situation: Peggy and Fairy are going to visit the gallery on the weekend and Peggy's years-old friend Gina is coming to town.

情境：Peggy 和 Fair 這週末要去參觀畫廊。Peggy 的多年老友 Gina 也要來鎮上。

Peggy	Have you heard of Gina? Peggy, you remember her? We met her at Sara's high school graduation party two years ago. She is coming back this weekend.	妳有聽說 Gina 的消息嗎？Peggy，你還記得她嗎？兩年前，我們在 Sara 的高中畢業派對上遇過她。她這週末要回來。
Fairy	Gina is in town? Well, I do not quite remember her. What does she look like?	Gina 要回鎮上？嗯，我不是很記得她。她長得怎樣？
Peggy	She has blond hair, she is kind of slender, and she is about your height.	她一頭金髮，人瘦瘦的。她大概跟你一般高。
Fairy	She wears eyeglasses, right?	她有戴眼鏡，對不對？

Peggy	Yes, and she was playing the piano off and on during the party.	對！她在派對上還有彈鋼琴啊！
Fairy	I remember her now. Yes, do bring her along with us to the gallery on the weekend. She is such a nice person, and funny too.	我現在記起來了。好，請妳這週末帶她一起來畫廊。她是一個好人，也很有趣。
Peggy	She graduated last June, and she will start her teaching career next week when the new school term begin. I think she will be happy to meet you again.	她去年六月畢業，然後她從下週起就要開始教書了。我想妳再見到她一定會很開心。

單字與實用例句

- plan *(n.)* 計畫

  Successful people tend to make plans before they set out to anything.

  成功人士傾向於在著手處理任何事物前先做計劃。

- cinema *(n.)* 電影，電影院

  Ang Lee has devoted all his life to cinema.

  李安把一生奉獻於電影。

- grab a bite *(v. phr.)* 隨手抓些東西來吃

  Because Jim got up too late, he just grabbed a bite before going to work.

  因為 Jim 太晚起床，他去上班前先隨便抓些東西來吃。

- beforehand *(adv.)* 事先

  Please set everything ready beforehand.

  請先事先把所有事情準備好。

- gallery *(n.)* 畫廊

  The gallery is having an exhibition of Chinese water and ink painting.

  這間畫廊現正展出中國水墨畫。

- remember *(v.)* 記得

  Do you remember having your assignments done?

  你記得把作業寫完嗎？

- graduation *(n.)* 畢業

  Ur was invited to deliver a speech in the graduation ceremony in a local junior high school.

  Ur 受邀在當地國中的畢業典禮上演講。

- career *(n.)* 生涯

  Jane is a career woman. She tries to strike the balance between work and her family.

  Jane 是位職業婦女。她努力要在工作與家庭間取得平衡。

好用主題用語，用法解說

> Cinema Max on Walnut Boulevard is showing "Maggie".
> She is coming back this weekend.

進行式 be Ving：

在英文對話中，當我們要表達一個動作正在持續進行或是代替未來式時，我們會用現在進行式：be Ving。

- 某個動作正在持續進行：

  The old lady is waiting for the train to Edinburgh.

  （這位老太太正在等往愛丁堡的火車。)

  The patient is recovering after the surgery.

  （這位病人術後正在復原中。）

  The economy is improving slowly.

  （經濟正緩慢復甦。）

- 代替未來式：

  My parents is returning home from Kyoto tomorrow.

  （我父母明天將從京都回來。）

  I am starting my new job next week.

  （我下週要展開新工作。）

  Vivian is going to Brazil next month.

  （Vivian 下週要去巴西。）

Unit 07 過去式

勵志篇 故事

One day, a donkey fell into a well. The animal cried for hours as the farmer tried his best to figure out a way to get him out. Finally, the farmer decided it was just not possible; besides, the donkey was pretty old and the well was dry anyway. So instead of saving the donkey, the farmer asked his neighbor to help him fill up the well.

They both grabbed a shovel and began to shove dirt into the well.

Realizing what was going to happen, the donkey cried horribly, but after a few minutes, he just quieted down and didn't make a sound.

After shoveling some loads of dirt, the farmer looked down. To his surprise, the donkey was not buried under the dirt! Instead, with every shovel of dirt hit his back, the donkey just shook it off and stepped on it.

As the farmer and his neighbor continued shoveling dirt on top of the donkey, he continued to shake it off and take a step up. Shortly after, to everyone's amazement, the donkey stepped up over the edge of the well and walked away.

有天，一頭驢子掉進井裡。當農夫想破了頭要把牠從井裡救出來的同時，牠不停地在井底哀號著。最後，農夫便放棄了，反正這頭驢子也老了，井也乾了啊；所以農夫便找了他的鄰居打算將井給填平，而不是想要將驢子救出來。

他們各拿了一把鏟子，開始將土給鏟到井裡去。

意識到即將要發生什麼事，驢子開始在井底發出淒厲的哀號，但幾分鐘之後，牠就安靜下來，不再發出任何聲音了。

鏟了一些土到井裡之後，農夫探頭往井裡一看，出乎他意料之外，驢子不但沒有被土給埋起來，反而是將每一鏟掉到牠身上甩開，然後踩上去。

隨著農夫和鄰居不斷地將土往井裡鏟到驢子身上，驢子也不停的將土甩開，然後踩上去。不出一會兒，在眾人的驚嘆之下，驢子一腳踩過井的邊緣，然後漫步離開了。

文法重點

過去簡單式 (Past Tense)

Realizing what was going to happen, the donkey cried horribly, but after a few minutes, he just quieted down and didn' t make a sound.
（意識到即將要發生什麼事，驢子開始在井底發出淒厲的哀號，但幾分鐘之後，牠就安靜下來，不再發出任何聲音了。）

英文句子裡的時態主要分成：現在式、過去式與未來式。其中，過去簡單式用於表示過去發生的一般動作或狀態，並且這個動作在過去某一時間點已經結束。

- 過去簡單式的句子常與表示過去時間的副詞，如 yesterday, last year, three years ago 等一起使用。

  The general manager did not come to the office this morning.
  （總經理今天早上沒進辦公室。）

  What do you eat for dinner last night?（你昨天晚上吃什麼？）
- 表示過去的習慣或過去頻繁的動作（但是現在已經沒有了。）
- Eric was a therapist in his thirties.
  （Eric 在 30 幾歲時曾是個治療師。）

Linda used to go jogging on Sundays.

（Linda 以前在星期天時都會去健行。）

- 主要句子的動詞為過去式時，從屬子句的動詞也要用過去式。

I thought she was happy with the result.

（我想她對結果感到高興。）

Jean pointed out that the economic situation could be worse.
（Jean 指出經濟狀況可能會更糟。）

- 強調與現在事實相反的假設語氣句型，需用過去式代替現在式。

I wish that I were a millionaire.（我希望我是個百萬富翁。）

If I were a bird, I could fly away from my work.

（如果我是一隻鳥，我就能飛離我的工作。）

句型解析

The animal cried for hours as the farmer tried his best to figure out a way to get him out.

1. The animal (S) cried (V) for hours (Adv. Phr.) [as the farmer tried his best... to get him out.] (Adv. Cl.)

2. 本句的 as 是連接詞，意為「正當……」(=while=when)。

3. 句型 try one's best to V 意為「盡全力去(做)……」。

例句：The scientist tried his best to complete the experiment.

（這位科學家盡全力完成實驗。）

4. 動詞片語 figure out 意為「想出…(的方法)」。
例句：The single father figured out the best way to tend his baby.
（這位單親父親想出照顧小寶寶最好的方法。）

So instead of saving the donkey, the farmer asked his neighbor to help him fill up the well.

1. So instead of saving the donkey, the farmer asked his neighbor to help him fill up the well.

instead of saving the donkey	the farmer	asked	his neighbor	to help him fill up the well
Adv. Phr.	S	V	O	Infinitive Phr.

2. 片語 instead of 意為「而不是……」，其後須接名詞，動詞則須變成動名詞。以本句為例，save the donkey 需變化成 saving the donkey。
3. fill *(v.)* 填補。fill up the well 意為「填滿水井」。
4. 本句用到 ask + O + to V 的句型，意為「要(某人)去做……」。

To his surprise, the donkey was not buried under the dirt!

1. To his surprise, the donkey was not buried under the dirt!

To his surprise	the donkey	was	not	buried	under the dirt
Adv. Phr.	S	BeV	Adv.	Vpassive	Adv. Phr.

2. 本句用到片語 to one's surprise 意為「令某人驚訝的是，……」。本句亦可改寫成 "He was surprised that the donkey was not buried under the dirt!"

心情小語

In our life, we are sure to confront difficult situations when people throw troubles to us. Faced with those unpleasant and unfair moments, we can choose to be upset, furious, or even keep complaining over and over again. However, those complaints and negative thoughts can never really improve those unpleasant situations. If we can try to act like a donkey in the story, changing the dirt used to bury it into stairs to climb upwards, we can see opportunities to turn the table. That is, when we face unfair situations where people dump hot potatoes to us, we should not complain first but rather calm down and face the music. That is the key for us to success.

我們一生當中，一定會遇到很多不斷地將一些麻煩事往我們身上丟的人事物。這時我們可以為自己所遭受的不公平待遇抱怨、難過，甚至生氣、憤怒；但這些都只是宣洩一時的情緒，並沒有辦法真正的對我們有幫助。但如果我們可以像故事中的驢子一樣，將那些原本應該是要用來埋他的土，化成幫助牠往上爬的階梯。所以如果當我們遇到有人將麻煩的事往我們身上丟的時候，先不要急著哭天搶地地哀號，這時應該冷靜下來，面對問題；因為這很可能就是幫助我們成功的階梯。

One Sunday afternoon, Joe was in his front yard mowing grass when suddenly he saw his neighbor, an attractive blonde girl, came out of the house and went straight to the mailbox.

She opened it, slammed it shut and stormed back to the house.

Joe didn't know what happened to her, so he kept on mowing the lawn.

A little later, she came out of her house again. She walked to the mailbox, opened it, slammed it shut, again and then walked straight back to her house angrily.

As Joe was getting to the last part of the lawn, the girl came out again! This time she looked really mad as she marched to the mailbox, opened it and then slammed it shut harder than ever.

Extremely puzzled by her action, he finally asked her, "Is something wrong?"

The girl rolled her eyes and said. "It's my stupid computer! It keeps giving me a message saying "YOU'VE GOT MAIL", but there was none!"

一個星期天下午，喬正在院子裡除草。突然間，他看見住在隔壁的美麗金髮女鄰居從屋子裡走出來。

她走到信箱，打開來，然後用力將信箱關上，便悻悻然地走了回去。

一會兒之後，她又從屋子裡走出來。

她再次地走到信箱，打開它，然後在用力地關上，最後氣呼呼地走回去。

當喬已經幾乎快要把草除完的時後，這女孩又出來了！這次她看起來真的超火大！她大步地走到信箱、打開它，然後再用力地關上。

喬已經被她的舉止弄的滿腦子問號，終於開口問了她：「請問是有什麼問題嗎？」

女孩翻了個白眼說道：「是我的笨電腦啦！它一直跳出一個訊息跟我說『你有信件』，但明明就沒有啊！！」

文法重點

過去進行式 (Past Progressive)

> As Joe was getting to the last part of the lawn, the girl came out again!
> （當喬已經幾乎快要把草除完的時後，這女孩又出來了！）

除了粗分過去式、現在式與未來式，英文文法裡的時態還可以細分為：一般事實（簡單式）、正在或持續發生（進行式）以及已經發生（完成式）。其中，過去進行式用於表示過去某時間點正在發生或持續的動作。

- 過去進行式經常與另一過去簡單式的子句並用。強調在過去的某個時間裡某一個動作突然發生時，另一個動作正在進行。

  The doorbell rang while I was taking a shower.

  （當我在洗澡的時候，門鈴響了。）

  When Sandy arrived, Henry was cooking the dinner.

  （當 Sandy 抵達時，Henry 正在煮晚餐。）

  Ur called his friend while he was watching TV last night.

  （Ur 昨天晚上在看電視時打電話給他的朋友。）

  What were you doing when the earthquake struck last Friday?

  （上星期五地震的時候你在做什麼？）

- 如果副詞子句與主要子句的動作都是在過去時間點同時在進行的話，兩個子句皆可用過去進行式。

While my mother was looking for me at the airport, I was calling her.

（當我媽在機場找我的時候，我正在打電話給她。）

While Nina was preparing the luncheon, one guest after another was arriving at hers.

（當 Nina 正在準備午宴時，一個接著一個的賓客陸續抵達。）

句型解析

Joe didn't know what happened to her, so he kept on mowing the lawn.

1. Joe did n't know [what happened to her],

S Aux. Adv. V N. Cl.→ O

[so he kept on mowing the lawn].

Adv.Cl.

2. 本句的"what happened to her"為名詞子句當 know 的受詞用。

happen *(v.)* 發生。只有主動式，沒有被動式。

例句：Kate burst out crying when she learnt that a car accident happened to her son.

當 Kate 知道她兒子發生車禍，她突然哭了出來。

3. 動詞片語"keep on + Ving"，意為「繼續（做）…」。

This time she looked really mad as she marched to the mailbox, opened it and then slammed it shut harder than ever.

1. This time she looked really mad

   Adv. Phr. S V Adv. Adj.→ SC

   [as she marched to the mailbox, ... ever.]

   Adv. Cl.

2. 本句的 as 是連接詞，意為「正當……」(=while)。
3. 本句的“she marched to the mailbox, opened it and then slammed it shut harder than ever”意為「她大步地走到信箱、打開它，然後再用力地關上」這句 S +V1,V2, and V3 句構，強調先做 V1，再做 V2，然後再做 V3，三個順序的動作。

Extremely puzzled by her action, he finally asked her, “Is something wrong?”

1. Extremely puzzled by her action, he finally asked her,

   Participial Construction S Adv. V I.O.

   “Is something wrong?”

   D.O.

2. 本句“Extremely puzzled by her action, ...”是分詞構句，可還原成“Because he was extremely puzzled by her action, ...”。
3. puzzle *(v.)* 使……困惑。

   例句：The complex math formula puzzled all the students.
   複雜的數學公式使所有學生困惑。

心情小語

While computers have been a common necessity in each household nowadays, the design and parts of computers are complicated to most ordinary people and they are not familiar with the design and parts of computers. In fact, computers are designed by people from science and engineering departments who pay less attention to the using method than to its multifunctions. For example, we common people think iPad useful mainly because of its convenience rather than because of its possible super functions. However, many computer companies in Taiwan do not understand this simple fact: what users want is not a fast and multifunctional super computer, but a user-friendly and easy-to-use computer.

電腦雖然是現在很普及，家家戶戶都有的東西，但很多人即使每天都在用，對電腦的一切還是完全陌生。這些都是因為電腦對很多人來說還是太複雜了。由於設計電腦的人都是理工科出身，而理工科的人是不會去考慮太多這類使用上的問題，因為他們在意的只有「把功能做出來」。所以為什麼我們會覺得 iPad 很好用，那就是因為它的出發點從來就不在強調它超強的功能上，而是在其「便利性」上。這也是許多台灣科技大廠都一直搞不懂的；絕大多數的使用者並不想要一個處理速度超快、功能強到只差自己不會獨立思考，但卻很難用的超級電腦；大家想要的其實就是一台「就算我隨便亂玩它也不會輕易掛掉」的超簡單電腦而已啊。

生活篇 對話 1

Situation: Jason is discussing plans for Winter break with his friend Brian while they are driving home from their basketball game.

Situation: 籃球賽後，Jason 開車回家並和朋友 Brian 聊寒假計畫。

Brian	Hey Jason, hop on in and throw your stuff in the back.	嗨，Jason。把東西丟在後座然後上車吧！
Jason	OK, Brian. Thank you for giving me a ride home. All my family went to JJ's Café for my grandma's birthday.	好啊，Brian。謝謝妳載我回家。我家人都去 JJ's 咖啡館慶祝我祖母的生日了。
Brian	JJ's Café? That place has the best bagels in town! The atmosphere is also nice. Good food and a good setting, what more could you ask for? We should eat there after our next basketball game.	JJ's 咖啡館？那裡有鎮裡最好的貝果耶！那裡氣氛不錯。有好吃的食物跟漂亮的擺設，你還能再要求什麼？我們下場籃球比賽後應該在那裡吃東西的。
Jason	Yes, that sounds like a good plan. When is our next game by the way?	好，那聽起還不錯。那我們下次比賽是什麼時候？
Brian	I think it is after Winter break, which is a long way off.	我想會在寒假之後吧，還要很久。
Jason	Then, it's a deal. We will come to enjoy watching games after Winter break!	那一言為定，我們寒假之後去那裏看比賽。
Brian	Okay.	好啊。

生活篇 對話 2

Brian	Do you have any plans set up for the upcoming vacation?	接下來的寒假你有什麼計畫嗎？
Jason	Well, besides basketball practices, I'll most likely be working.	嗯，除了練習籃球之外，我可能會去工作。
Brian	Oh, working? Did you get a new job or are you still working at Starbucks?	喔，工作？你有新工作還是繼續在星巴克工作？
Jason	I loved the people I worked with. However, my work schedule was definitely very difficult and a conflict to my class schedule.	我喜歡跟那裡的人共事。但是我在排班上有困難，而且會跟我的課表衝突。
Brian	What's your new job?	那你新工作是什麼？
Jason	I am an Administrative Assistant for a company called Multi-Soft.	我現在是 Multi-Soft 公司的行政助理。
Brian	When did you start this new job?	你什麼時候開始新工作的？
Jason	I have been with Multi-Soft since December 1st. What about you? Do you have any plans?	我從12月1日就開始在那工作。你呢？有什麼計畫呢？
Brian	I think I am just going to hang out at home. I am planning a snowboarding trip though.	我想我就在家待著。我也在計畫滑雪行程。
Jason	Oh, that sounds like fun!	喔，聽起來好像很有趣！

單字與實用例句

- ride *(n.)* (一趟)車程、船程

  Vivian gave me a ride to the local market.
  Vivian 載我一程去當地市場。

- atmosphere *(n.)* 氣氛

  The atmosphere in the meeting is weird.
  會議的氣氛怪怪的。

- enjoy *(v.)* 享受

  Olivia enjoyed listening to the music played in the store.
  Olivia 享受店裡播放的音樂。

- upcoming *(adj.)* 接下來的，即將要來的

  The weather bureau warned the public of the upcoming typhoon.
  氣象局警告大家會有颱風來臨。

- schedule *(n.)* 行程表

  I will give you a reply once I check my schedule.
  一旦我查了我的行程表之後，我會給你回覆。

好用主題用語，用法解說

I think it is after Winter break, which is a long way off.
I think I am just going to hang out at home and read some books.

在口語中，表示陳述個人意見時，我們可以用 S think/consider/ suppose/ reckon that S + V （我認為…）這個句型。

I suppose the economic recession will slow down.
（我認為經濟衰退會趨緩。）

Dylan thought that he did not work hard enough to achieve his goal.
（Dylan 認為他並不夠努力以達成他的目標。）
除了 S think/consider/ suppose/ reckon that S + V 這個句型可以用來表示陳述意見，在口語中還有以下常見用於意見陳述的句型：

- In one's opinion/view, S V

  In my opinion, that red dress doesn't suit you.

  （在我看來，紅洋裝與你不相稱。）

  In Oliver's view, bananas are the best fruit in the world.

  （Oliver 認為香蕉是這世上最棒的水果。）

- Personally (speaking), S V

  Personally speaking, Isabelle is a reliable helper.

  （就我個人而言，Isabelle 是個可靠的助手。）

  Personally, I think it is just a matter of time.

  （就我個人而言，我認為這只是遲早的問題。）

- As far as one's be concerned, S V

  As far as the manager's concerned, it is the time to invest the oversea market.

  （就經理看來，現在該是要投資海外市場的時候。）

  As far as I am concerned, no trip to Maldives will be complete without snorkeling.

  （我認為去馬爾地夫旅遊怎麼可以少了浮潛。）

Unit 08 未來式

勵志篇 故事

Once upon a time, there was a king who was a cruel dictator. Anyone who had differed from him in opinions was executed without any trial. However, one day, he surprised everyone in the country by announcing that he had decided to change.

"There will be no more cruelty and no more injustice", he promised. The king kept his promise and became a gentle and loving king.

Months after his transformation, one of his ministers plucked up enough courage to ask him what had made him change.

The king answered, "As I was riding my horse across the forest, I saw a fox being chased by a dog. The fox escaped into its hole but the dog had bitten into its leg. Then a farmer came, and the dog went running towards the farmer, barking at him. The farmer took a rock and threw at the dog, and broke its leg. The farmer walked for a while and a horse accidently kicked his knee. His knee was shattered and wouldn't be able to walk. The horse began to run but it fell into a hole and broke its leg. Seeing all this made me realize that evil might lead to evil. If I continue to be evil, I will be overtaken by evil one day. Therefore, I decided to change."

很久以前有個國王，他是個殘忍的獨裁者。任何人只要意見跟他不一樣，就會在未經任何審判之下被處死。然而有一天，他突然出乎所有人意料之

外，宣佈説從今以後他會開始改變。

「今後將不再會有任何暴政和不公。」他承諾道。這個國王也信守自己的承諾，變成了一個勤政愛民的好國王。

在他轉變之後的幾個月，其中一個首長鼓足了勇氣問他到底是什麼導致了他的改變。

國王回道：「就在我騎著馬要穿越森林的時候，我看到一隻狐狸被狗追。狐狸雖然逃進他的洞，但腿卻被狗咬了一口。接著來了一個農夫，那隻狗又跑來對著農夫吠叫，農夫拿起石頭丟向狗，打斷了牠的腿。農夫走了一會兒被一隻馬意外的踢到他的膝蓋，他膝蓋整個碎掉，以後再也無法行走。而那隻馬則開始狂奔，卻踩到一個洞，摔斷了腿。看到這一切讓我頓悟，邪惡只會招來邪惡。如果我繼續這麼邪惡下去，總有一天我也會被邪惡吞噬。因此我決定改變。」

文法重點

未來簡單式 (Future Tense)

There will be no more cruelty and no more injustice.
（今後將不再會有任何暴政和不公。）

英文句子裡的時態主要分成：現在式、過去式與未來式。其中，未來簡單式用來表示未來可能發生的事與狀態或對未來想要做的事。
它有兩種形式：第一種句型形式為：will + V。助動詞 will 意為「將要、將會」。
Kate will go to Turkey this Friday.（Kate 這個星期五要去土耳其。）
Will you help me with my assignment?（你要幫我做作業嗎？）
I won't forgive John if he officially apologizes to me.（如果 John 不公開的向我道歉，我不會原諒他。）→ will not 可以略縮寫成 won't

- 未來式常與表示未來的時間副詞，如 tomorrow, next day, next year...連用。

Will you go to see the movie tomorrow?

（你明天要去看電影嗎？）

Olivia will finish her house chore by 9 a.m.

（Olivia 將會在早上 9 點完成她的家事。）

- 在連接詞 when, before, after, if...所引導的副詞子句中，常用現在簡單式來表示未來式。

If the typhoon hit Taiwan tomorrow, we will have a day off.

（如果颱風明天侵襲台灣，我們就會放一天的假。）

When I see Kelvin, I will tell him that you called him.

（我看到 Kelvin 時，我會告訴他你打電話給他。）

句型解析

Anyone who had differed from him in opinions was executed without any trial.

1. Anyone [who had differed from him in opinions] was executed

S　　Adj. Cl.　　V Passive

without any trial.

Adv. Phr.

2. 本句的“who had differed from him in opinions”是形容詞子句，修飾先行詞anyone。

differ (*v*)　與……不同。

3. 動詞execute 原意是「執行」，但在本句是「處死」的意思。本句亦可改寫成：Anyone who had differed from him in opinions would receive death penalty/ capital punishment without any trial. 或是Anyone who had differed from him in opinions was put to death without any trial.

Months after his transformation, one of his ministers plucked up enough courage to ask him what had made him change.

1. Months after his transformation, one of his ministers

   Adv. Phr. S

   plucked up enough courage

   V Phr.→ V

   to ask him what had made him change.

   Infinitive Phr.

2. pluck up courage (*v. phr.*) 鼓起勇氣。

   例句：Sometimes you need to pluck up courage to make the right decision.

   （有時候你需要鼓起勇氣來做對的決定。）

3. 本句的what had made him change是名詞子句做動詞ask的直接受詞用。

As I was riding my horse across the forest, I saw a fox being chased by a dog.

1. [As I was riding my horse across the forest], I saw a fox

   Adv. Phr. S V O

   being chased by a dog.

   Ving→ O.C.

2. 本句的as是連接詞，意為「正當」(=when=while)。

3. 本句用到see+ O + OC 的句型，being chased by a dog當作受詞補語，修飾受詞a fox。

心情小語

Some people think that "an eye for an eye" is the best solution to a problematic situation. Therefore, whenever they confront problems, all they think of is to resort to violence. However, violence will lead to a lose-lose situation. The fox and the dog in the story seemed to win at first, but in the end both of them got hurt and defeated. The gain never covers the loss when we use violence. Like the farmer in the story, thinking that "I will make you pay for what you have done to me since you hurt me in advance", people who tend to resort to violence always think that they are acting for God to perform righteous acts. Then, there is only hatred in their hearts and there is no room for forgiveness. When there are only negative feelings, negative things will be attracted to you. Then, you will gradually forget what forgiveness is and think that everyone owes you something. To take your revenge, you will lose yourself at last. Unless you change and start to learn to think positively and to forgive, you will become a tyrant in your lonely kingdom.

有些人認為以暴制暴是最快的解決方法，因此，遇到問題時只想用暴力解決，卻不知道以暴制暴的下場往往是兩敗俱傷，沒有贏家。就像是故事中的狐狸跟狗。而有些人雖然表面上贏了，卻是輸了裡子，根本得不償失，就像是故事中的農夫。「既然你對不起我，我也不用對你客氣」這些人往往理直氣壯地說著。久而久之，這些人的心裡只有仇恨，沒有原諒，只有厭惡，沒有包容。當你的心裡被這些負面的情緒佔滿，所有的事情在你眼中也會變成負面的，漸漸地，你不知道什麼叫做寬容，漸漸地你會覺得所有人都對不起你，漸漸地，你就會失去了自己，除非你知道改變，不再讓這些負面的情緒影響你，

否則，終究，你會變成一個獨裁者，而不是一個仁君。

幽默篇 故事

After turning 18, a young cannibal is allowed to go hunting with his father for the first time. Since it's his first hunting, the father told the son to follow his lead.

They walked deep into the jungle, hid there and waited patiently for their prey to appear.

Before long, there came a skinny old man.

"Hey, dad, there's one!" said the son.

"No," said the father, "There's not enough meat on that one to even feed the dogs. We'll just wait."

A little while later, along came a really fat man.

"Hey, dad, this one got plenty of meat!" said the son.

"No," said the father "We'd all die of heart attack from the fat in that one. We'll just wait."

Few hours later, came a really beautiful woman.

The son said, "Well, there's nothing wrong with this one! Let's eat her!"

"No," said the father "We're not going to eat her either."

"Why not?" asked the son.

"Because we're going to take her home, and eat your mother."

在滿 18 歲之後，一個年輕的食人族首度被准許和父親一起去打獵。由於這是他的第一次狩獵，所以父親要他跟在後面，聽他的指示。

他們深入到叢林裡，躲了起來，並耐心地等待獵物的出現。

不久之後，一個瘦小的老人走了過來。

「嘿，爸，這邊有一個！」兒子說道。

「不，」父親說道：「這個身上的肉連餵狗都不夠了，我們再等等。」

過了一會兒，走來了一個非常胖的人。

「嘿，爸，這個人身上的肉夠多了！」兒子說道。

「不，」父親說道：「吃了這傢伙的肥肉，我們全部的人都會因為心臟病而死的！再等等。」

幾個小時之後，一個非常漂亮的女人走了過來。

「好了，這個應該沒什麼問題了吧，爸？我們吃她吧！」兒子說道。

「不，」父親說道：「我們也不能吃她。」

「為什麼不？」兒子問道。

「因為我們要把她帶回家，然後把你媽給吃了！」

文法重點

未來簡單式(Future Tense)

Because we're going to take her home, and eat your mother.
（因為我們要把她帶回家，然後把你媽給吃了。）

英文句子裡的時態主要分成：現在式、過去式與未來式。其中，未來簡單式用來表示未來可能發生的事與狀態或對未來想要做的事。
除了 will + V 的形式之外，第二種表示未來式的句型形式為：BeV going to + Vr。跟第一種形式 will + Vr 相比，will 表示有意願或比較有可能發生的事； 而 BeV going to 強調的是預定或打算。此外，BeV about to + Vr 也可以用來替換 BeV going to + Vr。

例句：Vicky is going to take a sick leave because she has a stomachache today.
（因為Vicky今天肚子痛，所以她要請病假。）
Mick is about to visit his parents this afternoon.
（Mick 今天下午可能會去看他爸媽。）

句型解析

After turning 18, a young cannibal is allowed to go hunting with his father for the first time.

1. <u>After turning 18,</u> <u>a young cannibal</u> <u>is</u> <u>allowed</u> <u>to go hunting</u>
   Participial Construction S BeV Vpassive Infinitive Phr.
   <u>with his father for the first time.</u>
   Adv. Phr.
2. 本句的"After turning 18, ..."是分詞構句，可以還原成"<u>After a young cannibal turned 18, ...</u>"。
3. allow *(v.)* 允許。其用法為 "allow + O + to V"。

例句：Smokers are not allowed to smoke indoors in this gallery.
（吸菸者不准在這間畫廊內吸菸。）

Since it's his first hunting, the father told the son to follow his lead.

1. Since it's his first hunting, the father told the son
   Adv. Cl. S V O
   to follow his lead.
   Infinitive Phr.
2. 本句的 since 是連接詞，意為「因為」(=as=because)。
3. lead *(n.)* 引導。本句 the father told the son to follow his lead 意為「他父親叫他小孩跟著他走」。

We'd all die of heart attack from the fat in that one.

1. We' d all die of heart attack from the fat in that
   S Aux. Adv. V Adv. Phr. Adv. Phr.
   one.
   動詞片語 die of 意為「死於……(的原因)」。
   例句：The alcoholic died of liver cancer.
   （那位酗酒者死於肝癌。）
2. heart attack (*n. phr.*) 心臟病。

心情小語

As Facebook becomes more and more popular, the common problem emerges: you may feel sad about your dull and miserable life when you saw pictures taken by your friends when they are travelling abroad and having feasts. While others can go out and play, you may have to work overtime. Sad, isn't it? Through these comparisons, many people may start to think of themselves as useless and even some got depressed. However, the fact may be that those who have afternoon teas at department stores probably will be fired at any time. Those who go abroad and have feasts may be having husbands who only send their salary home and never go back. What I mean is not to despite others' happiness. We can give our best wishes to them while we value our own worth. No one is perfect. Between those happy pictures may be poor and harsh situations. We can envy others and work hard for that but never think lowly of ourselves, or that would be too silly.

隨著臉書的流行，最常見的問題就是：看著上面一個個幸福又快樂的動態，突然覺得自己的生活好無趣、好悲慘；為什麼那個誰誰誰每天請假去喝下午茶，自己卻連放假都要加班？還有那個誰，三天兩頭就出國玩，要不就吃大餐，為什麼我連去個百貨公司都沒空？在這樣不斷的比較之下，就開始覺得自己一無是處，甚至還有人因此得了憂鬱症。可是當我們在羨慕這些人的時候或許不知道，那個每天請假喝下午茶的，是因為在公司根本不受重視，隨時準備要被資遣了，才會那麼有空；又例如那個三天兩頭出國、吃大餐的，其實老公每個月只有把錢寄回家，但是根本每天都在外頭跟小三玩得樂不思蜀的，完全不管家人的死活，所以她才豁出去不把老公賺的錢當錢用。這不是要大家見不得別人好；別人好，我們還是可以開心的給予祝福，但在這同時也不要忽視了自己的好。沒有人的人生是十全十美的，就算可以營造出讓人羨慕的表象，背後一定也有難以為外人道的痛苦。我們可以羨慕別人，並且以此為努力的目標，但千萬不要因此而妄自菲薄、喪失鬥志，那就太傻了！

生活篇 對話 1

Situation: Winnie has not been feeling well lately. Today she goes to see her doctor for a physical checkup.

情境：Winnie 最近身體不舒服。今天她去看醫生作檢查。

Winnie	Good morning, I have an appointment with Doctor David at 9:30.	早安，我跟 David 醫生約九點半的診。
Clerk	Let me pull your record. Have a seat, please.	我拿一下你的紀錄。請坐。
Nurse	Winnie Johnson.	Winnie Johnson。
Winnie	Here.	在這。
Nurse	Follow me to Room A please.	請跟我到診間 A。
Nurse	Here we are. What are your reasons for seeing Doctor David today?	我們到了。你今天是為什麼來看 David 醫生呢？
Winnie	Well, lately I have had really bad headaches and an upset stomach. On top of that, I have had this persistent cough for the last two weeks.	嗯，最近我頭很疼，然後胃也不舒服。此外，我這兩週也持續地咳嗽。
Nurse	Are you taking any medications?	你有在接受任何藥物治療嗎？

Winnie	I am only taking a multi-vitamin tablet and extra Vitamin C every day.	我每天只有吃綜合維他命跟維他命 C 而已。
Nurse	OK, let me take your vital signs.	嗯，我來量量你的體溫及血壓（生命徵兆）。
Winnie	How am I doing?	我怎麼了嗎？
Nurse	Everything is good- normal blood pressure and no high temperature. Please wait here for a minute. Doctor David will be with you in a moment.	大致上良好一血壓跟體溫都正常。請在這裡等一下，David 醫生一會兒就來了。

生活篇 對話 2

Doctor	Good morning, Winnie. Did you run a fever?	早啊，Winnie。你有發燒嗎？
Winnie	No, doctor.	沒有，醫生。
Doctor	Were there any changes in your diet or your weight lately?	你最近飲食上跟體重上有任何改變嗎？
Winnie	I ate the usual things, but I lost five pounds recently.	我吃得跟以往一樣，但我掉了五磅重。
Doctor	Did you suffer from insomnia?	你有失眠嗎？
Winnie	It is pretty hard for me to fall asleep when I go to bed. I also woke up many times during the night.	我睡覺很難入睡。我晚上也會醒來好幾次。

Doctor	How are things at work?	最近工作怎麼樣？
Winnie	There was a change of ownership three months ago, and I had to work overtime, even during the weekend.	最近公司所有權有所轉變，於是我開始加班工作。甚至週末都要加班。
Doctore	It looks like you have pneumonia. Are you allergic to any medicine?	看起來你得了肺炎。你對什麼藥物過敏？
Winnie	Not to my knowledge.	據我所知沒有。
Doctore	OK, take this medication three times a day after you eat. Also, I want you to have some blood tests. Stop by the laboratory on your way out and have the nurse draw your blood.	好的，那就一天三次飯後服藥。此外，我要你做一些血液測試。妳出診間後請到檢驗室那裡去一下，護士會幫你抽血。
Winnie	Thank you, Doctor.	謝謝，醫生。

單字與實用例句

- well *(adj.)* （身體）舒服的

  Grandma caught a cold so she did not feel well.
  祖母感冒了，所以身體不舒服。

- physical *(adj.)* 生理的

  The teacher puts great emphasis on physical education.
  那位老師高度重視體育教育。

- appointment *(n.)* 約會

  If you want to meet our manager, please make an appointment in advance.

  如果你想見我們經理，請您事先預約。

- follow *(v.)* 跟隨

  Randy is courageous and insightful so many people would like to follow him.

  因為 Randy 很勇敢有深具慧眼，所以很多人想要追隨他。

- fever *(n.)* 發燒

  Put on more clothes since it gets colder and older. Otherwise, you may get a fever.

  當天氣越來越冷時，多穿些衣服。否則你會發燒的。

- suffer *(v.)* 承受（痛苦）

  Many people have to suffer from great pressure from work to make their ends meet.

  為了收支平衡，許多人必須承受工作的壓力。

- overtime *(adv.)* 超時地

  To save money for her house, Mia often works overtime.

  為了存房子的錢，Mia 常常加班。

- allergic *(adj.)* 過敏的

  Sandy is allergic to seafood.

  Sandy 對海鮮過敏。

好用主題用語，用法解說

Have a seat, please.
OK, take this medication three times a day after you eat.

祈使句

在英文對話中，當我們要請求、命令對方或是表示勸告、禁止時，我們常常會以動詞原型起頭，省略主詞「你」的祈使句句型來表示。

- 表示請求：

  Please turn on the air conditioner.

  （請開冷氣。）

  Please pass the salt.

  （請把鹽遞過來。）

- 表示命令：

  Take off your shoes.

  （把鞋脫掉。）

  Go and wash your hands!

  （去洗手！）

- 表示勸告：

  Be kind to your brother.

  （對你弟弟要好一點。）

  Watch your steps.

  （走路小心。）

- 表示禁止：

  Don't touch the painting.

  （請不要用手觸摸這幅畫。）

  Keep off the grass.

  （請勿踐踏草坪。）

Unit 09 完成式

勵志篇 故事

Rick went into a flower shop to order a dozen of roses. He asked the flower shop to deliver those flowers to his mother, who lived two hundred miles away. Rick hadn't seen his mother for a while. He was just too busy to actually visit her.

As he got out of the shop, he saw a young girl sitting on the sidewalk crying.

"What's wrong?" Rick asked.

"I wanted to buy a red rose for my mother, but I don't have enough money... I don't know what to do."

Rick smiled and said, "Don't you worry now, come on, I'll buy you a rose."

He bought the young girl a rose, and asked if she needed a ride home.

"Yes! Please! You can take me to my mother." The young girl said.

Rick followed her direction, and found that they were at the cemetery. The young girl ran to a newly dug grave, and placed her rose in front of it.

Rick quickly picked up his cell phone and called the flower shop "Hi, I've just made an order to deliver a dozen of roses... yes, I'd like to cancel that order... no, I still want those roses, but I'll be delivering it myself."

瑞克走進一家花店去訂了一打的玫瑰花。他要花店幫他把花送給他住在兩百哩外的母親。瑞克其實已經好久沒有見過自己的母親，但他實在是忙到抽不出時間來。

當他從店裡出來的時候，他看到一個小女孩坐在人行道上哭泣著。

「怎麼了嗎？」瑞克問道。

「我想要買一朵玫瑰花給我媽媽，但是我身上的錢不夠，不知道該怎麼辦才好。」

瑞克笑著說：「別擔心了，來吧，我買一朵玫瑰花給妳。」

他買了玫瑰花給小女孩，並且問她需不需要搭便車回家。

「好的！拜託您了！請您帶我到我媽媽那邊。」小女孩說道。

瑞克順著她所指的路開啊開，結果竟然來到一座墓園。小女孩跑向一個新建的墳墓，然後將玫瑰花放在墓前。

瑞克立刻拿起手機撥給花店說道：「嗨，我剛有去訂了一打玫瑰花要託運的……是的，我想取消這個訂單……噢不，我一樣需要那些玫瑰，只是我要親自送過去。」

文法重點

過去完成式 (Past Perfect Tense)

Rick hadn't seen his mother for a while.
（瑞克其實已經好久沒有見過自己的母親。）

除了粗分過去式、現在式與未來式，英文文法裡的時態還可以細分為：一般事實(簡單式)、正在或持續發生(進行式)以及已經發生(完成式)。其中，當我們要表達過去某一時間或某一動作之前已經完成的動作或經驗。我們會用過去完成式，其句型形式為：had + Vpp.，其中 had 是表示過去完成式的助動詞。

- 過去完成式用於表示在過去某個時間點之前，有另一個動作已經持續進行了一段時間，或是已經結束在過去的某個事件之前。

  Lisa had never learned how to cook before she got married.

  （在 Lisa 結婚之前，她從來沒有學過怎麼做菜。）

  Before Peter rushed to the railway station, the train had already departed.

  （在 Peter 趕到火車站之前，火車就已經開走了。）

- 過去完成式常見於故事或報導中的轉述句裡。

  The researcher wondered if the medication had had significant effect on the patient.

  （研究人員在想也許這個藥在病人身上會有顯著的效果。）

  The secretary said that Elaine had left the company already.

  （秘書說 Elaine 已經離開公司了。）

- 過去完成式也會用在表示與過去事實相反的假設語氣句子裡。

  If I had worked hard, I would have gained more bonuses this year.

  （如果我努力工作的話，我今年就可以拿到多一點的獎金。）

  If it had not rained last night, Ray could have come and visited us.

（如果昨天晚上沒有下雨的話，Ray 可能會來拜訪我們。）

- 過去完成式也有進行的形式：had + been Ving，用以強調在過去某一時刻，有一個動作已經持續一段時間，且該動作在那時刻仍持續進行中。

  The student had been chatting before the teacher came into the classroom.

  （學生在老師進教室之前一直在聊天。）

  The pollution had been worsening even if the mayor took tough measures to stop it.

  （污染持續地惡化當中，儘管市長已採用強硬手段來阻止了。）

句型解析

He asked the flower shop to deliver those flowers to his mother, who lived two hundred miles away.

1. He asked the flower shop to deliver those flowers to his

   S V O Infinitive Phr.

   mother, [who lived two hundred miles away].

   Adj. Cl.

2. 本句的“He asked the flower shop to deliver those flowers to his mother”用到 ask sb. to V 的句型。

   ask *(v.)* 問；要求。

3. 本句的“who lived two hundred miles away”是形容詞子句，修飾先行詞 his mother。因為母親這世上只有一個，所以需用「非限定形容詞子句」，也就是關係代名詞前需接逗號，讓形容詞子句只是表示補充說明。

He was just too busy to actually visit her.

1. He was just too busy to actually visit her.

   S BeV Adv. Adv. Adj.→SC Infinitive Phr.

2. 本句用到 too+ adj. + to V 的句型，意為「太…以致於不能」。

   例句：Peter was too short to reach the cabinet.

   Peter 太矮以致於不能碰到櫃櫥。

As he got out of the shop, he saw a young girl sitting on the sidewalk crying.

1. [As he got out of the shop], he saw a young girl

   Adv. Cl. S V O

   sitting on the sidewalk crying.

   Ving → Adj. Phr.

2. 本句的 as 是連接詞，意為「正當……」(=when=while)。
3. 本句的“he saw a young girl sitting on the sidewalk crying”用到了 see (看到；感官動詞)+ O + Vr/Ving 句型。

心情小語

This story teaches us an important lesson: to show filial obedience does not mean spending a lot of money or doing something great to make our parents feel touched and proud. Actually, all we need to do to make them touched is give them a hearty phone call or a warm regard. Making them know that we are doing well is the best comfort to them. It may be too exaggerating if we tell them how much we love them on the phone like what happens in a commercial (sometimes it may be seen as a fraud in our own culture). We do not necessarily do things like that. We can chat about anything with our parents on the phone. Our parents will be happy to receive our calls. Of course, it will be very nice if we can visit and accompany them by ourselves. Please note that we have to seize every opportunity to show our gratitude and love to our parents since we have little time to do that while they have taken good care of us since we were born.

這個故事告訴了我們一件很重要的事：孝順父母親其實並不一定要花很多錢，或是做什麼轟轟烈烈的事來讓父母感動；只要一通電話，或是偶爾關心一下父母，讓父母知道你現在過得很好，就是對父母最大的安慰了。當然像某電信廣告這樣沒事打電話回去對父母說「我愛你」是有點太矯情（而且還可能被認為是詐騙），不需要做到這種地步；就算沒有要幹嘛，打個電話回家跟父母天南地北亂聊也沒關係，父母親還是會很開心的。當然，能夠親自出現在他們面前就更好了。要記得，父母親花了他們大半的人生在照顧我們，而我們能夠回報的時間其實只有一點點，要好好把握才行。

Keith was walking along a beach when suddenly he found a lamp.

Not sure what to do, he rubbed it, and then a genie appeared.

"Greetings mortal, thank you for freeing me. I will grant you one wish..."

"Only one? What happened to three wishes?"

"Look pal, it's been millenniums since I've been trapped inside this lamp, and all I do is granting people's wishes! So either you take the offer and get this over with quickly or just leave it for someone else." The genie retorted impatiently.

"OK, OK... I get it... geez." Keith replied, "Oh, I got one. I'd really like to visit Hawaii, but can't afford the plane ticket. Therefore, I'd like you to build a bridge from California to Hawaii."

"Your wish has to be practical! Do you know the engineering to design such bridge, and the materials it would take? Not to mention the workers needed for such a huge project..."

"Fine, I got your point!" Keith thought for a while, "Oh, I do have a practical wish. You see, I've always wanted to understand women..."

"How would you like your bridge? Two lanes or four?" the genie responded.

基斯有天在海邊走著，突然發現一個神燈。

不知道該怎麼做才對，他便把神燈拿來擦了擦，一個精靈從裡頭冒了出來。

「你好，凡人，謝謝你放我出來，我可以給你一個願望……」

「一個？不是三個嗎？」基斯問道。

「聽著，我已經被困在這燈裡幾千年了，一天到晚都只能幫人家完成願望。所以要嘛你就快點許一許，不然就把機會留給其他人好了。」

「好啦好啦……我知道了啦……天啊。」基斯回道：「有了！我一直很想去夏威夷，但是機票實在是太貴了，我要你蓋座從加州通到夏威夷的大橋。」

「你的願望應該要實際一點啊！你知道光是要設計這座大橋需要多複雜的工程學嗎？還有耗費的材料？更別提這樣大工程所需的人力……」

「好啦！我知道你的意思了啦！」基斯想了一會兒：「噢，我是有個比較實際一點的願望啦；你知道的，我一直想要能夠瞭解女人……」

「這座橋你要幾線道？雙線道還四線道？」精靈回答道。

文法重點

現在完成式 (Present Perfect Tense)

Look pal, it's been millenniums since I've been trapped inside this lamp...
（聽著，我已經被困在這燈裡幾千年了……）

除了粗分過去式、現在式與未來式，英文文法裡的時態還可以細分為：一般事實(簡單式)、正在或持續發生(進行式)以及已經發生(完成式)。其中，當我們想要表示過去的某個動作，到現在已經完成，或是某一個動作從過去的某一個時間點開始，一直持續到現在的時間剛好完成，我們會用現在完成式，其句型形式為：have/has + Vpp，而 have/has 是表示現在完成式的助動詞。值得一提的是，現在完成式通常會與時間副詞 already, lately, recently，或是帶有 for 或 since 表時間的介系詞片語一起連用。

- 表示過去某一時刻開始的動作持續到現在，或是過去的某個動作，不久前才剛剛完成。

What have you been doing lately?

（你剛剛在做什麼？）

Have you finished your assignments?

（你寫完功課了嗎？）

I have just completed the mission.

（我剛剛才完成任務。）

- 強調從過去到現在的經驗。

Have you been to Japan?

（你曾去過日本嘛？）

Have she ever talked to you?

（他曾經跟你說過話嗎？。）

- 指某個動作從過去到現在，已經累積多少的次數或時間。這個表示句中動作，在往後的時間裡，有可能還會繼續下去。

Jane has lived here since 1988.

（Jane 從 1988 年起就住在這兒了。）

Eric has read the documents for two hours.

（Eric 已經讀這一份文件讀了兩個小時了。）

- 過去完成式也有進行的形式：have/ has + been Ving，用以強調在過去某一時刻，有一個動作已經持續一段時間直到現在，且該動作在那時刻仍持續進行中。

David and Fion have been seeing each other for one month now.

（David 和 Fion 已經約會一個月了。）

I have been waiting for you since 5 o'clock.

（我從 5 點就一直在等你。）

句型解析

Not sure what to do, he rubbed it, and then a genie appeared.

1. Not sure what to do, he rubbed it, and then a genie appeared.

   Participial Construction S1 V2 O Conj. Adv. S2 V2

2. 本句的"Not sure what to do"是分詞構句，可還原為 "Because he was no sure what to do,⋯"。

I'd really like to visit Hawaii, but can't afford the plane ticket.

1. I 'd really like to visit Hawaii, but can 't afford the ⋯ ticket.

   S Aux. Adv. V Inifinitve Phr. Conj. Aux. Adv. V O

2. 本句的"I'd really like to visit Hawaii"是"I would like to visit Hawaii"。句型 would like to + V，意為「（比較委婉客氣的語氣）想要去⋯」(=want to+ V= feel like + Ving)。

Do you know the engineering to design such bridge, and the materials it would take?

1. Do you know the engineering to design such bridge, and

   Aux. S V O Conj.

   the materials [it would take]?

   O ← Adj. Cl.

2. 本句"to design such bridge"是不定詞片語，修飾 the engineering。
3. "the materials it would take"可還原成"the materials which it would take"，這裡的 which it would take 是形容詞子句，修飾 the materials。

心情小語

When a woman says to a man, "I do not like gifts. Gifting would only be money wasted", it doesn't mean she really thinks it is fine that you do not send her any gifts. That is, she does not want to be regarded as a childish material girl. However, if a man does believe what his girlfriend said and does not send any gifts, he has to get ready to face the huge disaster 100 times more powerful than the comet attack. Most women expect their men can discern their innermost thoughts and do what they really want them to do. However, men and women have different ways of thinking, Men are linear, so they take no as no when women say no to them. Therefore, rather than say indirectly and give many hints, women have to express what they want clearly when they communicate with men. Likewise, men have to learn to read what women mean between the lines. It takes time and consideration to understand each other. However, only through this, men from the Mars and women from the Venus can live in peace on earth.

當一個女人對男人說「我不喜歡禮物，送禮物真的很浪費錢」的時候，並不是她真的認為你不要送沒關係，而是她不希望被認為是個很物質、膚淺、隨便送點東西就可以討好的幼稚小女孩；但如果你信了這種話然後真的沒送的話，那就準備迎接比彗星撞地球還恐怖一百倍的地球浩劫吧。因為女人通常會期望男人可以了解她內心真正的想法，然後做出她「想像中」應該出現的反應。只是男人的思考是很直線的，妳自己都說不要，那當然就不要囉！所以如果女人希望男人怎麼樣的時候，可以盡量明顯一點地表達出來，而不要講得不清不楚，或是刻意裝死然後自己在那邊演腦內小劇場，覺得男人會懂妳的「暗示」；那是不可能的，別傻了。而男人也要學著去理解女生每一句話都一定有某種含意，不是字面上看到的那麼簡單，必須多花很多的時間和心思去理解她的個性才有辦法解讀；唯有這樣，來自火星的男人和來自金星的女人，才有辦法在地球上和平共存。

生活篇 對話 1

Situation: Sarah's mother had asked her to go grocery shopping before she went to work this morning. Since Sarah is still busy with her homework, she asks her brother, Clark, to go to the market for her.

情境：Sarah 的母親今天早上出門時要她去買些日常用品。因為 Sarah 還在忙作業，她要她弟弟 Clark 幫她去市場。

Sarah	Mom had asked me to go grocery shopping before she left for work this morning, but I need to finish my school project. Can you go for me, Clark?	媽今天早上出門時要我去買些日常用品，但我還沒寫完學校作業。Clark，你能幫我去嗎？
Clark	I can. I am done with my homework. What did mom want you to buy?	我可以。我已經寫完作業了。媽要你買什麼？
Sarah	Well, she wanted me to buy enough groceries for the whole week. Besides meat, some fish and vegetables, we can buy whatever else we want for snacks and breakfast.	嗯，她要我買整個禮拜的雜貨量。除了肉、魚還有菜，我們還可以買任何我們想要吃的零食和早餐。
Clark	What do you want for breakfast?	你早餐想吃什麼？
Sarah	I guess some cereal as usual.	我想跟平常一樣，穀物就好了。

Clark	I do not want cereal every day. I will buy some pancakes and syrup then.	我不想要天天吃麥片。我要買一些鬆餅跟糖漿。
Clark	Do we still have enough coffee and cream for mom and dad?	爸媽要喝的咖啡和奶精還有嗎？
Sarah	Yes, we do. Speaking of coffee and cream, you'd better buy some milk also. We almost ran out of it.	還有。說到咖啡和奶精，你最好也買些牛奶。我們快喝完了。

生活篇 對話 2

Situation: Sarah and her brother, Clark, are discussing what they are going to buy at the market.

情境：Sarah 和她弟弟 Clark 正討論要去市場買些什麼。

Clark	What do you want for snacks?	妳零食要買什麼？
Sarah	Some chips would be fine with me. You probably want your chocolate cookies.	我想要一些洋芋片。你可能想要些巧克力餅乾吧。
Clark	I'd better write down all these things; otherwise, I will forget them by the time I get to the market. I would hate to make two trips to take care of things.	我最好把要買的東西寫下來。否則，我到市場時會忘記我要買什麼。我不喜歡再回頭去將東西買齊。
Clark	Do we need anything for dessert?	我們要買什麼甜點嗎？

Sarah	I am on a diet so except those delicious pastries you can buy anything you want.	我在節食中，所以除了那些好吃糕點之外，你可以買你想要的東西。
Clark	Just asking.	我只是問問。
Sarah	You have quite a few items to take care of. You need to get going.	你有許多東西要買，你最好快去。
Clark	Yes, the list is quite long. By the time I get to the cashier to pay, I will probably have a full shopping cart. OK, I am all set to go. I will be back soon.	對啊，清單真的很長。要去櫃檯付錢時，我大概會有快滿出來的推車吧。好，我要出門了，一會兒就回來。
Sarah	Drive carefully please!	小心開車！

單字與實用例句

- grocery *(n.)* 雜貨

  Frank usually goes to the nearby supermarket and buys a box of groceries once in a month.
  Frank 常常每月一次去附近的超市買一箱的食物雜貨。

- busy *(adj.)* 忙碌

  William is busy with his project.
  William 正在忙著他的計畫。

- buy *(v.)* 購買

  Think twice before you buy anything: do you just want it or really need it.
  你買任何東西前要先多再想一想：你只是想要它還是真的需要它。

- guess *(v.)* 猜想

  It is hard to guess what is in a woman's mind.
  猜女人心裡在想什麼是件難事。

- probably *(adv.)* 或許

  Do not underestimate yourself. You will probably be somebody some day in the future.
  不要小看自己。你或許未來有一天會成為知名人物。

- forget *(v.)* 忘記

  Emily forgot to email these important notices to our clients.
  Emily 忘記用電郵寄出這些重要通知給我們的客戶。

- delicious *(adj.)* 可口的

  The café offers delicious cake and desserts as well.
  這間咖啡店也提供可口的蛋糕跟甜點。

- take care of *(v. phr.)* 照顧

  The caring mother took good care of her sick children.
  這位慈愛的母親細心照顧她生病的孩子們。

好用主題用語，用法解說

Besides meat, some fish and vegetables, we can buy whatever else we want for snacks and breakfast.

I am on a diet so except those delicious pastries you can buy anything you want.

除了…之外：在英文中，besides 與 except 都是「除了…之外」，但是 besides 表示「除了…之外，還有…」是一種附加的關係；except 表示「除了…之外，不再有…」是一種排他的關係。

- 除了…之外，還有…：

  Besides English, I major in math and physics.

  （除了英文，我還主修數學與物理。）

- 除了 besides，in addition to 也可以表示「除了…之外，還有…」。

  In addition to fried fish, I had chips for lunch.

  （除了炸魚，我午餐還吃了薯條。）

- 除了…之外，不再有…：

  Jane eats anything except durians.

  （除了榴槤之外，Jane 什麼都吃。）

  The museum is open every day except Monday.

  （這間博物館禮拜一休館。）

- 除了 besides 與 except 表示「除了…之外」，還有 apart from 與 aside from 這兩個常見的片語可用來表示「除了…之外」。但這兩個片語的用法皆可表示「除了…之外，還有…」與「除了…之外，不再有…」，必須從文句語意中去理解區分它們正確的意思。

  Marilyn was a weird girl; she wore nothing apart from white dresses.

  （Marilyn 是個奇特的女孩；她只穿白色的洋裝。）

  Alice likes travelling. Aside from London, she has been to Amsterdam, Dublin, and Barcelona.

  （Alice 喜歡旅遊。除了倫敦，她還去過阿姆斯特丹、都柏林與巴塞隆納。）

Unit 10 假設語氣

勵志篇 故事

A professor held up a glass of water in his class one day. He held it up for everyone to see and asked "What would happen if I held it up like this for a few minutes?"

"Nothing.", the students replied.

"OK, what would it happen if I held it up like this for an hour?" the professor asked.

"Your arm would begin to ache." said one of the students.

"That's correct, now what would happen if I held it up for a day?"

The students looked at each other, and one of the students said "Your arm could go numb, you might have severe muscle stress, and you might be paralyzed and have to go to hospital."

The professor said "Very good, but during all this, did the weight of the glass change?"

"No...?" said the students.

"Then what caused the pain and muscle stress?" asked the professor.

"Because you wouldn't put the glass down." The whole class burst into laughter.

The professor smiled and said, “Exactly! Then why let the problem of life stay in your head when you can simply put it down?”

有一天，一位教授帶著一杯水到課堂上。他將水杯舉高讓大家都看得到，然後問道：「如果我把這杯子舉個幾分鐘會怎樣？」

「不會怎樣？」學生們回答。

「好，那如果我這樣舉個一小時呢？」

「你的手會開始痛。」一個學生説道。

「沒錯，那如果我舉一整天呢？」

學生們面面相覷，其中一個學生説道：「你的手會麻掉，你可能還會有嚴重的肌肉緊繃，也有可能會癱瘓到需要送醫的地步。」

「非常好！但在這些過程之中，杯子的重量減輕了嗎？」

「沒有……」學生們説道。

「那是什麼導致這些疼痛和肌肉緊繃？」教授問道。

「因為你就一直不把杯子放下去啊。」全班哄堂大笑。

教授微笑著説道：「完全正確，那麼為什麼要讓人生中的煩惱一直困擾著你，當你明明可以很簡單地放下它？」

文法重點

假設語氣 (Subjunctive Mood)

"What would happen if I held it up like this for a few minutes?"
「如果我把這杯子舉個幾分鐘會怎樣？」

在英文文法中，主要有三種語氣：一般直述的陳述語氣、表示命令或建議的祈使句、以及與事實相反的假設語氣。其中，假設語氣句型是利用動詞變化來表示與現在或與過去事實相反的的一種形式。
與現在事實相反的假設語氣，會用過去式來表示假設語氣。

- 在最常見的 If (假如)副詞子句，與現在事實相反的假設語氣句型為：If S were/Vpt, S would/could/should/might Vr；或是 If S were/Vpt, S would/could/should/might Vr 。

  If I were you, I wouldn't go out this afternoon.

  （如果我是你，我今天下午就不會出去。）

  If he knew the truth, he would be furious.

  （如果他知道真相的話，他一定會生氣的。）

- wish (希望)引導與現在事實相反假設語氣名詞子句的句型：S wish that S were + SC / would/could/should/might Vr 。

  I wish that I were a handsome man.

  （我希望我是一個帥哥。）

  Kate wishes that she could go on a trip.

  （Kate 希望她可以去旅行。）

- 表示提議、要求、命令等動詞（suggest, advise, recommend, maintain, request, demand）後面的名詞子句為與現在事實相反的假設語氣句型：S suggest that S (should) Vr 。

  The expert suggested that more strict measures be taken to improve the city's environment.

（這位專家建議，需採取更嚴厲的手段來改善這一個城市的環境。）

The manager demands that the secretary should see him immediately.

（經理要秘書應該要立刻去見他。）

句型解析

"Your arm could go numb, you might have severe muscle stress, and you might be paralyzed and have to go to hospital."

1. "Your arm could go numb, you might have
   S Aux. Vr. Adj.→SC S Aux. Vr.
   severe muscle stress, and you might be paralyzed
   O Conj. S Aux. BeV V Passive
   and have to go to hospital."
   Conj. Vr Infinitive Phr.
2. 這裡 go numb 意為「變得麻木，失去知覺」。
   numb *(v.)* 麻木。
3. paralyze *(v.)* 使…麻痺；使…癱瘓。
   例句：The power failure paralyzed the public transit of the city.
   停電癱瘓了城市的大眾運輸。

The whole class burst into laughter.

1. The whole class burst into laughter.

   S　　　　　V Phr.V

2. 片語 burst into laughter 意為「突然大笑出來」；亦可改寫為 burst out laughing。常見的用法還有：「突然哭出來」burst into tears 或 burst out crying。

"Exactly! Then why let the problem of life stay in your head when you can simply put it down?"

1. "Exactly! Then why let the problem of life stay in your head

   Adv. Adv. V　　O　　Vr　Adv. Phr.

   [when you can simply put it down]? "

   Adv. Cl.

2. exactly *(adv.)* 正是；正確地(=correctly)。
3. 本句副詞 simply 不是指「簡單地」，而是另一個意思「只是」(=just)。

心情小語

Worries and vexations in life are just like that cup of water in the professor's hand. If we give it a second thought, we will find the situations are not as bad as we think. However, if we put them in our heart for a few more days, they sting. Later, these worries will paralyze you, making you unable to do anything. Thinking and taking challenges are two important things in life while "letting it go" is another important lesson we have to learn. We have to learn to let our worries go before we go to bed each night. Actually, many worries will grow larger if we think it over and over again in our mind. It turns out to be that we will become tired and more anxious while worries still exist there in our mind. Therefore, it is better that we put them aside first and take some rest. It is possible that we will figure out the solutions after we have sufficient rest.

人生中的煩惱就像教授手中的那杯水一樣。在腦子裡想個幾分鐘，還好嘛！但放在心裡多想個幾天，它就開始會痛了；再想久一點，煩惱就會開始癱瘓你，讓你什麼事也做不了。在人生中去思考和挑戰困難是很重要的，但更重要的是要學會每天在睡覺之前，「放下」心裡頭的煩惱。很多煩惱其實你一直去想它、一直在那邊不知道該怎麼辦，只會讓自己更亂、更累、更焦慮而已，煩惱並不會因此消失。所以這時不如先將它暫時放下，讓自己好好休息，說不定經過充足的睡眠，讓大腦重開機之後，就會立刻靈光一閃想到解決方法了也說不定！

Jill invited her father over for dinner one evening. Her father was suspicious that Jill and her roommate, Jack, were having a relationship.

He watched the two of them interact over the course of the evening and getting more and more convinced that there was something between them.

Knowing only too well what her father was thinking, Jill said, “Dad, I know what you’re thinking, but rest assured, Jack and I are strictly roommates, nothing else.”

A few days later, Jack went to Jill and said, “Have you seen my blue mug? Well, ever since your father visited us, I can’t seem to find it. You don’t think he would have taken it, do you?”

“I doubt it, but I’ll text him, just be sure.”, replied Jill.

Jill took her cell phone and texted, “Dear Dad, while I’m not saying you ‘did’ take away a blue mug from my house, and I’m not saying you ‘didn’t’, but that fact remains that it’s missing since you were here for dinner that evening. Love, Jill”

Few minutes later, Jill received a reply from her father, “Dear Jill, while I’m not saying you ‘do’ sleep with Jack, and I’m not saying you ‘don’t’, but the fact remains that he would have found his mug by now if he was sleeping in his own bed. Love, Dad.”

一天晚上，吉兒邀請她爸爸來共進晚餐。她的爸爸一直在懷疑吉兒和她的室友傑克兩個人在一起。

一整個晚上，他都在觀察兩人的互動，然後越來越確信兩個人之間一定有什麼。

太了解自己的爸爸在想什麼，吉兒便開口説道：「爸，我知道你在想什麼，但是請放心好了，我和傑克只是純粹的室友關係，其他什麼都沒有。」

幾天之後，傑克問吉兒：「妳有看到我的藍色馬克杯嗎？自從妳爸來過之後我就找不到那個杯子了。妳覺得會不會是妳爸拿走了？」

「我很懷疑，不過我會發個簡訊問他看看。」吉兒回答道。

吉兒拿出手機，並且打著：「親愛的老爸，當然我不是説你『有』從我們這裡拿走一個藍色的馬克杯，但我也不是説你『沒有』。但事實就是，自從你那個晚上來吃過晚餐之後，它就不見了。愛你的 吉兒。」

幾分鐘之後吉兒收到了她爸爸的回覆：「親愛的吉兒，當然我不是説妳『有』跟傑克睡在一起，但我也不是説妳『沒有』。但事實就是，如果他是睡在自己房間裡的話，那他現在早就找到那個馬克杯了。愛妳的 老爸。」

文法重點

假設語氣 (Subjunctive Mood)

You don't think he would have taken it, do you?"
（妳覺得會不會是妳爸拿走了？）

在英文文法中，主要有三種語氣：一般直述的陳述語氣、表示命令或建議的祈使句、以及與事實相反的假設語氣。其中，假設語氣句型是利用動詞變化來表示與現在或與過去事實相反的一種形式。
與現在事實相反的假設語氣，會用過去完成式來表示假設語氣。

- 在最常見的 If (假如)副詞子句，與現在事實相反的假設語氣句型為：If S had Vpp, S would/could/should/might have Vpp。

  If Gary had quitted smoking, he would not have come down with lung cancer last year.

  （如果 Gary 有戒煙的話，那他去年就不會因為肺癌而倒下了。）

  If I had been more careful, I would not have been robbed of the purse.

  （如果我更小心的話，我的錢包就不會被搶走了。）

- wish (希望)引導與過去事實相反假設語氣名詞子句的句型：S wish that S had Vpp；或是 S wish that S would/could/should/might have Vpp。

  Fanny wishes that she could have studied harder when she was a high school student.

  （Fanny 希望當她還是高中生的時候，有好好地用功讀書。）

  Leo wishes that he would have proposed to Mary before she left for Japan last week.

  （Leo 希望在上星期 Mary 離開去日本之前，他就已經跟她求婚了。）

- 表示過去該做而未做的假設語氣句型：S should/would/could have Vpp。

  Peter should have fully prepared for the concert, but he fooled around last night.

  （Peter 應該要對這場音樂會有充分的準備，但他昨晚浪費太多時間了。）

  I could have won the race, but I sprained my ankle.

  （我本來在這次賽跑可以贏的，但是我扭傷了我的腳踝。）

句型解析

Her father was suspicious that Jill and her roommate, Jack, were having a relationship.

1. Her father was suspicious [that Jill and her roommate... a relationship].

   S BeV Adj.→SC N. Cl.

2. suspicious *(adj.)* 懷疑；起疑心的。

   本句亦可寫成：Her father suspected that Jill and her roommate Jack were having a relationship.

   suspect *(v.)* 懷疑。

3. 名詞子句 Jill and her roommate, Jack, were having a relationship 用到進行式，意為「他們正在交往中」。

   本句亦可寫成：Jill and her roommate, Jack, were seeing each other.（正在交往中）

He watched the two of them interact over the course of the evening, getting more and more convinced that there was something between them.

1. He watched the two of them interact

S V O Vr

over the course of the evening, getting more... between them.

Adv. Phr. Participial Construction

2. 本句的“He watched the two of them interact over the course of the evening”用到了 watch (觀看；感官動詞)+ O + Vr/Ving 句型。

3. 本句的“getting more and more convinced that there was something between them”是分詞構句，可還原成“and got more and more convinced that there was something between them”。

convince *(v.)* 說服。句型 S be convinced that S+V 意為「……相信……」(=S believer that S+V) 。

... that fact remains that it's missing since you were here for dinner that evening.

1. ... that fact remains [that it's missing since you were...

S V N. Cl.→ SC

that evening].

2. remain *(v.)* 保持，仍是(=stay=keep)。

例句：The air-conditioned room remained cool even in a hot summer day.
（這一間有空調的房間，僅管是在炎炎夏日仍能保持涼爽。）

心情小語

"Just see what you have done! What a great embarrassment!" If Jill now were in front of me, I would say that to her. Honesty is the best policy. If Jill had confessed to her father, she would not have made herself so embarrassed. Those businessmen in the food industry who put additives into their products thought their wrongdoing would not be disclosed. However, when their wrongdoing is disclosed, their credits and reputation will be greatly damaged no matter how many apologies or confessions they made. Therefore, we have to understand that there is no "perfect crime" in the world. Traces will be left once one does something. Following the traces, we can find out the truth. Therefore, we should choose not to commit crime at the beginning. If we do, we have to take the consequences and responsibility.

「糗大了吧？啊哈哈，妳看看妳」，如果現在吉兒在我面前，我應該會這樣跟她說。誠實是最好的策略。如果吉兒可以對自己的爸爸坦承一點，說不定不會搞到現在這麼難堪。就像那些在食物裡摻了添加物的廠商，剛開始一定也以為反正神不知鬼不覺，沒有人會注意到，等到有一天爆出來，這時再多的道歉、再多的懺悔，也挽不回失去辛苦建立多年的商譽和信用了。所以我們必須認清一個事實，就是這個世界上並不存在著什麼「完美犯罪」這種事；任何事只要是人做的，就一定會留下痕跡，只要有跡可循，就一定會被找到破綻。與其這樣，那我們不如一開始就不要做；要是做了，就要有勇於承擔後果的心裡準備，而不要心存僥倖。

生活篇 對話 1

Situation: Jim is having problems with his homework. His friend Tom is having problems with building a jet model. They are seeking each other's help.

情境：Jim 寫作業有些困難。他的朋友 Tom 也不是很會組噴射機模型。他們正在尋求彼此的協助。

Tom	Jim, what are you doing?	Jim，你在做什麼？
Jim	I have been trying to solve this physics problem for the last half hour, and I still have no idea how to do it.	我剛半小時都在解這道物理題目，但到現在我還是不知道怎麼解。
Tom	When do you have to turn it in?	你什麼時候要交？
Jim	It is due at the end of this week.	這週末前要交出去。
Tom	Well, it is only Monday. Why don't you get some after-school-tutoring tomorrow?	嗯，現在才禮拜一。你明天何不去找課後輔導中心幫忙？
Jim	I have to sign up for it first. I guess I will go sign up for the Wednesday session tomorrow.	我得先登記啊。我想我明天應該會去登記星期三的時段吧。
Tom	You should reread the chapter before you show up for the session. It will help you understand the subject matter better.	你去課後輔導中心前應該先讀過該章節。那將會幫你更清楚的瞭解題目內容。
Jim	OK, I will do that.	好吧，我會的。

生活篇 對話 2

Tom	Now that your problem is solved, I need you to lend me a hand with my problem.	既然你的問題解決了，我要你幫我解決我的問題。
Jim	What is up?	怎麼了？
Tom	I need to build a new jet model for John. I was putting his jet model away, and somehow I accidentally dropped it. It was broken into pieces.	我需要幫 John 蓋一個噴射機模型。我本來想把他的噴射機模型收好，但卻不知怎麼地把它摔壞了。它現在支離破碎。
Jim	How clumsy of you! Does she know?	你真是破壞大王啊！他知道了嗎？
Tom	I told him about it. I could not lie to him. Ah, I wish I have not touched his jet model! What should I do then?	我跟他說了。我不想騙他。啊，我真希望不要碰他的噴射機模型，現在我是要怎麼辦呢？
Jim	Get help from somebody who knows how to build a jet model. I would not be of any help to you in this project.	去找你知道會蓋噴射機模型的人幫忙啊。我其實幫不了你什麼忙。
Tom	Who do you suggest I ask?	你建議我找誰？
Jim	How about Mr. Brown? He will be glad to help you out. Why don't you give him a call?	Brown 先生開過玩具店。他會很高興幫你的。你何不打電話給他？
Tom	You are right.	你說的真對。

單字與實用例句

- seek *(v.)* 尋找

  The lady is seeking her lost purse.
  這位女士在尋找她丟失的包包。

- turn in *(v.)* 繳交

  All of the students have to turn in a term paper at the end of the semester.
  所有的學生學期末都必須要交一份期末報告。

- due *(adj.)* 到期的

  The book you borrowed from the library is due. You had better return it as soon as possible.
  你從圖書館借來的書到期了。你最好儘快歸還。

- subject *(n.)* 科目

  How many subjects do you have in your senior high school?
  你高中有多少科目要學？

- solve *(v.)* 解決

  Zoe is an optimistic person; she thinks there are no problems but be solved.
  Zoe 是一個樂觀的人；她認為沒有問題不能解決。

- jet *(n.)* 噴射機

  Ray has a whole collection of jet models.
  Ray 有一整組噴射機模型。

- clumsy *(adj.)* 笨拙的

  Professor as Victor is, he is clumsy at household chores.
  雖然 Victor 是位教授，但是他卻拙於家事。

好用主題用語，用法解說

Why don’t you get some after-school-tutoring tomorrow?
How about Mr. Brown?

表示建議的句型：當我們要在英文口語會話中提出建議或邀請，有下列幾種常見的句型。

句型	例句
Why not V ?	• Why not go to see the movie with me? （何不和我一起去看電影呢？） • Why not take a break? （何不休息一下？） • Why not give her a chance? （不妨給她一次機會？）
Why don’t you V?	• Why don’t you ask for help? （你為什麼不找人幫忙？） • Why don’t you go to see a doctor? （你為何不去看醫生呢？） • Why don’t you follow the advice? •（你為什麼不聽勸呢？）
How about?	• How about fried chicken? （炸雞如何？） • How about Friday? （星期五好嗎？） • How about Taipei? （台北好嗎？）
Let’s V.	• Let’s go shopping.（我們去逛街吧。） • Let’s enjoy the show.（讓我們享受這一場秀吧。） • Let’s do it.（我們來做吧！）

Unit 11 祈使句與被動式

勵志篇 故事

There was a farmer who had a horse and a goat. One day, the horse became ill; the veterinarian checked the horse and said "Your horse was infected by a virus. He needs to take this medicine for three days. If he doesn't get any better, I think you need to put him down."

The goat heard their conversation. After they gave the horse the medicine and left, the goat came and said to the horse "Be strong, my friend! Get up or they're going to kill you!"

The next day, after the horse took the medicine, the goat came back again.

"Come on! Get up! I'll help you, let's go!"

The third day, the vet came and gave the horse medicine.

"Unfortunately, we're going to put him down tomorrow. Otherwise the virus will infect other animals."

After they left, the goat approached the horse and said "Listen pal, it's now or never! Get up! Come on! That's it, slowly! You can do it! Don't give up on yourself now! Come on!"

The horse slowly stood up and began to walk! Within a few minutes, the horse could run again!

The farmer came back, seeing the horse running in the field. He yelled with excitement “It’s a miracle! Let’s kill the goat and celebrate!”

從前有個農夫，他養了一匹馬和一隻羊。有一天，馬病了，獸醫檢查過後說道：「你的馬被病毒感染了，讓他吃這個藥三天，如果病情沒改善的話，我想你就得撲殺他了。」

羊聽到了這個對話。在他們餵完藥走掉之後，羊走過來對馬說道：「堅強一點，我的朋友。趕快站起來，不然他們就要殺死你了。」

第二天，在馬吃完藥之後，羊又過來。

「加油！起來！我來幫你！快點！」

第三天，獸醫過來餵完藥之後說道：「很不幸的，我們明天就必須要撲殺他了。否則病毒可能會傳染給其他動物。」

當他們離開之後，羊走到馬的身邊說道：「聽著老兄，現在再不做就永遠沒機會了！站起來！加油！就是這樣！慢慢的，你辦得到！千萬不要放棄喔！加油！」

馬緩緩的站起來走了幾步，幾分鐘之後，他又再次健步如飛了！

農夫回來剛好看到馬在田野中奔跑著，他興奮的大喊著：「這真是個奇蹟啊！我們把羊宰來慶祝吧！」

文法重點

祈使語氣 (Imperative Mood)

Be strong, my friend! Get up or they're going to kill you!
（堅強一點，我的朋友。趕快站起來，不然他們就要殺死你了。）

英文文法中，除了表示陳述的直述語氣以及與事實相反的假設語氣之外，還有用來表示請求、命令、禁止、或勸導的祈使語氣。祈使句的句型中常見主詞(you)省略，please 的出現，以及句中動詞須用原形動詞。

例句：Have a seat, please.
（請坐。）
Be careful when you cross a road.
（過馬路的時候要小心。）
Don't tease the dog.
（不要去逗狗。）
Let's go.
（我們走吧。）

此外，祈使句後也常見由 and 或 or 連接另一個表示條件的句子。

例句：Get up early, <u>or</u> you will miss the first train.
（早一點起床，<u>否則</u>你會錯過第一班火車。）
Work hard, <u>and</u> you will make it someday in the near future.
（努力工作，<u>那麼</u>你在不久的將來就達成的。）

句型解析

There was a farmer who had a horse and a goat.

1. <u>There</u> <u>was</u> <u>a farmer</u> [<u>who had a horse and a goat</u>].

   Adv. BeV O Adj. Cl.

2. there + BeV + S 的句型是地方副詞在句首的倒裝句，主詞在 BeV 之後。以本句為例，因為主詞是 a farmer，所以 BeV 須用第三人稱的 was。

3. 本句“who had a horse and a goat”是形容詞子句，修飾先行詞 a farmer。

If he doesn't get any better, I think you need to put him down.

1. [If he doesn't get any better], I think [(that) you need to put him down].

   Adv. Cl. S V N. Cl.→ O

2. 本句的副詞子句“If he doesn't get any better”，表示「條件」。

3. 本句的“(that)you need to put him down”是名詞子句作 think 的受詞。

4. 動詞片語 put down 原意為「將……放下」，在本句衍生為「將……處死」。

The farmer came back, seeing the horse running in the field.

1. The farmer came back, seeing the horse running in the field.

   S V Adv. Participial Construction

2. 本句的“..., seeing the horse running in the field”是分詞構句，可還原為“..., and he saw the horse running in the field”。

3. 本句的“seeing the horse running in the field”用到了“see (看見)+ O+ V/Ving”的句型。

心情小語

We used to be taught that only hardworking staff who focused on their own share in the company would be noticed and promoted by the boss. In reality, the situation is the other way around. Most bosses do not care how much effort we make; what they pay attention to is the result. Thus, those who could claim the results will be favored by bosses. However, many people despite those who claim credits but blame on others. To solve the dilemma, we have to figure out some smart ways to make our bosses aware of our efforts and credits during our "hard" work, such as regular reports, or frequent comments in meetings. Otherwise, we will be like the silent goat in the story, working the hardest, but got killed in the end. Whether these strategies work or not, if we say something at work at least our bosses will not have the impression that we do not make any contribution. On the contrary, they will think we really make some effort.

以往長輩都會教我們說，工作時不要刻意求表現，只要默默努力，主管一定會注意到。但這其實是理想狀態；現實是，大多數的主管根本不可能會注意到這些。因為通常主管都只看結果，所以誰能夠在最後表現說「都是我的功勞」，就容易受到主管的青睞。只是大家都很看不起爭功諉過的人，偏偏不爭功諉過的話，又很難生存下去，那怎麼辦呢？所以我們就必須想辦法讓主管在過程之中就注意到，誰是付出最多、最認真的那個人。這方法很多，例如定時提出報告，或是在開會時多多發言，不管有用沒用，只要多表示自己的意見，主管就不會有那種「都不知道你在幹嘛」的感覺；而當最後問題解決或是案子成功之後，他也一定會記得，你為這個案子也付出不少心力，就不會像故事中的羊一樣，明明付出最多的是他，最後卻還是被犧牲掉。

幽默篇 故事

Bill Gates died and went up to Heaven. Saint Peter showed him a beautiful 20-room house with a tennis court. Bill Gates was pleased, and spent several months there.

One day, while he was enjoying one of Heaven's many beautiful parks, he ran into a man dressed in a fine tailored suit.

"That's a nice suit, sir." Said Bill Gates, "Where did you get it?"

"It was given to me." The man replied, "I was given a hundred of these when I get here, along with a mansion on the hill overlooking a beautiful lake, with a golf course and a Porsche."

Bill Gates was really surprised "Were you the Pope or some really famous doctor who invented medicine to cure cancer?"

"No," the man replied, "I'm Edward Smith, Captain of the Titanic."

Hearing this made Bill Gates quite angry; he went to see St. Peter immediately.

"How could you only give me a house, when you gave this guy a mansion, fancy suits and expensive car? He's just the captain of the Titanic! I invented the Windows operation system! Why does he deserve better?"

"Well yeah, "said St. Peters, "but the Titanic only crashed once."

比爾蓋茲死了之後上天堂，聖彼得給他一棟有著 20 個房間和私人網球場的大房子。比爾蓋茲很滿意，並在那邊生活了好幾個月。

有一天，當他正悠閒地在天堂其中一個美麗的公園中享受時，他遇到一個穿著高級訂製西裝的人。

「這真是套好西裝啊，這位先生。」比爾蓋茲說道：「你是在哪弄到的？」

「他們給我的。」那人說道：「他們給了我好幾百件這種西裝，還有一棟位於山丘上可以俯瞰整個美麗湖畔和私人高爾夫球場的大豪宅，以及一輛保時捷。」

比爾蓋茲吃驚地問道：「你是教宗嗎？還是某個發明治療癌症藥物的名醫？」

「不是，我是鐵達尼號的船長，愛德華史密斯。」那人回道。

一聽到這個比爾蓋茲整個很不爽，他立刻跑去找聖彼得。

「你怎麼可以只給我一棟房子，卻給這傢伙一棟豪宅、華麗的西裝、和名車？他也只不過是鐵達尼號的船長而已，我發明了 Windows 作業系統耶！為什麼他待遇就比我好？」

「是沒錯啦，」聖彼得說道：「但鐵達尼號只撞毀（crash 另有『當機』的意思）過一次。」

文法重點

被動語態 (Passive Voice)

I was given a hundred of these when I get here, along with a mansion on the hill overlooking a beautiful lake, with a golf course and a Porsche.
（他們給了我好幾百件這種西裝，還有一棟位於山丘上可以俯瞰整個美麗湖畔和私人高爾夫球場的大豪宅，以及一輛保時捷。）

在英文文法中，有兩種語態：主動語態與被動語態。主動語態(S + V + O)十分常見，例句： Jill washed her car every Sunday.

（Jill 每個星期天都會洗她的車。）

而如果我們將句型改成：S + BeV + Vpp by N 即為被動語態，則為下列的寫法。

例句： Jill's car was washed by her every Sunday.

（Jill 的車每個星期天都被她洗。）

- 被動語態句型可用於彰顯主動語態中的受詞。

  The book was written in 1930.

  （這本書是在 1930 年時寫的。）

  I was born and raised in Taiwan.

  （我在台灣出生及長大。）

- 被動語態句型可用於動作的執行者不是那麼重要或不知是誰的情況。

  The museum is closed every Monday.

  （博物館每個星期一休館。）

  The United States was established in 1776.

  （美國是在 1776 年時建國的。）

- 被動語態句型可用於表示客觀

  It is reported that the case was solved.

  （據報導這一件案件已經破案了。）

  It is predicted that the new medicine will treat cancer.

  （據預測這一種新藥將能治癒癌症。）

- 被動語態句型可用於表示客氣委婉

  You proposal was rejected.

  （你的提案被駁回了。）

句型解析

One day, while he was enjoying one of Heaven's many beautiful parks, he ran into a man dressed in a fine tailored suit.

1. One day, [while he was enjoying... parks], he ran into

   Adv. Phr   Adv. Cl.   S V. Phr.→ V

   a man dressed in a fine tailored suit.

   O   Adj. Phr.

2. 動詞片語 run into + N，意為「突然遇見……」(=bump into=come across)。

3. 本句的形容詞片語"dressed in a fine tailored suit"可還原為形容詞子句"who was dressed in a fine tailored suit"，修飾先行詞 a man。

   dress *(v.)* 使……穿上。「穿上(衣服)……」的用法為：S be dressed in + N (= wear)。

I was given a hundred of these when I get here, along with a mansion on the hill overlooking a beautiful lake, with a golf course and a Porsche.

1. "I was given a hundred of these [when I get here],

   S BeV V Passive   O   Adv. Cl.

   along with a mansion... a beautiful lake,

   Adv. Phr.

   with a golf course and a Porsche."

   Adv. Phr.

2. 片語 along with 意為「連同……一起」(=together with)。

例句：Tina escaped from the explosion along with her pet dog.

Tina 還有她的愛犬一起逃離爆炸。

3. 本句的形容詞片語“overlooking a beautiful lake”可還原為形容詞子句“which overlooked a beautiful lake”，修飾先行詞 a mansion。

overlook *(v.)* 俯視；鳥瞰。

Hearing this made Bill Gates quite angry; he went to see St. Peters immediately.

1. Hearing this... quite angry, he went to see St. Peters immediately.

Hearing this... quite angry,	he	went	to see St. Peters	immediately.
Adv. Phr.	S	V	Infinitive Phr.	Adv.

2. 本句的“Hearing this made Bill Gates quite angry”是的主詞是動名詞 hearing this。

3. “Hearing this made Bill Gates quite angry”用到了“make (使) + O + OC”的句型，這裡 angry 為受詞補語與修飾受詞 Bill Gates。

Windows in fact is a system which leaves a lot to be desired. It wastes too many resources, takes up too much storage, and has poor efficiency. Most of people choose this system because they have been used to it. It's easy for human beings to fall into their habits. Often, we have known the consequences of our doings, but we still choose to do what we are used to. Why don't we have another choice? That is because we are the creatures of our habits. However, it is weird because we can never predict what will become. Making changes is a stimulus for improvement. Only when we are willing to change can we improve. Doesn't life evolve because of changes? If we deny changes and stay in our comfort zone, we will confine ourselves in our own comfort zone where we paralyze ourselves with a false sense of security and certainty. When we are afraid of changes and talk ourselves into maintaining the current situations, we then dare not change and in the end bind ourselves in our own mental cocoons.

Windows其實是個很爛的作業系統，它耗費資源太多、吃硬碟空間，而且執行效率又差；那為什麼我們還要用？因為我們已經習慣了。人是很容易習慣的動物，很多事情我們都知道這樣不好，但為什麼不做出別的選擇？因為我們習慣了，我們害怕改變會帶來無法預知的後果，所以我們寧可繼續爛下去，而不想做任何改變。可是這其實是個很弔詭的想法，我們如何能夠去預測自己根本還沒做的事呢？改變是進步的動力，只有勇於改變，才能進步，生命不就是這樣演化過來的嗎？如果我們一直拒絕改變，就只能在原地踏步，就像日本那些足不出戶的繭居族一樣，因為害怕外在環境帶來的不安和不確定感，所以乾脆就不出門，成天把自己關在房裡。我們想要當這樣的人嗎？很遺憾的，當我們因為習慣某件事而害怕改變，不停的用「維持現狀」來自我麻醉時，我們其實就已經成了不折不扣的心靈繭居族了。

生活篇 對話 1

Situation: Sean and Leo will start their first semester at the University soon, and they are trying to find an apartment before school starts.

情境：Sean 和 Leo 的大學第一個學期即將要開始了。他們想要在開學前找到出租公寓。

Sean	Hey, Leo. What are you doing here?	嗨，Leo。你在做什麼啊？
Leo	I am looking for an apartment to rent. Looking for an apartment also?	我在找有沒有出租公寓。你也在找出租公寓嗎？
Sean	Yes. Since my parents' house is so far away, I need to find an apartment closer to school. I thought you were going to stay at the school dormitory.	是啊，因為我家其實很遠，我需要找一間離學校近的公寓。我還想說你會住學校宿舍咧。
Leo	I still have not decided whether to stay at the dormitory or not. I am looking at different options to find the cheapest lodging.	我還沒有決定是不是要住學校宿舍。我在看有沒有可能找到最便宜的住宿。
Sean	So, what are you looking for?	那你在找什麼房子呢？
Leo	All I need is a place big enough for my bed, my desk and my television. Of course, the place should have a kitchen so that I can cook my meals. I will have to watch every dime.	我需要一間能放床、書桌與電視的房間。當然，最好有個廚房，那麼我就可以煮三餐。我得把錢花在刀口上。

Sean	Me too. I will be living on a very tight budget. So, a safe and decent apartment is all I need.	我也是。我生活開支很緊。所以，只要是安全舒適的公寓就可以了。

生活篇 對話 2

Leo	It is not easy to find an apartment to your liking that does not cost a lot. I have been looking at the ads in the newspapers for two weeks, and I still have not found anything yet.	要找到我喜歡又不貴的公寓不容易。我已經看廣告找了兩個禮拜，但是我還沒有看到我喜歡的。
Sean	Really? Is it that difficult to find an apartment?	真的嗎？找一間公寓有那麼難嗎？
Leo	No, it is just that everything I like so far is too expensive.	沒有啦，只是現在看到的都好貴。
Sean	Is it because they are very close to school? I heard that the closer they are to school, the higher the rental cost.	是因為要離校近嗎？我聽說越靠近學校，房租就會越昂貴。
Leo	Maybe that is the problem. Since I do not have a car, I need to find something close to school.	或許這就是問題了。因為我沒有車，所以我必須找離學校近的房子。

Sean	Have you thought about sharing an apartment? If you want, we can find a two bedrooms apartment and share it.	你有想過共租嗎？如果你願意，我們可以找一間有兩間房間的公寓一起共租。
Leo	It seems that sharing an apartment with you may work. Do you want to try it?	跟你共租公寓似乎可以解決問題耶。你要試試看嗎？
Sean	Yes. Let's go in and take a look at this one.	好嗎，我們來去看看這間吧。

單字與實用例句

- apartment *(n.)* 公寓

  Many young people cannot afford high prices of houses. They can rent apartments only.

  許多年輕人無法負擔高房價。他們只能租公寓。

- look for *(v. phr.)* 尋找

  Kathy is looking for her missing cat.

  Kathy 正在尋找她走失的貓。

- rent *(v.)* 租

  It is convenient to rend a motorcycle when you travel to the countryside.

  當你去鄉下旅行，租一台機車是方便的。

- dormitory *(n.)* 宿舍

  George decided to live in the dormitory with his classmates rather than live alone in a flat.

  George 決定跟同學住在宿舍而不要自己一個人住在公寓。

- budget *(n.)* 預算

  Amy had a low-paying job as an assistant so she had to live on a tight budget.

  Amy 的助理工作薪水很低，所以她得掐緊預算過生活。

- cost *(v.)* 花費

  The new recreational van cost Leo a fortune.

  這台新休旅車花了 Leo 許多錢。

- expensive *(adj.)* 昂貴

  A cruise trip to Hong Kong is very expensive.

  去香港的遊輪行程十分昂貴。

- share *(v.)* 分享

  Claire likes to share everything in life with her husband.

  Claire 喜歡跟她先生分享生活中所有事情。

好用主題用語，用法解說

> Since my parents' house is so far away, I need to find an apartment closer to school.
> Since I do not have a car, I need to find something close to school.

表示因果關係的副詞子句：在英文文法中，當需要表示因果關係時，我們會使用 because、since、as、now that、for（因為…，所以…）等從屬連接詞來引導副詞子句與主要子句型形成因果關係。

- because（因為……，所以……）：

  I am tired because I have run 6 miles.

  （因為跑了六哩路，我現在很累。）

  要注意，一個複雜句裡只需要一個從屬連接詞來連接副詞子句與主要子句。上面那個句子也可以改寫成：I have run 6 miles so I am tired.

- since, as, now that（既然……，所以……）：

  Since it is raining, I have to go now.

  （既然正在下雨，我必須得走了。）

  As John was seriously ill, he took a day off.

  （John 病得很嚴重，所以他請了一天假。）

  Now that you are busy, I will call you later.

  （既然你在忙，我等下再打過來。）

- for（因為……，所以……）：

  Henry must be late for work for he is running now.

  （看到他在跑，想必 Henry 一定是上班遲到了。）

Unit 12 助動詞

勵志篇 故事

Jim had a very bad temper. His father tried everything to teach him to control his temper, but none of them worked. One day, his father gave him a bag of nails and a hammer. He told Jim that every time when he's losing his temper, hammer a nail into the fence.

The first day, Jim hammered 40 nails into the fence. Over the next few weeks, the nails hammered into the fence were gradually decreased, for he had learned that it's easier to hold his temper than to drive those nails into the fence.

Finally, he told his father, he didn't lose his temper all day. Jim's father was very happy, and told him from now on, he could pull out one nail each day that he was able to control his temper.

Days passed and one day, Jim finally removed all the nails on the fence. As he told his father proudly, his father took him to the fence and said "You've done well, Jim, but look at the holes in the fence. The fence will never be the same."

吉姆的脾氣很差。他爸爸試著用各種方法要教他控制住脾氣，但都沒辦法。有一天，他爸爸給了他一袋釘子和一支鐵鎚。他告訴吉姆說，每次當他覺得要發脾氣的時候，就把一根釘子釘到籬笆上。

第一天，吉姆釘了四十根釘子到籬笆上。接下來的幾個星期，釘在籬笆上的釘子數量漸漸地減少，因為吉姆已經學會控制自己的脾氣，比把釘子釘進籬笆裡要容易多了。

終於，他告訴他爸爸，他已經一整天都沒發脾氣了。他的父親非常高興，並且告訴他說從現在開始，只要他一天沒發脾氣，就可以從籬笆上拔下一根釘子。

日子一天天過去，有一天，吉姆終於把籬笆上所有的釘子都拔下來了。當他驕傲的告訴他父親的時候，他的父親便帶著他到籬笆旁說：「你做得非常好，吉姆，但看看籬笆上的坑坑洞洞，它再也回不去原本的樣子了。」

文法重點

助動詞 (Auxiliary Verbs)

...he could pull out one nail each day that he was able to control his temper.
（……只要他一天沒發脾氣，就可以從籬笆上拔下一根釘子。）

在英文文法中的助動詞，主要是幫助主要動詞形成疑問句，否定句或是肯定句中的加強語氣，甚至還可以表示各種時態與語氣。最常使用來表示時態的助動詞有 have (have, has, had)，do (do, does, did) 和 will (will, will, will)。

have	現在完成式	I have completed my mission. （我已經完成我的任務。）	
has	現在完成式 (第三人稱單數)	She has won the race. （她贏了這一次賽跑。）	
had	過去完成式	He had gotten the information before he came to the office. （他在到辦公室之前就已經得到消息了。）	
do	現在簡單式	I do go jogging every morning. （我每個早上都有去慢跑。）	加強語氣
does	現在簡單式 (第三人稱單數)	He does not like swimming. （他不喜歡游泳。）	否定句

did	過去簡單式	Did you bring an umbrella with you this morning?（你今天早上有帶雨傘嗎？）	疑問句
will	未來式	Will I see you tomorrow? （我明天早上會見到你嗎？）	疑問句

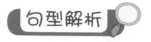

句型解析

His father tried everything to teach him to control his temper, but none of them worked.

1. His father tried everything to teach him to control his temper,

   S V1 O Infinitive Phr. Infinitive Phr.

   but none of them worked.

   Conj. S2 V2

2. 本句的"to control his temper"可還原為"in order to/ so as to control his temper"。片語"in order to/ so as to + V"意為「為了……」，表示目的。

3. 代名詞 none 為否定代名詞，意為「沒有一人/一個/一件……」。注意，當前面名詞為三件東西以上，我們用 none 作否定代名詞；當前面名詞為兩件東西而已，我們用 neither 作否定代名詞。

   例句：The mother asked her three sons to help her, but none of them responded to her.
   那位母親叫她小孩來幫忙，但卻沒有一人回應。

   例句：John and Mary have a lot in common; neither of them likes durians.
   John 和 Mary 有許多共同點；他們都不喜歡榴槤。

He told Jim that every time when he's losing his temper, hammer a nail into the fence.

1. He told Jim [that every time when he's losing... a nail into the fence].

   S V I.O. N. Cl.→ D.O.

2. 句型 "every time when S + V, S+V"意為「每一次……」，when 可省略(=each time when= whenever)。

   例句：Every time (when)/Each time (when)/ Whenever the boss has an argument with Luis, he always loses in the end.
   每次老闆跟 Luis 吵架，他最後總是會輸。

3. 動詞片語 lose one's temper 意為「發飆、生氣」(=get very angry)。反義為 hold one's temple 意為「控制脾氣」。

Over the next few weeks, the nails hammered into the fence were gradually decreased, for he had learned that it's easier to hold his temper than to drive those nails into the fence.

1. Over the next few weeks, the nails hammered into the fence

   Adv. Phr. S

   were gradually decreased, [for he had learned that it's easier to

   BeV Adv. V Passive Adv. Cl.

   hold... those nails into the fence].

2. 本句的形容詞片語"hammered into the fence"可還原成形容詞子句"which were hammered into the fence"，修飾先行詞 the nails。

3. 本句的 for 是連接詞，意為「因為…」(=because=as=since)。

心情小語

Whenever we have a fight, we will try everything we can to hurt each other, wishing him or her to shut up. Indeed, saying bitter words to hurt others makes us feel good when we lose our temper. Since most of us do not like to lose the fight, we will try to use harsh words to hurt each other while proving we are absolutely right. However, we often overlook the consequences and the painful results those stagger-like harsh words coming out of our mouths may bring about. Although they seem harmless in appearance, the wounds they cause are hard to heal. Although we usually do not mean to hurt people, these harsh words do lead to irreversible damage to others. Therefore, the best solution to preventing ourselves from losing our mind is to hold our temper. Whenever we are going to lose our temper, leave the place right away, take a few deep breaths, and then clam ourselves down. We will find that when we are calm and cool, we can make others convinced by our words easily.

吵架的時候，想辦法用最尖銳的言詞讓對方閉嘴，的確是非常有快感的一件事。因為誰不喜歡贏的感覺？當雙方意見不同的時候，自己能夠讓對方講不下去，似乎就表示自己是對的，別人是錯的。但是我們卻往往忽略了這些所謂的「氣話」可能造成的傷害有多大。這些傷害雖然不像是用刀子捅人家一刀這樣嚴重，但卻也不是用線縫個幾針般的這樣容易癒合。很多時候我們在氣頭上說的話其實並不是真的帶著惡意，只是在那個當下講出這樣的話，很爽、很痛快，但事後這些話卻很可能對自己或別人造成無法彌補的傷害。所以最好的辦法，就是不要讓自己陷入「氣昏頭」的情緒中，以免在失控之中說出會讓自己後悔的話。每當氣話要脫口而出時，離開現場，或者做幾個深呼吸，讓自己冷靜下來。我們就會發現，有時心平氣和講出來的話，

不僅不會造成傷害，反而比氣話更容易說服別人。

幽默篇故事

One day, a blonde girl went into a shop.

She browsed for a while and said "I'd like to buy this TV." she said.

"I'm sorry," the shopkeeper said "I can't sell this to you."

"It must be the hair!" She thought, "The shopkeeper must assume I'm too stupid to use that TV and won't sell it to me because I'm blonde!"

So the next day, she dyed her hair and went back to the shop again.

"I'd like to buy this TV.", she pointed at the same TV she saw yesterday.

"I'm sorry. I can't sell this to you." The shopkeeper gave the same reply as yesterday.

Finally, she shaved her head and went back, but the shopkeeper refused her, for the third time.

"How on earth do you know I'm blonde?" She exclaimed.

The shopkeeper sighed, "First of all, this is a microwave oven."

有一天，一個金髮女子走進一家店。

她在店裡逛了一會兒然後說：「我想要買這台電視。」

「很抱歉，」店員說道：「我不能把這個賣給妳。」

「一定是因為我的頭髮的關係！」女子想著：「這店員一定是因為看我一頭金髮就認為我太笨不會用而不肯賣給我！」

於是第二天，她就把頭髮染黑，走回那家店。

「我想要買這台電視。」她指著和昨天同一台的電視機說道。

「很抱歉，我不能把這賣給妳。」店員給了和昨天同樣的答覆。

最後，她把頭髮都給剃光了，但是店員卻還是第三次的拒絕賣給她。

「怎麼可能這樣你還知道我是金髮？！」女子喊道。

店員嘆了口氣：「首先呢，這是台微波爐。」

文法重點

助動詞 (Auxiliary Verbs)

It must be the hair!
（一定是因為我的頭髮的關係！）

在英文文法中的助動詞，主要是幫助主要動詞形成疑問句，否定句或是肯定句中的加強語氣，甚至還可以表示各種時態與語氣。最常使用來表示語氣的情態助動詞有 would, should, ought to, can, could, may, might 和 must。

would	可以…	Would you close the door for me? （你可以幫我關門嗎？）
	想要… （請求允許）	Would you like to have some tea? （你想要來點茶嗎？）
should	應該…	We should pay the tax. （我們應該要納稅。）
ought to	應該…	Students ought to hand in their assignments in time. （學生應該要準時的交作業。）
can	能夠…	Can you speak English? （你會說英文嗎？）
could	能夠…	Could he catch the train in time this morning? （他今天早上能趕得上火車嗎？）
	可以… （請求允許）	Could pass the salt, please. （請把鹽巴遞過來。）

may	可能…	The diamond ring may be real. （這個鑽戒可能是真的。）
	可以… （請求允許）	May I leave now? （我現在可以離開嗎？）
might	可能…	The drawing might be a fake. （這一幅畫可能是贗品。）
must	必定…	The antique vase must be genuine. （這一個古董花瓶一定是真的。）
	必須…	Kate must arrive the airport before 6 a.m. （Kate 一定要在早上 6 點之前抵達機場。）

句型解析

"The shopkeeper must assume I'm too stupid to use that TV and won't sell it to me because I'm blonde!"

1. "The shopkeeper must assume [I'm too stupid to use that TV] and

   S Aux. V N. Cl.→ O Conj.

   wo n't sell it to me [because I'm blonde]!"

   Aux. Adv. V D.O. Prep. I.O. Adv. Cl.

2. assume *(v.)* 假設；猜想。

   例句：Many people assume that women are more vulnerable than men.

   許多人認為女性比男性脆弱。

3. 本句的名詞子句"I'm too stupid to use that TV"中用到了"too adj./adv. to V"的句型，意為「太……以致於不能……」。

   例句：Natasha was too young to vote.

   Natasha 年齡太小，不能投票。

The shopkeeper gave the same reply as yesterday.

1. The shopkeeper gave the same reply as yesterday.

   S V O Adv. Phr.

2. 本句可還原為："The shopkeeper gave the same reply as he gave yesterday." 這裡

   用到 the same N as S V 的句型，意為「與……一樣」。這裡 as 是準關係代名詞，意為「如同……」。

   例句：Zoe has the same bag as Cathy does.
   Zoe 有個跟 Cathy 一樣的包。

"How on earth do you know I'm blonde?"

1. "How on earth do you know [(that) I'm blonde]?"

   Adv. Adv. Phr. Aux. S V N. Cl.→ O

2. 副詞片語 on earth 意為「到底……；究竟……」。

   例句：What on earth are you thinking?
   你到底在想什麼？

心情小語

People often do some things to prove they are smart. However, these acts actually make them look really dumb. In fact, we clearly know who we are, but we often hope to be identified by others. In fact, we do not have to care how other people think of us too much. As long as we know what we are doing and stick to our principles, our virtues will shine someday. When we want to prove us what we are with things against our nature, we will lose ourselves. A friend of mine often thought herself tasteless in clothes. To prove herself trendy and in, she spent tens of thousands of dollars on clothes in department stores. Moreover, she would show off her expensive clothes to her friends by asking questions like "Do you know which brand it is?", or "Do you know how much this coat cost?", and so on. However, all those efforts did not make people think her trendy; people started to think it was she herself that disgraced the value and taste of the branded products on her. In short, just be ourselves. If we change ourselves for others and even do things against our nature, we may lose ourselves sooner or later.

很多人常常會做一些事，想要向大家證明他一點都不笨；但往往做的這些事都只是更讓大家覺得，他的確是個笨蛋無誤。其實我們自己是怎麼樣的人，自己最清楚了，但往往都會陷入一種「希望別人能夠認同自己」的迷思，而在裡頭打轉，繞不出來。別人怎麼看我們，真的不需要太在意，只要我們知道自己這樣沒有錯，堅持著自己的步調走，總有一天他們會發現我們真正的優點。最怕就是為了證明自己，而去做一些違背我們本性的事，最後反而得不償失。身邊有個朋友，常被認為她穿著很沒品味，於是她為了證明自己很會穿衣服，便到百貨公司，花了幾萬塊治裝。隔天一來就對大家說，「你知道這件上衣什麼牌的嗎？你知道這件外套多少錢嗎？」。但是這樣真的有讓大家對她改觀嗎？完全沒有，反而讓大家覺得原來不是她沒品味，而是根本她整個人就是沒氣質，才會連這些穿在身上的名牌都跟著 low 掉。所以，做自己就好了，不要為了別人而改變自己，勉強自己去做一些不適合自己的事，只會更得不償失而已。

生活篇 對話 1

Situation: Zoe, Vicky, and Jo just finished their etiquette lesson and now they are having lunch at the restaurant.

情境：Zoe，Vicky 和 Jo 剛上完她們的禮儀課程。現在她們正在餐廳用餐。

Zoe	Vicky, may I borrow your cell phone to call my mother after we finish lunch?	Vicky，用完餐後我可以跟妳借用手機打電話給我母親嗎？
Vicky	Yes, of course, Zoe. And please, do not forget to ask your mother whether you may go to the movies with us afterwards.	好的，當然可以，Zoe。請也別忘了跟你母親詢問妳待會兒是否可以跟我們去看電影。
Jo	Zoe, could you pass the salt, please?	Zoe，可以請你把鹽遞過來嗎？
Zoe	Sure, here you are.	好的，在這。
Jo	And the pepper too, please. Thank you.	還有，請把胡椒也遞過來好嗎？謝謝。
Zoe	You are welcome.	別客氣。
Vicky	I ordered too many French fries. Would anybody care for some?	我點了太多的薯條。有人願意再多些薯條嗎？
Zoe	Yes, I would like some.	好的，請給我一點。
Vicky	How about you, Jo?	Jo，你呢？
Jo	No, thank you. I have enough food already.	不用了，謝謝。我已經吃得夠多了。

Zoe	Vicky, would you like some of my fried rice?	Vicky，我的炒飯可以給你一點嗎？
Vicky	Yes, please. Just a little bit.	好的，謝謝，我只要一些些。
Zoe	Here you go.	喏，這些給你。
Vicky	Oh, that is enough! No more, please.	喔，這些夠了！不用再多了，謝謝。

生活篇 對話 2

Situation: Zoe, Vicky, and Jo are now having lunch at the restaurant and talking about gifts for Jo's mother.

情境：Zoe，Vicky 和 Jo 。現在在餐廳用餐，並討論著要給 Jo 母親的禮物。

Vicky	Would both of you mind if I stop by Mercury bookstore after the movie?	等會兒看完電影，我想要在水星書店停一下，不知道妳們兩個是否介意？
Zoe	No, not at all. I would love to take a look at their Top 10 New Books selection. So, I would like to stop there also.	不會，一點兒也不。我想要在十大新書排行榜那看看。我也想在那裡繞繞。

Vicky	I would love to spend some time with you in that well-decorated bookstore. That must be very nice, but I need to be home by 5:00 o'clock.	我也喜歡跟妳們在那間裝潢美麗的書店待一會兒。那會很有趣，但我必須 5 點前回到家。
Jo	You can go if you want.	妳隨時想離開都可以。
Vicky	Thank you, Jo. Why would you want to do at Mercury bookstore?	謝謝妳，Jo。妳怎麼會想去水星書店呢？
Jo	I need to pick up a gift for my mother. Her birthday is on Sunday next week. What would you recommend, Zoe?	我要幫我母親挑一個禮物。她下週日生日。Zoe，你會推薦什麼呢？
Zoe	Just a moment please. Let me think. How about a brooch since she loves wearing scarves?	等會兒，讓我想想。既然她喜歡披圍巾，那麼送她一個胸針好了。
Jo	What a clever suggestion! My mother will thank me for the lovely gift. I hope there is a lovely brooch in the store.	真是一個明智的建議！我母親一定會很喜歡這個禮物的。我希望書店裡有個可愛的胸針才好。
Vicky	That's great!	這真是太好了！

單字與實用例句

- etiquette *(n.)* 禮儀，禮貌

  Etiquette is important in a formal situation.
  正式場合中禮儀是很重要的事。

- borrow *(v.)* 借用

  May I borrow a pen from you?
  我可以跟你借一枝筆嗎？

- pass *(v.)* 遞

  Can you pass me that bag over there?
  可以請你遞那邊的那個包包給我好嗎？

- care *(v.)* 在意，在乎

  The selfish boss did not care if his workers lived or died.
  那自私的老闆不在乎他員工的死活。

- mind *(v.)* 介意

  Do you mind if I smoke here?
  你介意我在這裡吸菸嗎？

- recommend *(v.)* 推薦

  The therapist Mary recommended to me is really good.
  Mary 推薦給我的治療師不錯。

- suggestion *(n.)* 提議，建議

  The expert made a lot of suggestions as to how to improve the current poor economic situation.
  這位專家對於如何改善當今不良經濟局勢做出許多建議。

- lovely *(adj.)* 可愛的

  The baby girl is lovely and adorable.
  這個女娃娃真是可愛。

好用主題用語，用法解說

Zoe, could you pass the salt, please?
I would love to spend some time with you in that well-decorated bookstore.

用英文表示客氣與禮貌：英文中的語氣常常是用助動詞來表現。最常見的就是 would 與 could 這兩個助動詞除了可以當作是 will 與 can 的過去式之外，還可以用來表示「客氣」與「禮貌」的語氣。以下介紹幾種常見的表示「客氣」與「禮貌」的英文會話句型：

- Would/Could you please + V ?「請您……可以嗎？」

  Could you please move your car?

  （請您把車挪動一下可以嗎？）

  Would you please be quiet for a few minutes?

  （請您安靜幾分鐘好嗎？）

- Would you like/love N ?

  Would you like/love + to V...?「您要……嗎？」

  Would you like a cup of coffee?

  （您要一杯咖啡嗎？）

  Would you love to have the dinner with me?

  （您要跟我一起吃晚餐嗎？）

- Would you mind + Ving...?

  Would you mind if S+V?「您介意……嗎？」

  Would you mind closing the window?

  （您介意關上窗戶嗎？）

  Would you mind if I smoke here?

  （您介意我在這抽根菸嗎？）

Unit 13 分詞

勵志篇 故事

A doctor, a lawyer, a little boy and a priest were on a plane, when suddenly the pilot announced that the plane have problems with the engine, and would be crashed soon.

The pilot asked everyone to grab a parachute and jump for their lives, but unfortunately, there were only three parachutes left, and there are four of them left.

The doctor grabbed one and said "I'm a doctor, I save lives, so I deserve to live." and jumped out.

The lawyer quickly grabbed another one "I'm a lawyer and lawyers are the smartest people in the world, so I deserve to live as well!" and jumped out.

The priest looked at the little boy and said "My son, I've live long enough. You are young and have a bright future ahead of you. Take the parachute and go."

The little boy handed the parachute to the priest and said "Don't worry, Father. The smartest man in the world just took off with my backpack."

一個醫生、一個律師、一個小男孩和一個牧師在一架飛機上。突然之間，飛機駕駛宣佈說飛機因為引擎有問題即將墜毀。

駕駛員要大家拿著降落傘趕快跳機逃生，但不幸的是，最後只剩三個降落傘，但卻還有他們四個人。

醫生抓起了一個降落傘說：「我是醫生，我可以拯救生命，我應該活下去！」便跳了出去。

律師立刻抓了另外一個：「我是律師，律師們是世界上最聰明的人，所以我也應該活下去。」說完他也跳了出去。

牧師看著小男孩說道：「我的孩子，我已經活得夠久了。你還年輕，還有光明的未來在等著你，快拿降落傘走吧。」

小男孩將降落傘遞給牧師：「不用擔心，牧師。那個全世界最聰明的人剛背著我的背包跳下去了。」

文法重點

分詞 (Participles)

There were only three parachutes left...
（最後只剩三個降落傘……）

在英文文法中，分詞由動詞變化而來主要分為：現在分詞(Ving)與過去分詞(Vpp)。分詞的主要功能像是形容詞，用來修飾「名詞」或「代名詞」，或是當主詞或是受詞補語使用。

- 現在分詞當形容詞用，強調動作的正在進行或是主動狀態，如 boiling water （正在煮的水），falling leaves（正在飄零的樹葉），burning car（著火的車），developing country（發展中國家），English-speaking people（說英文的人）……。過去分詞當形容詞用，強調動作的已經發生或是被動狀態，如 boiled water（燒開的水），fallen leaves（落下的樹葉），burnt car（燒毀的車），developed country（已發展國家），English-written book（英文寫的書）

• 分詞也可以與 BeV 與助動詞形成不同時態。

進行式：Be V + Ving		
	進行式	完成進行式
現在	am/are/is leaving	have/has been leaving
過去	was/were leaving	had been leaving
未來	shall/will be leaving	shall/will have been leaving

完成式：have/ has/ had + Vpp	
	完成式
現在完成式	have/has left
過去完成式	had left
未來完成式	shall/will have left

被動式：BeV + Vpp	
現在	am/ are /is Vpp
過去	was/ were Vpp
未來	will be Vpp
完成	have/ has/ had + been Vpp

句型解析

A doctor, a lawyer, a little boy and a priest were on a plane, when suddenly the pilot announced that the plane have problems with the engine, and would be crashed soon.

1. A doctor, a lawyer, a little boy and a priest (S) were (BeV) on a plane (Adv. Phr.),

   [when suddenly the pilot announced that the plane have problems …be crashed soon.] (Adv. Cl.)

2. 本句的“that the plane have problems with the engine, and would be crashed soon”是名詞子句，作動詞 announce 的受詞。

   announce *(v.)* 宣布。

3. 動詞片語 have problems/trouble/difficulty with + N 意為「……有問題/困難」。

   例句：Jennings had problems with her project.
   Jennings 在這件計畫上有困難。

I'm a lawyer and lawyers are the smartest people in the world, so I deserve to live as well!

1. “I' (S1) m (BeV1) a lawyer (N.→SC) and (Conj.) lawyers (S2) are (BeV2) the smartest people (N.→SC) in the world (Adv. Phr.), [so I deserve to live as well!] (Adv. Cl.)”

2. deserve *(v.)* 值得；應得。

例句：Frank worked so hard on the project so he deserved the promotion.
Frank 在這個案子上努力許多，所以他值得升職。

3. as well (adv. phr.) 也(=too= also)。

例句：Emma booked a ticket to the concert, and her sister did as well.
Emma 預訂了音樂會的票，她妹妹也是。

The smartest man in the world just took off with my backpack.

1. The smartest man in the world (S) just (Adv.) took off (V. Phr.→V) with my backpack. (Adv. Phr.)

2. 動詞片語 take off 在本句意為「跳下去（離開飛機）」。

3. 本句的 with 是介系詞，意為「有……；帶著……」。

例句：You can take your carry-on luggage on the plane.
你可以帶著隨身行李上飛機。

心情小語

Why are people fond of watching disaster films? In addition to its spectacular scenes, the storyline of disaster films usually clearly demonstrate the bright side and the dark side of humanity: not only the heroes who sacrifice themselves and save others but also selfish people who care about nothing but their own survivals are depicted in those films. As we all know, those selfish people are unlikely to have a happy ending. Like the lawyer in the story, he may be the smartest person in the world. However, he ignored the little boy on the plane. If the lawyer had given his parachute to the little, the priest might have thought that he should give his parachute to the lawyer because he was old. In fact, the lawyer's selfishness beat his mentality at that moment so that he made a wrong judgment. Therefore, when making any important decisions, we can try to exclude ourselves from other factors and think which choice can most benefit everyone concerned. Maybe we'll find the answer is clear.

為什麼大家都喜歡看災難片？除了壯觀的特效外，災難片通常最能夠明顯的表達出人類的光明面和黑暗面。每次那種災難片總會有那種捨身救人的英雄，當然也就有那種只要自己可以獲救，把別人踹下去都無所謂的傢伙。但在每部電影中我們都會發現，那些太過自私只想著自己逃命的人，最後下場都不會太好。故事中的那位律師，他也許真的就是全世界最聰明的人；只是他卻忽略了，飛機上還有個更需要得到救援的小男孩在。或許他當時如果先把降落傘給小男孩，牧師會認為自己年紀已經很大了，便將降落傘讓給他，但是在那一刻，他的自私卻戰勝了理智，致使他做出錯誤的判斷。所以當我們要做個重大的決定不知該如何是好時，試著先把自己排除在外，想想怎麼樣的決定可以讓所有人都得到美好的結果，或許答案就很清楚了。

幽默篇 故事

Matt came home from work and found his two children outside, playing in the mud, with empty food boxes and cookie crumbles all around the front garden.

The front door to the house was open, and there was no sign of their dog. Proceeding into the hall, Matt found that the lamp had been knocked over, and the rug was covered with mud. In the living room, the TV was turned on and playing cartoon loudly. The floor was covered with toys and clothes.

What happened here?

Matt quickly headed upstairs, stepping over toys and lots of clothes, looking for his wife. He was worried that she might be ill, or something even worse happened to her.

As he went upstairs, he found that the faucet in the bathroom was turned on, and the water was flooding the bathroom floor. Also, the toilet was jammed with roll of toilet paper.

As he rushed into the bedroom, he found he wife lying on the bed, reading novels. She looked at him and smiled.

"What happened today?!" Matt asked.

His wife said, "Do you remember what you asked me with great contempt yesterday, about what in the world did I do all day?"

"Yeah?"

"Well, today, I didn't do it.", his wife said with a bigger smile on her face.

麥特下班回到家，發現他的兩個小孩在屋外玩著泥巴。空的食物盒子和餅乾屑撒滿了整個花園。

房子的前門大開著，他們養的狗不知去向。繼續往大廳前進，麥特發現檯燈被弄倒在地，地毯上也佈滿了泥巴。客廳裡，電視正大聲的播放著卡通，地板上也堆滿了玩具和衣物。

這裡到底發生了什麼事？！

麥特，一邊不斷的踩過許多玩具和衣物，一邊快步上樓尋找他的太太。他擔心太太會不會生病了，或是發生更糟糕的事情了。

當他上樓後，他發現浴室的水龍頭被打開，水流滿了一地。馬桶也被一大綑衛生紙給塞住。

他衝進臥室，看到太太正躺在床上看小説。她看著他笑了笑。

「今天發生什麼事了？」麥特問道。

他的太太説：「你還記得你昨天用鄙視的口氣問我説一整天到底都在做什麼嗎？」

「記得啊。」

「唔，我今天就是沒有做了而已。」他的太太説道，給了他一抹更大的微笑。

文法重點

分詞 (Participles)

Matt came home from work and found his two children outside, playing in the mud, with empty food boxes and cookie crumbles all around the front garden.
（麥特下班回到家，發現他的兩個小孩在屋外玩著泥巴。空的食物盒子和餅乾屑撒滿了整個花園。）

在英文文法中，分詞由動詞變化而來主要分為：現在分詞(Ving)與過去分詞(Vpp)。分詞的主要功能像是形容詞，用來修飾「名詞」或「代名詞」，或是當主詞或是受詞補語使用。

英文中使用到分詞作補語的句型十分常見，下面介紹幾個常見的句型：

- There+BeV+S+ Ving/ Vpp 那裡有……

  There are many children playing in the field.

  （那裡有許多小孩在原野上玩耍。）

  There were several boxes left in the room.

  （那裡有許多的箱子被留在房間裡。）

- S + V + with + O + OC 有……

  The girl rode her bike in the park with her hair blowing in the wind.

  （這個女孩在公園裡騎腳踏車，她的頭髮隨風飄揚著。）

  My grandpa sat on the armchair with his eyes closed.

  （我的祖父閉著眼睛坐在搖椅上。）

- S + leave (讓)/ keep(讓)/ find (發覺) + O + OC

  Fay left the window closed.

  （Fay 讓窗戶關著。）

  Peter found the baby crying.

  （Peter 發現這個嬰兒在哭。）

- S + remain (依然)/ stay (保持)/ keep (保持)

  Cindy remained interested in what Teresa was talking about.

  （Cindy 對 Teresa 在說的事情依然有興趣。）

句型解析

Proceeding into the hall, Matt found that the lamp had been knocked over, and the rug was covered with mud.

1. Proceeding into the hall, Matt found

   Participial Construction S V

   [that the lamp had been... with mud].

   N. Cl.→ O

2. 本句的"Proceeding into the hall, ..."是分詞構句，可還原為副詞子句"When Matt proceeded into the hall, ..."。

3. 句型 S + be covered with + N，意為「(被)覆蓋著……」。

   例句：The summit of the mountain has long been covered with snow.

   這座山的山頂常年被雪覆蓋。

In the living room, the TV was turned on and playing cartoon loudly.

1. In the living room, the TV was turned on and playing

   Adv. Phr. S BeV V Passive Adv. Conj. Ving

   cartoon loudly.

   O Adv.

2. 動詞片語 turn on 意為「打開(電器用品)」。

例句：It is so hot. Please turn on the air condition.

好熱喔。請開一下空調嘛。

3. 本句"the TV was turned on and playing cartoon loudly"的 play 意為「播放……」。

He was worried that she might be ill, or something even worse happened to her.

1. He was worried

S BeV V Passive

[that she might be ill, ...worse happened to her].

N. Cl.→ O

2. 本句的"that she might be ill, or something even worse happened to her"是名詞子句，作 BeV worried(擔心……)的受詞。

3. happen *(v.)* 發生。當 happen 意為發生時，主詞需為事物，且只有主動的型態。

例句：Good things will happen to you if you always look on the bright side.

只要你看著事情的光明面，好事就會發生在你身上。

心情小語

Father works hard to bring home the bacon while Mother takes care of all the household chores at home every day...Does this scenario sound familiar to you? Trivial and ordinary as it is, those who work hard for us are who make us what we are today. However, it is a pity that we often take them and even what they did for granted, just as the husband in the story easily ignored the contribution his wife made for their family. At first, he thought he was greater since he worked hard to bring home the bacon while his wife just seemed to idle around at home. However, not until his wife took a day off did he realize how much his wife had contributed to their family. Of course, it did not turn out that the husband worked on his own to clean up the house; the couple cooperated to finish the chores. Yet, it is not hard to imagine that the husband would not think that what his wife did every day was just eating chips, watching TV, and sleeping on a couch at home every day.

爸爸每天出去辛苦工作賺錢、媽媽在家煮飯、洗衣服打掃家裡；看起來好像很天經地義、理所當然。可是常常就因為這樣，我們都忽略了這些工作的重要性，而忘了對辛苦付出的家人心存感激。像故事中的丈夫，他認為自己每天在外工作，然後太太好像每天在家休息無所事事，因而覺得不平衡；卻沒想到當有一天太太罷工了之後，全家就頓時變得像剛剛被核子彈炸過一樣。當然我們並不知道最後是這個丈夫負責去收拾殘局，還是又得靠太太出馬才能搞定，但可想而知的是，經過這次之後，這個丈夫應該再也不敢質疑太太每天在家是躺在沙發上吃東西看、電視、睡覺而已了。

生活篇 對話 1

Situation: Olivia just graduated with a Bachelor degree in Finance. Now, she is looking for a job in her field of studies instead of continuing to hold her current Payroll position.

情境：Olivia 才剛拿到財務系學士學位畢業。現在她正打算尋找相關領域的工作，不再做她現在出納的職位。

Nathan	Hi. It is good to see you, Olivia.	嗨，很高興見到妳，Olivia。
Olivia	Same here, Nathan. It has been a long time since I last saw you.	我也是，Nathan。上次見面已經好久了。
Nathan	Yes, the last time we saw each other was New Year's Eve. How are you doing?	對啊，上次我們見面是新年除夕夜了。妳近來如何？
Olivia	I am doing OK. It would be better if I have a new job right now.	我還可以啦。如果我有份新工作就更好了。
Nathan	You are looking for a new job? Why?	妳在找新工作，為什麼？
Olivia	I already finished my studies and graduated last week. Now, I want to get a job in the Finance field. Payroll is not exactly Finance.	我上週已經完成學業畢業了。現在我想要找一個跟財政相關的工作。出納職務跟財務不太相關。
Nathan	How long have you been looking for a new job?	妳找新工作找多久了？
Olivia	I just started this week.	這一週才開始。

生活篇 對話 2

Situation: Olivia's friend, Nathan, is giving her some advice.

情境：Olivia 的朋友 Nathan 正在給她建議。

Nathan	Don't worry, Olivia. The job market is pretty good right now, and all companies need financial analysts.	不用擔心，Olivia。現在就業市場還不錯，而且每間公司都需要財務分析人才。
Olivia	I hope so.	但願如此啊。
Nathan	Did you mail your resume to a lot of companies? How about recruiting agencies?	妳有把履歷寄給很多公司嗎？妳有寄給人力銀行嗎？
Olivia	Yes. I have sent it to a dozen companies already. No, I have not thought about recruiting agencies. But, I do look closely at the employment ads listed in the newspaper every day.	有啊，我已經把履歷寄給很多公司了。不過我到現在還沒想過人力銀行。但是，我每天都有認真仔細看報紙上的就業廣告。
Nathan	My friends told me that it helps to do some homework before you go to an interview. You need to know the company well—what kind of business is it in? What types of products does it sell? How is it doing lately?	我朋友告訴我面試前先做些功課是好的。你必須要清楚了解這個公司一它是屬於什麼企業？它主要是在銷售什麼產品？它最近的表現如何？

Olivia	I can handle that. Thank you for your advice.	這些我會做。謝謝你的建議。
Nathan	Good luck in your job search, Olivia.	祝妳找工作順利喔，Olivia。

單字與實用例句

- finance *(n.)* 財務，財政

  The former Finance Minister was relieved of his post last month.

  前任的財政部部長在上個月被卸職了。

- continue *(v.)* 繼續

  Owen decided to continue his study after graduation from college.

  Owen 決定大學畢業之後繼續他的學業。

- hold *(v.)* 握住，持有

  The two political parties held totally different ideas over the issue.

  這兩個政黨在這件事情的觀點大相逕庭。

- current *(adj.)* 目前的，當今的

  The current financial situation of that company is quit unstable.

  那間公司現今的財務情勢相當不穩定。

- mail *(v.)* 郵寄

  Please mail me the contract.

  請把合約寄給我。

- recruit *(v.)* 招募

  The international company offers high salaries to recruit real talents.

  這間跨國公司祭出高薪來招募真正人才。

- agency *(n.)* 代理商，代理所

  If you want to save time, you can join the package tour offered by that travel agency.

  如果你想省時間，你可以參加那間旅行社推出的套裝行程。

- lately *(adv.)* 最近

  Have you heard of Helen lately?

  你最近有聽說 Helen 的消息嗎？

好用主題用語，用法解說

Yes, the last time we saw each other was NewYear's Eve.
Did you mail your resume to a lot of companies?

過去式：在一般生活對話中，我們常常會描述過去的事情。英文中描述過去的事情，動詞需變化成過去式。過去式主要是描述過去發生的而已經結束的動作或是過去某個時間裡發生的動作或狀態。以下說明動詞過去式的變化。

- Be 動詞的過去式：was/ were

  Judy was once a teacher, but now she is a writer.

  （Judy 以前曾經是老師，但現在是位作家。）

  Mike was at the meeting yesterday.

  （Mike 昨天有出席會議。）

  We were exhausted after jogging 42 kilometers.

  （慢跑完 42 公里後，我們累壞了。）

- 一般動詞的過去式（不規則變化）：英文中有許多常用的動詞，如 take、get、come、run 等的過去式是不規則變化。

- 一般動詞的過去式（規則變化）：V-ed

  I never met Yvonne.

  （我從未見過 Yvonne。）

  Kelvin bought the bike last month. Kelvin.

  （上個月買了一台腳踏車。）

  Gina visited her parents one a week last year.

  （Gina 去年每週拜訪父母親兩次。）

  Iren walked her dog last night.

（Irene 昨晚遛狗。）

- 過去式的問句與否定句：did 這個助動詞協助動詞形成過去式的問句與否定句。

  Did you send the letters?

  （你寄信了嗎？）

  Fred did not catch a cold.

  （Fred 並沒有感冒。）

Unit 14

比較級與最高級

勵志篇 故事

Long time ago, there was an Emperor who told one of his knights that if he could ride his horse and cover as much land as he liked, the Emperor would give him the area of the land he covered.

The knight quickly jumped onto his horse and rode as fast as possible to cover as much land area as he could. He kept on riding the horse, whipping the horse to go as fast as possible. When he felt hungry and tired, he didn't stop to rest because he wanted to cover more land area.

Finally, after several days of horse riding without any rest, the knight had covered a huge amount of land. But suddenly he stopped and fell from the horse because he was too exhausted and dying.

The knight asked himself, "What's the point when I have so much land, but the only land area I could use is a small place to bury myself?"

很久以前，皇帝告訴他的一個騎士説，如果他可以騎著他的馬，經過他所能經過的所有土地，皇帝就會把他所經過的這些範圍內的土地都賜給他。

騎士迅速地跳上馬，然後以最快的速度騎了出去，為了要儘可能的經過更多的土地。他不斷的騎馬、用鞭子抽馬，讓牠盡可能的以最快速度奔馳。當他覺得餓了、累了的時候，他也不停下來休息，因為他想要經過更多的土地。

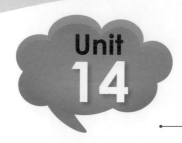

最後，在不眠不休連續騎了好幾天之後，騎士已經涵蓋了很大面積的土地，但他卻突然停下來，然後從馬上跌落。因為他已經太過疲倦，瀕臨垂死邊緣了。

騎士問自己道：「當我擁有了那麼大片土地，但我現在能用得到的只有用來埋我自己的那一小塊，這樣到底有什麼意義呢？」

文法重點

形容詞的比較 (Comparison)

The knight quickly jumped onto his horse and rode as fast as possible to cover as much land area as he could.
（騎士迅速地跳上馬，然後以最快的速度騎了出去，為了要儘可能的經過更多的土地。）

在英文文法中，形容詞主要的功能主要在與修飾名詞或是做為主詞或受詞補語用。而當形容詞所要修飾程度與等級的不同，則有原級(positive)、比較級(comparative)、最高級(superlative)三種區分。
例如：

	原級	比較級	最高級
高的	tall	taller	tallest
乾淨的	clean	cleaner	cleanest
美麗的	beautiful	more beautiful	most beautiful
好的	good	better	best
糟的	bad	worse	worst

這裡需要注意比較級與最高級的形分為規則變化與不規則變化。規則變化的比較級通常在原級形容詞字尾加 -er 或字前加 more；而最高級則是在字尾加 -est 或字前加 most。
就語意上而言，原級比較以及比較級屬於兩者之間的比較。
原級比較的句型為：S Be V + as adj. as + S BeV。

例句：John is as tall as Frank.
（John 比 Frank 高。）

The shirt is as expensive as that one.
（這一件襯衫比那一件貴。）
而比較級的句型為：S BeV + adj. er/ more adj. /less adj. + S BeV。

例句：Linda is shorter than Miranda.
（Linda 比 Miranda 矮。）
Oliver is more handsome that Peter.
（Oliver 比 Peter 帥。）
The cake is less delicious than that one.
（這一塊蛋糕跟那一塊比起來沒那麼好吃。）

句型解析

Long time ago, there was an Emperor who told one of his knights that if he could ride his horse and cover as much land as he liked, the Emperor would give him the area of the land he covered.

1. Long time ago, (Adv. Phr.) there (Adv.) was (BeV) an Emperor (S) [who... the land he covered]. (Adj. Cl.)
2. 在本句 there was an Emperor... 的主詞是 Emperor，所以動詞為第三人稱單數 was。
3. 本句的"who told one of his knights that if he could ride his horse and cover as much land as he liked, the Emperor would give him the area of the land he covered"是形容詞子句修飾先行詞 an Emperor。
4. 本句的"that if he could ride his horse and cover as much land as he liked, the Emperor would give him the area of the land he covered"是名詞子句作 told 的直接受詞用。

5. 本句的 if 是連接詞，意為「假如……」，引導表示條件的副詞子句。

He kept on riding the horse, whipping the horse to go as fast as possible.

1. He / kept on / riding the horse,

   S / V.Phr.→ V / Ving →O

   whipping the horse to... possible.

   Construction Participial

2. 動詞片語 keep on，意為「繼續(做)……」，其後需接 Ving。

3. 本句的“..., whipping the horse to go as fast as possible”是分詞構句，可還原為 “..., and he whipped the horse to go as fast as possible”。

   whip *(v.)* 鞭打。

Finally, after several days of horse riding without any rest, the knight had covered a huge amount of land.

1. Finally, / after several days of horse riding without any rest,

   Adv. / Adv. Phr.

   the knight / had / covered / a huge amount of land.

   S / Aux. / V Passive / O

2. finally *(adv.)* 終於(=at last=in the end)。

3. 本句“a huge amount of land”因為 land（土地）是不可數名詞，所以要用 amount *(n.)* 數量來修飾。

心情小語

Greed has no boundaries. When one is poor, he or she will think: if only I had one million dollars! However, when he or she does have one million dollars, he or she then will wish for 10 million dollars. Yet, when he or she really has 10 million dollars, he or she will wish that they would have 100 million dollars. Greed seems like a bottomless pit which one can ever fill up. Only when he or she is dying will he or she realize the importance of health. Many things in our life cannot be taken back once we lose them. Therefore, we have to make choices and strike the balance all the time. However, health should always be our top priority. We can lead a happy life even though we do not have much money, but without good health we would lose everything in our life. Therefore, we should take good care of our well-being through exercising, balanced diet, regular hours, and no alcohol. It will be better to be a poor happy healthy man rather than to be a sick ill rich man.

人類的貪心是沒有極限的；當你沒錢的時候，就想說我要是有一百萬就好了；當你有一百萬的時候，就會想說要是我有一千萬就好了；當你有一千萬的時候，就會想說我要是有一億就好了。唯有在你快死的時候，才會想到說，我這時什麼都不要，只要身體健康就好了。人生有很多東西，是犧牲掉之後就再也換不回來。有時我們必須要取捨，是不是在這中間找到一個平衡；但只有健康，是不管怎麼樣都不應該被犧牲掉。很多人沒有錢，照樣可以活得很愉快；但失去了健康，卻是再多的錢都買不回來的。所以我們從現在開始，就要時時刻刻，好好的照顧自己的身體；每天多運動、保持均衡飲食、不熬夜、不酗酒。寧可錢當一個身體健康、心靈愉快的窮人；也不要當個看著存摺裏的天文數字，卻沒命花的有錢人。

幽默篇故事

One day, Count Dracula decided to carry out a competition to see which is the finest vampire on his side. So he asked all the vampires to go out and whoever drank most blood won.

All the vampires turned into bats and flew out to look for blood. 3 minutes later, first vampire came back with his mouth full of blood.

"Congratulations, how did you do that?" asked Dracula.

"Do you see that tower? Behind it is a house. I went in and sucked the blood of the whole family."

"Very good." said Dracula.

5 minutes later, the second vampire came back with his face covered in blood.

"How did you do that?" asked Dracula.

"Do you see that tower? Behind it is a school. I went in and sucked the blood of all the students."

"Very impressive!" Dracula said with astonishment.

10 minutes later, the third vampire came back with his whole body covered in blood!

"Wow! You must tell us how you did that!" said Dracula.

"Do you see that tower?" The vampire pointed at the tower.

"Yes." Dracula replied.

"Well, I didn't."

有一天，德古拉伯爵決定舉辦一個比賽，看看誰才是他身邊最強的吸血鬼。所以他要求所有吸血鬼都出去，然後看誰吸到最多的血回來就贏了。

三分鐘之後，第一隻吸血鬼滿嘴都是血的回來了。

「你是怎麼做到的呢？」德古拉問道。

「你有看到前面那座塔嗎？在它後面有間房子，我就進去把全家人的血都吸光了。」

「非常好！」德古拉説道。

五分鐘之後，第二個吸血鬼滿臉是血的飛了回來。

「你又是怎麼做到的呢？」德古拉問道。

「有看到那座塔嗎？在它後面是間學校，我就進去吸了所有學生的血。」

「太了不起了！」

十分鐘之後，第三個吸血鬼全身是血的飛回來。

「哇塞！你一定要告訴我你是怎麼做到的！」德古拉説道。

「你有看到那座塔嗎？」吸血鬼指著那座塔説道。

「有啊。」德古拉回道。

「我就是沒看到。」

文法重點

形容詞的比較 (Comparison)

One day, Count Dracula decided to carry out a competition to see which is the finest vampire on his side.
（有一天，德古拉伯爵決定舉辦一個比賽，看看誰才是他身邊最強的吸血鬼。）

在英文文法中，形容詞主要的功能主要在於修飾名詞或是做為主詞或受詞補語用。而當形容詞所要修飾程度與等級的不同，則有原級(positive)、比較級(comparative)、最高級(superlative)三種區分。

就語意上而言，最高級的比較適用於三者以上的比較。

最高級比較的句型為： S Be V + the adj. est/ the most adj. / the least adj. + S BeV。

例句： Tina is the tallest student in her class.
（Tina 是她班上最高的。）
Tom is the least hardworking worker in the office.
（Tom 是辦公室裡最不努力工作的員工。）

值得注意的是，在一般句子裡，我們用 very 來修飾原級形容詞，如 very tall 或是 very fascinating。而到了比較級與最高級裡，我們不可以再用 very 去修飾比較級與最高級，對於比較級形容詞，我們只能用：a little/a lot/even/still/much/far；而最高級形容詞則須用：much the/the very/by far 。

例句： Dian is far smarter than her brother.
（Dian 比她的弟弟要聰明多了。）
The weather in Yilan is a little more humid than that in Taipei.
（宜蘭的天氣比台北還要再潮濕一點點。）
The movie is by far the most interesting film that I've ever seen.
（這一部電影是我目前看過最有趣的。）

句型解析

So he asked all the vampires to go out and whoever drank most blood won.

1. So he asked all the vampires to go out and
   S1 V1 O Infinitive Phr. Conj.
   whoever... blood won.
   S2 V2
2. 本句的“whoever drank most blood”可還原為“anyone who drank most blood”，意為「任一個吸到最多血的」。

3 minutes later, first vampire came back with his mouth full of blood.

1. 3 minutes later, first vampire came back with his mouth full of
   Adv. Phr. S V Adv. Adv. Phr.
   blood.
2. 本句的“with his mouth full of blood” 用到了 with + O + OC 的句型，意為「伴隨著……」。形容詞 full of blood 作為是受詞補語修飾受詞 his mouth。在這個句型裡的受詞補語可以是形容詞、現在分詞（表主動或進行）、過去分詞（表被動或已經）或表示地方的副詞片語（表示位置）。

   例句：Mia fell asleep on the couch with her mouth open.
   Mia 在躺椅上睡著了，嘴巴張開開。
   The dog watched the food with its mouth watering.
   小狗看著食物，嘴裡口水直流。
   Tom enjoyed the music with his eyes closed.
   Tom 闔上雙眼，享受著音樂。

The suspect looked indifferent, with his hands in his pocket.
嫌疑犯看起來漠不關心，雙手插在口袋裡。

3. 句型 S + be full of + N 意為「充滿著⋯⋯」。

10 minutes later, the third vampire came back with his whole body covered in blood!

1. 10 minutes later, the third vampire came back with his whole...

10 minutes later,	the third vampire	came	back	with his whole... in blood!
Adv. Phr.	S	V	Adv.	Adv. Phr.

2. later *(adv.)* 稍後。

例句：Vicky kept on exercising every day and, one month later, she lost 10 pounds!
Vicky 堅持每天運動，一個月後，她竟然減了 10 磅重！

3. 本句的“with his whole body covered in blood” 用到了 with + O + OC 的句型，意為「伴隨著⋯⋯」。過去分詞 covered in blood 作為是受詞補語(表示被動)修飾受詞 his whole body。

We often see in TV serials that the male lead is hit by a car when he is attentively chasing after the female lead. Whenever I see the scene, I can't help myself to stop satirizing. The coming car is not that small actually, why he would not notice it? However, in reality, it is often seen that we may pay so much attention to a certain point of an issue that we ignore the potential risks. Like the vampire in the story, he rushed over without seeing anyone around. He did not even notice the high tower in front of him. The blind spots exist everywhere. The best solution is to think twice before we jump. To avoid these risks, we have to give the issues we are facing with a second thought. A second thought won't take us much time; however, just because of the second thought, we can prevent many possible hazards. As the above-mentioned male-lead, when he sees the female lead rushing out of the door, he would choose to hold on and make sure the traffic condition before he starts to chase after the female lead (well, then we will lose the dramatic scene). As the saying goes, "A slow fire makes sweet malt." When we are in haste, we tend to ruin what we are doing. Therefore, take our time and handle the situation step by step, and we will have a satisfactory results.

連續劇常有這樣的情節，男主角只顧著追跑走的女主角，眼看著就快要追到了，卻被旁邊不知道什麼時候冒出來的車子給撞了。每次看到這種情節就讓人很想吐槽，車子那麼大台從旁邊過來，最好是事先不會注意到啦！可是有很多時候，我們真的會太專注在問題的某個點上，而忽略了存在旁邊潛在的危險。像故事中的吸血鬼，他就是看到旁邊有人可以吸，立刻毫不考慮衝過去，而沒注意到前面的高塔。這些盲點無時無刻存在於我們的四周，而要迴避它們最好的辦法，就是看到目標在毫不考慮衝過去之前，先等一下！這「一下」要不了我們太多的時間，但或許就因為這「一下」，我們可以避免掉許多傷害。像前面提到的連續劇男主角，在看到女主角衝出去時，能夠先停住，馬路左右看一下確認沒有車子再衝出去，也許就不會被車撞了（當然戲不能這麼演就是了）。所謂事緩則圓，就是這個道理。當我們操之過急的時候，往往只會把事情搞砸；放慢腳步，慢慢的設法應付，反而可以得到圓滿的解決。

生活篇 對話 1

Situation: Sintel, a computer chip manufacturing company, currently has a job opening in its Finance department. John is the first applicant to be interviewed this morning by Sintel's Finance Manager, Ian Gates .

情境：電腦晶片製造公司 Sintel 最近財務部門有個職缺。今天早上，John 是第一位要接受 Sintel 財務經理 Ian Gates 面試的應徵者。

Ian	Let's start the interview. Are you ready?	我們開始面試吧。你準備好了嗎？
David	Yes, I am.	好的，我準備好了。
Ian	First of all, let me introduce myself. I am the Finance Department Manager. As you know there is an open position in my department, and I need to fill this position as soon as possible.	首先，讓我介紹一下我自己。我是財務部經理。就你所知，我們部門有個職缺，而我必須儘快地找到適合這個職務的人。
David	Please, tell me a little bit about the position.	那麼請多告訴我一些關於這個職位的訊息。
Ian	The new employee will have to work closely with the Accounting department. He will also have to deal with the bank on a daily basis.	新的員工必須與會計部門緊密合作。他也得每天處理銀行的事務。
David	What type of qualifications do you require?	這個職務需要什麼資格？

Ian	I require a four-year college degree in Finance. Some working experience would be helpful.	我需要財務領域大學畢業的人才，有些工作經驗是最好的。
David	What kind of experience are you looking for?	你指的工作經驗是？
Ian	Doing office work is good. I am willing to train the new person.	能處理辦公室文書工作。我也願意訓練新進人員。
David	That is great!	那太好了！

生活篇 對話 2

Situation: The Finance Department Manager of Sintel, Ian Gates, is interviewing John now.

情境：Sintel 的財務部經理 Ian Gates 現在正在面試 John。

Ian	David, tell me about yourself.	David，說說你自己吧。
David	I just graduated with a Bachelor degree in Finance. I have been working part-time as a payroll clerk for the last two years.	我是財務系大學畢業生，我已經兼職出納員兩年了。
Ian	What are you looking for in a job?	你對工作的期望是什麼?
David	The job should help me see what Finance is all about. I have learned a lot of Finance theories at school, and now it is time for me to put them into practice.	工作能幫助我看到財務是什麼吧。我在學校學了許多財務理論，然後現在該是我把這些理論付諸實踐了。
Ian	What are your strengths? Why should I hire you?	你的強項是什麼？我為什麼要僱用你？
David	I am a hard-working person and a fast learner. I am very eager to learn, and I get along fine with people.	我是一個努力的人，而且學得很快。我很渴望學習，我也擅長與人相處。
Ian	Do you still have any questions for me?	你還有什麼問題要問我嗎？

David	No, I think I have a pretty good understanding of the job. I hope to have the opportunity to work for you.	沒有，我想我已經很了解這個職務的情形。我希望我有機會能與你共事。
Ian	David, thank you for coming.	David，謝謝你來面試。
David	Thank you for seeing me.	謝謝你面試我。

單字與實用例句

- applicant *(n.)* 應徵者，申請者

  Applicants for this job position must have a good command of English and French.
  這個職缺的應徵者必須有良好的英文跟法文的能力。

- ready *(adj.)* 準備好的

  It took Fiona to get ready for her date with Sean.
  Fiona 花了許多時間準備跟 Sean 的約會。

- introduce *(v.)* 介紹

  May I introduce you Nancy, my classmate in junior high?
  我可以向您介紹我國中同學 Nancy 嗎？

- position *(n.)* 職位，方位

  The professor left his teaching position and ran a small shop in the downtown.
  那位教授離開教職並在市區開了間小店。

- clerk *(n.)* 職員

  The clerk helped Miranda try on the clothes she picked up.
  那位店員幫 Miranda 試穿她所挑選的衣服。

- theory *(n.)* 理論

  The theory is based on the results of numerous experiments carried out by that scientist.
  這個理論是基於那位科學家所做的實驗結果。

- strength *(n.)* 強項，優勢

  Before making your career plan, you have to consider your strengths and weaknesses.
  在你做任何生涯計劃時，你必須要考慮你的強項與弱點。

- eager *(adj.)* 急切的，渴望的

  The athlete is eager to win the championship.
  那位運動員很想要贏得冠軍。

好用主題用語，用法解說

I am willing to train the new person.
I am very eager to learn, and I get along fine with people.

表示意願的英文句型：在一般對話中，我們常常要表達自己對於某件事的意願程度。以下介紹幾種常用於表達意願的句型：

	例句
表示意願程度高	• I am happy to team up with your company. （我很高興能和你們的公司合作。） • I am willing to take few more jobs. （我願意接受更多的工作。） • I am eager/keen/ excited to visit the gallery. （我熱切的/強烈的/興奮的想要參觀藝廊。） • I am looking forward to your visit. （我期待著你的來訪。） • I can't wait to go hiking with you. （我等不及要跟你去遠足了。） • I am dying for a cold drink. （我真想要喝杯冷飲。）
表示意願程度低	• I am unwilling to go on this business trip. （我不想去出差。） • I am reluctant to lend my cell phone to Robin. （我不想借 Robin 我的手機。）

Unit 15 副詞

勵志篇 故事

Every year, Lisa and Hans would go to the State Fair, and every year, Hans would say, "Lisa, I'd like to ride in that airplane."

And Lisa would always said, "I know, Hans, but the airplane ride cost a hundred dollars, and a hundred dollars is a hundred dollars."

One year, Hans finally said "Lisa, I'm 75 years old. If I don't have a ride on that plane this year, I may never get another chance!"

The pilot overheard them and said, "Hey, tell you what, if you can keep absolute silent during the flight, you can ride it for free. But if you said one word, you have to pay me one hundred dollars."

Lisa and Hans agreed, so the ride began. The pilot did all kinds of rolls and dives, twists and turns over and over again, but didn't hear a word.

When they finally landed, the pilot turned to Hans and said, "Gosh, I did everything I could to get you to yell, and you never said a word!"

"Well," Hans shrugged, "I was going to say something when Lisa fell out, but a hundred is a hundred dollars.

麗莎和漢斯每年都會到州立園遊會去玩，而每年漢斯都會說：「麗莎，我想搭那個飛機看看。」

而麗莎也總是這麼說：「我知道，漢斯，但是那個搭一次要一百塊，而一百塊不是小錢啊。」

有一年，漢斯終於說道：「麗莎，我今年已經 75 歲了，如果今年再不搭的話，我怕我以後再也沒有機會了。」

飛機的駕駛員剛好聽到他們的對話：「嘿，這麼著吧，如果整個飛行途中你們都可以保持絕對的安靜，你們就可以免費搭乘。但如果你們說了一個字，就得付我一百塊。」

麗莎和漢斯同意了，飛行也就展開了。駕駛員一再地做了各種的翻滾和俯衝、迴旋和轉彎，但卻一個字也沒聽到。

當飛機降落時，駕駛員對漢斯說道：「老天，我儘我可能的使出手段讓你們大叫，而你們卻一個字都沒講！」

「這個嘛，」漢斯聳聳肩：「當麗莎掉出機外時我本來想說點什麼的，但是一百塊不是小錢啊。」

文法重點

Every year, Lisa and Hans would go to the State Fair, and every year, Hans would say, "Lisa, I'd like to ride in that airplane."
（麗莎和漢斯每年都會到州立園遊會去玩，
而每年漢斯都會說：「麗莎，我想搭那個飛機看看。」）

在英文中，副詞是用來修飾動詞、形容詞與其他副詞的修飾語。就句型上來說，副詞的存在並不影響句子的完整性，但是副詞的存在，卻會增加文意的精確性。

以 The bird flies(S + V)為例，以下添加副詞以完整句義。

The bird flies slowly.（鳥飛得慢。）
The bird flies very slowly.（鳥飛得很慢。）
The bird flies very slowly in the sky.（鳥在天空上飛得很慢。）
The bird flies very slowly in the sky now.
（鳥現在在天空上飛得很慢。）

一般來說，副詞可以分成：時間副詞、地方副詞、程度副詞、頻率副詞與情態副詞。

- 時間副詞：如 now, already, yesterday, tomorrow, every day, next month, last year, in 2000, since 1998...

  例句：Robert went to Japan last week.
  （Robert 上禮拜去日本。）
  Daisy has moved to Turkey since 1998.
  （Daisy 從 1998 年時就搬到土耳其了。）

- 地方副詞：如 here, there, out, in, around, somewhere, in the room, in front of the house…

  例句：Sandy played games with her son in the living room.
  （Sandy 跟她的兒子在客廳裡玩。）

- 程度副詞：如 very, too, enough, quite, greatly, slightly, approximately, totally, completely, fully, wholly…

  例句：Lung cancer has greatly to do with smoking.
  （肺癌大多是抽煙所引起的。）

- 頻率副詞：如 always, usually, often, seldom, hardly, barely, never, sometimes…

  例句：Victor seldom visits his parents in the country.
  （Victor 很少拜訪他住在鄉下的父母。）

- 情態副詞：如 slowly, fast, easily, hard, loudly, quietly, carefully, deliberately, accidentally…

  例句：Yvonne ran fast out of the restaurant as soon as the baby cried.
  （娃娃一哭時，Yvonne 馬上快跑出餐廳。）

句型解析

If I don't have a ride on that plane this year, I may never get another chance!

1. [If I don't have a ride on that plane this year], I may never get another chance!

[If I don't have a ride on that plane this year],	I	may	never	get	another chance!
Adv. Cl.	S	Aux.	Adv.	V	O

2. 本句的 If I don't have a ride on that plane this year 是表示條件的副詞子句。if 是連接詞，意為「假如…」。
3. ride *(n.)* 乘（馬、車、船）一趟。

… if you can keep absolute silent during the flight, you can ride it for free.

1. ...[if you can keep absolute silent during the flight], you can ride it for free.

...[if you can keep absolute silent during the flight],	you	can	ride	it	for free.
Adv. Cl.	S	Aux.	V	O	Adv. Phr.

2. 本句的 if you can keep absolute silent during the flight 是表示條件的副詞子句。if 是連接詞，意為「假如……」。
3. keep *(v.)* 保持(=remain=stay)。其用法為 keep/remain/stay + adj.。

   例句：Steven tried to keep awake in the midnight by having cups of coffee.
   Steven 藉著喝許多杯咖啡，試著在午夜保持清醒。
4. 副詞片語 for free 意為「免費地……」。

The pilot did all kinds of rolls and dives, twists and turns over and over again, but didn't hear a word.

1. The pilot did all kinds of rolls and dives, twists and turns

   S1 V1 O1

   over and over again, but did n't hear a word.

   Adv. Phr. Conj. Aux. Adv. V2 O2

2. 片語 all kinds of + 複數名詞，意為「各種的……」(=various kinds of + N. pl.)。

   例句：You can see all kinds of things in a department store.

   你可以在百貨公司見到各式各樣的商品。

3. 副詞片語 over and over again 意為「一再地……」。

   例句：My girlfriend likes to nag about my clothing over and over again.

   我女朋友喜歡一再地嘮叨我的穿衣風格。

心情小語

"Seize the moment" is an important thing. However, many people end up discovering that they are not used to a relaxing life when they finally have some time to take a rest after hard work in their life. We used to be educated that playing is immoral and that playing means laziness. As it turns out, many Taiwanese work day and night and do not know how to manage their life. However, we do not have more income because of our sacrifices. Instead, most Europeans work hard at work and play hard after work. They do not have less income because of their playing. Well goes the saying, "All work and no play make Jack a dull person." Work hard and play hard. Life is short. Therefore, do not wait until we get old. When we are retired, we may have much time but will we have the energy to play? Maybe we cannot change the mindset of most bosses in Taiwan, but we can change our own attitude toward work: to be person who can play hard and work hard.

及時行樂，是很重要的一件事，很多人一輩子汲汲營營，等到好不容易可以休息了，卻發現自己根本沒那個命享福。因為我們從小就一直被教育說「玩」這件事是不好的、玩就是偷懶，所以台灣人非常努力工作，卻完全不懂得生活。結果台灣人這樣沒日沒夜的打拼，收入有比較多嗎？看看歐洲人，工作時努力工作，但下班時間一到就立刻走人，假日就算公司爆炸也不關他的事，結果人家這樣有賺得比我們少嗎？所以當我們有機會去玩，就好好的玩，不要去玩還一直想著工作，當一個工作沒效率、放假也不會玩的人。有多賣力的在工作，就要多賣力地去玩；人生苦短，千萬不要想說「等我老了、退休了有的是時間去玩」，因為，你確定到那個時候，還有那種體力和健康去玩嗎？也許我們改變不了老闆就是要把員工操死的想法，但我們可以改變自己那種一定要為公司沒日沒夜賣命的想法，當個認真工作，同時也認真在享受生活的快樂人吧。

A woman called her husband during work and asked him to pick up some organic vegetables for the dinner on his way home.

The husband arrived at the grocery store and began to look for organic vegetables, but he's not sure whether the ones in the store were organic vegetables. So he grabbed the vegetables and went to the storekeeper.

"Hi, can you tell me if these vegetables are organic or not?" he asked.

"I'm sorry, I don't know what you mean." The storekeeper looked confused.

"I'd like to buy some organic vegetables, but didn't seem to find any label or something on the vegetables. So I'm wondering if you can tell me. Are these organic vegetables?" The husband put the vegetables he got on the counter.

"These are absolutely fresh vegetables, just came in this morning directly from the field…if that's what you mean."

"No." the husband thought for a while and decided to explain to him in the simplest way, "Look, these vegetables are for my wife. I just need to know if they have been sprayed with poisonous chemicals."

"Of course not!" the storekeeper replied "You'll have to do that yourself."

一個女人在上班時間打電話給她先生，要他在回家時順便去買些有機蔬菜當晚餐。

丈夫到了雜貨店尋找有機蔬菜，但他並不確定這些到底是不是。所以他便抓了一把青菜到店員那邊。

「嗨，我想請問一下，這些是有機蔬菜嗎？」

「對不起，我不知道你的意思。」店員一臉疑惑地説道。

「我想要買有機蔬菜，但沒看到上面有任何標示或什麼的，所以才想請你跟我講一下説這些是有機的嗎？」丈夫説著，將手上的蔬菜放到櫃台上。

「這些是絕對新鮮的蔬菜，今天一大早才從產地直送過來的，你是要問這個嗎？」

「不，」丈夫想了一會兒，於是決定用最簡單的方式解釋給他聽：「聽著，這些蔬菜是要給我老婆吃的，我只是想要知道它們有沒有被噴上有毒的化學藥品而已。」

「當然沒有！」店員回答道：「這種事你得自己來才行啊。」

文法重點

So he grabbed the vegetables and went to the storekeeper.
（所以他便抓了一把青菜到店員那邊。）

在英文中，副詞是用來修飾動詞、形容詞與其他副詞的修飾語。就句型上來説，副詞的存在並不影響句子的完整性，但是副詞的存在，卻會增加文意的精確性。除了前一個單元介紹的時間副詞、地方副詞、程度副詞、頻率副詞與情態副詞之外，在英文中，還有表示語氣的副詞。

一般來説，常見的語氣副詞有：表示因果關係的副詞、表示轉折語氣的副詞、表示列舉的副詞、表示讓步的副詞、表示換句話説的副詞、表示加強語氣的副詞。

- 因果關係的副詞：如 therefore, thus, hence, accordingly, as a result...

例句：Oliver always complains; therefore, no one likes him.

（Oliver 總是抱怨，於是乎沒人喜歡他。）

- 表示轉折語氣的副詞：如 however, yet, still, nevertheless, nonetheless...

例句：Iris sent her resumes to 30 companies; however, none of them asked her for an interview.

（Iris 寄給 30 間公司她的履歷；但是，卻沒有任何一家叫她去面試。）

- 表示列舉的副詞：如 besides, in addition, moreover, furthermore, first, second, third...

例句：Leonardo Da Vinci was a famous artist. Moreover, he was a great scientist.

（李奧納多達芬奇是個知名的藝術家。此外，他也是個偉大的科學家。）

- 表示讓步的副詞：如 after all, though

例句：Many parents should not set high standards for their children. After all, they are still kids.

（許多家長不應該為自己的孩子設高標準。畢竟，他們還小。）

- 表示換句話說的副詞：如 in other words, that is to say, that is, namely, to put it differently...

例句：No one in Class 202 is taller than Polly; that is, she is the tallest!

（202 班沒人比 Polly 高；換句話說，她是最高的！）

- 表示加強語氣的副詞：如 certainly, absolutely, definitely, surly, really, of course...

例句：Your response to the incident is absolutely offensive.
（你對於這個事件的回應真的十分不禮貌。）

句型解析

The husband arrived at the grocery store and began to look for organic vegetables, but he's not sure whether the ones in the store were organic vegetables.

1. The husband arrived at the grocery store and began

   S1 V1 Adv. Phr. Conj. V2

   to look for... vegetables, but he' s not

   Infinitive Phr. Conj. S2 BeV Adv.

   sure [whether the ones in the store were organic vegetables].

   Adj. N. Cl.→ O
2. 動詞片語 look for+ N，意為「尋找……」(=search for=seek)。
3. 句型 S BeV sure that/if S +V 意為「某人確定……」。

   例句：Ben was not sure if he would be admitted to the university.
   Ben 不確定他是否能進入那間大學。

Hi, can you tell me if these vegetables are organic or not?

1. Hi, can you tell me [if these vegetables are organic or not]?

   Aux. S V I.O. N. Cl.→ D.O.

2. 本句的"if these vegetables are organic or not" 是名詞子句作 tell 的直接受詞用。

3. tell *(v.)* 說；告訴。是授與動詞，本句亦可以改成 can you tell if these vegetables are organic or not to me?

I just need to know if they have been sprayed with poisonous chemicals.

1. I just need

   S Adv. V

   to know if they have been sprayed with poisonous chemicals].

   Infinitive Phr.→ O

2. 本句的"if they have been sprayed with poisonous chemicals"是名詞子句作 know 的受詞用。

3. 本句"with poisonous chemicals"的 with 是介系詞，意為「用……」。

   chemicals *(n. pl.)* 農藥。

心情小語

Disputes are commonly seen in marriages. Although everyone knows that communication can settle the disputes, it is hard for couples to say words out of their bosom. Like snowballs, the disputes then accumulate in their hearts and grow larger and larger. Eventually, it will explore when there is no room for them to pile up their dissatisfaction. Many married friends of mine often complain to other friends that their couples never seem to change. However, complaints can never help you solve problems. Instead of nagging all the time, you can try to communicate with your spouse with patience. Sometimes, we may hear some unbearable or offensive words from our spouses; however, with patience we can calm them down. Or we can listen to what they really mean. Sometimes the problems are ours. If one wants to communicate and solve the problems, they can sort them out eventually. The worst situation is that they refuse to communicate and get angry with each other. You might think that "I hope he/she knows what he/she did!" Don't be silly. You will get nothing but an upset mood.

夫妻生活中會有很多的不滿，但其實只要能多溝通就可以解決了；但奇怪的是，有時候一些話對最親密的人，反而難以說出口。而這些不滿不說出口，堆積在心裡頭，就會像滾雪球一樣越滾越大，直到最後再也容不下這顆雪球而爆發，造成大雪崩。身邊有許多結婚的朋友，總是會跟其他朋友抱怨「我家老公就是這樣那樣，氣死我了」；或是「我家那個老太婆就老是這樣那樣」。只是跟朋友抱怨這些，有助於問題解決嗎？或者只是要取暖，找個可以同意自己意見的人來說「你沒有錯，錯的是你老婆/老公」而已？所以與其到處去抱怨這種事，不如找另一半坐下來，好好地溝通。有時另一半會很容易聽到某些字眼就生氣而不想聽，這時也只能耐著心安撫，放低姿態，慢慢地讓對方冷靜下來；或者就讓對方講，聽聽看對方的看法，因為說不定我們自己也有問題。只要有一方有心想要溝通，問題就一定可以得到解決。最怕就是都不講，然後自己在那邊生悶氣「希望對方自己知道自己做了什麼」，別傻了，這樣除了氣壞自己的身子，是什麼都得不到的！

生活篇 對話 1

Situation: David was hired as a financial analyst by Sintel. Today is David's first day at work.

Situation: David 已經錄取 Sintel 的財務分析師。今天是他第一天工作。

Ian	Good morning, David. Let me give you a tour of our facility. Let's go!	早安，David. 讓我帶你參觀我們的設施。我們走吧！
David	OK, I am ready.	好的，我準備好了。
Ian	Over there is Mary. She is our senior financial analyst. You will be working with her in the future. Let's go say hi to her. Mary, this is David, our department's new addition.	在那兒的是 Mary。她是我們資深財務分析師。你接下來會跟她共事。我們去跟她打聲招呼。Mary，這是 David，我們部門的新進員工。
Mary	Welcome aboard, David. I am very glad to see you. Boy! I was swamped with work the last couple of weeks. But, I can see myself going home at a more decent time from now on.	歡迎加入我們，David。很高興見到你，孩子！我這幾週都被工作淹沒了。但從現在起終於可以見到自己能在一個合理的時間下班回家了。
David	Thank you. I am very happy to be here. Just let me know whenever you need me. I am glad to be of any assistance.	謝謝，我很高興能來這裡工作。如果妳需要我，請儘管讓我知道。我樂意提供任何協助。

Ian	I am giving David a tour of our facility so that he knows his way around here.	我正在帶 David 參觀我們的設施，這樣他就會更熟悉這裡。
Mary	See you later, David.	待會兒見，David。
David	OK, Mary.	好的，Mary。

生活篇 對話 2

Situation: David was hired as a financial analyst by Sintel. Today is David's first day at work.

Situation: David 已經錄取 Sintel 的財務分析師。今天是他第一天工作。

Ian	We are now in the Finance department. Next to us, on your left, is the Accounting department. On your right is the Human Resources department. Go downstairs and we are in the Engineering department. Further down, at the end of the hallway is the Production area. You will be dealing with Steve, the Production manager. I will introduce you to him later because he is in a meeting at the moment.	我們現在在財務部。我們隔壁左邊是會計部。在你右邊是人力資源部。走下樓是工程部。而在走廊的盡頭是生產部門。你會跟生產部門經理 Steve 共事。因為他現在正在開會，所以我待會兒才會介紹你們認識。

	Let's go back to your desk so that we can talk about your duties.	我們回到你辦公桌去，然後來說說你的工作吧！
David	OK.	好的。
Ian	Yes, come see me whenever you have questions.	嗯嗯，如果你有任何問題，你可以來找我。
David	Thank you.	謝謝。
Ian	So, it is better that both of you start working on this project as soon as possible.	那麼，你們兩個如果可以儘早著手這個計劃會更好。
David	I will get together with Mary soon.	我會趕快跟 Mary 一起合作。
Ian	OK, that should be enough for now. I leave you on your own to get organized.	好，目前這樣應該差不多了。我就讓你自己去處理事情了。
David	Thank you, Ian.	謝謝，Ian。

單字與實用例句

- hire *(v.)* 雇用

  They hired a tour guide to lead them to visit the city.
  他們雇用一個導遊帶領他們參觀這個城市。

- facility *(n.)* 設備

  The facilities in that school are advanced and student-friendly.
  那間學校的設備很先進，且易於學生使用。

- senior *(adj.)* 資深的，高階的

  It is more polite to name an aged person “a senior citizen”.
  稱呼一個上年紀的人「資深公民」比較有禮貌。

- decent *(adj.)* 合宜的

  John leads a decent life by working as a lawyer.
  John 身為一個律師過著小康的生活。

- assistance *(n.)* 協助

  The final assistance for the sponsor solved the crisis of the company.
  贊助商的財務協助解決了公司的危機。

- hallway *(n.)* 走廊

  There are a lot of guests crowed in the hallway.
  走廊上擠滿賓客。

- deal with *(v. phr.)* 處理

  A multitasker is a person who deals with different things at the same time.
  多工處理者指的是同時間要處理許多不同事情的人。

- organize *(v.)* 組織

  The writer organized her thoughts and arranged a good plot for her next novel.
  那個作家組織她的想法並為她下一本小說安排了個好情節。

好用主題用語，用法解說

Over there is Mary.
On your right is the Human Resources department.

地方副詞為首的倒裝句：一般英文的句子語序為 S（主詞）+ V（動詞）。但是當我們想要強調地方副詞時，如 Here comes the bus（公車來了），我們會將地方副詞放句首，再接上動詞與主詞，形成 Adv-phr + V+S 的倒裝句型。

- there/ here 的倒裝：

  Here comes the train.

  （火車來了。）

  Here you are.

  （你來了。）

要注意，在此類倒裝句型中，主詞若為一般名詞時，須和動詞倒裝；但若主詞為代名詞時，主詞和動詞位置不倒裝。

- 介副詞(up, away, out, off)的倒裝

  Away flew my kite!

  （我風箏飛走了！）

  Out he went.

  （他走了。）

- 表位置副詞片語的倒裝

  On the right is a hotel.

  （右手邊是間旅館。）

  Behind the door hid a girl.

  （門後面躲了一個女孩。）

Unit 16 連接詞

勵志篇 故事

A doctor came running towards the surgery room after being called for an urgent surgery. The patient's father was pacing in the hall when he suddenly saw the doctor coming.

"What took you so long? Don't you know that my son's life is in danger? Don't you have any sense of responsibility?"

The doctor smiled and said "I'm sorry, I came here as soon as possible. Now please calm down so I can do my work."

"Don't tell me to calm down! What if it's your son in that room? Would you calm down? If your son dies now, what would you do? It's easier for you to say since it doesn't concern you." said the father angrily.

The doctor just simply smiled and walked away.

The surgery took several hours after which the doctor went out and said "Your son is saved! If you have any questions, ask the nurse."

Didn't wait for the father to retort, the doctor ran away.

"Why is he so arrogant? He couldn't wait a few minutes so "I can ask about my son's situation?" the father mumbled.

The nurse came out with tears on her face "His son had a serious accident yesterday. He was in the emergency room trying to save his son when we called him for your son's surgery. And now that he saved your son's life, he left running to save his son."

一個醫生接到緊急手術的電話，快步朝著手術室跑過來。病人的父親在走道上踱步，一看到醫生過來立刻走過去責問道：

「你怎麼這麼慢才來？！難道你不知道我兒子命在旦夕嗎？難道你一點責任感都沒有嗎？」

醫生笑著説道：「我很抱歉，我已經儘快趕過來了，請冷靜下來讓我做我的工作。」

「不要叫我冷靜下來！如果現在手術室裡的是你兒子呢？你冷靜的下來嗎？如果你的兒子現在就死了你會怎麼辦？因為跟你無關你才有辦法講得一副很輕鬆的樣子！」病人父親氣呼呼的説道。

醫生只是給他一個微笑，便走掉了。

手術歷經好幾個小時，醫生終於走出來説道：「你的兒子得救了，如果還有任何問題的話，去問護士。」

説完不等那位父親回話，醫生就又快步跑走了。

「他是在跩什麼啊？就不能多等個幾分鐘讓我問一下我兒子的狀況嗎？」病人父親不滿的咕噥道。

護士淚流滿面的走出手術室説道：「他兒子昨天發生嚴重的意外，當我們打電話告知他你兒子的手術時，他正在急診室搶救他兒子。而現在他已經救活你兒子了，才趕快要跑去救他的兒子。」

文法重點

連接詞 (Conjunctions)

It's easier for you to say since it doesn't concern you.
（因為跟你無關你才有辦法講得一副很輕鬆的樣子！）

在英文文法中，連接詞是用來連接句子中的字、詞、片語或是子句。連接詞依其功能區分有：對等連接詞、相關連接詞與從屬連接詞。其中，從屬連接詞(Subordinating Conjunctions)是連接從屬子句與主要子句形成為一個複雜句。因為從屬子句的功能在於修飾主要子句，所以它無法單獨存在，必須要跟主要子句形成為一個複雜句。要注意，當從屬子句放在句首時，需要加逗點在接上主要子句。常見的從屬連接詞有：

從屬連接詞	
時間	after, before, as soon as, while, when, by the time, the moment, since, until...
原因	as, because, since, now that...
條件	as long as, if, provided that, unless...
讓步	although, though, even though, even if...

例句：After John had his breakfast, he took his bag and went to school.

（John 吃完早餐之後，他拿著他的背包上學去了。）

I got up immediately the moment the alarm clock went off.

（當鬧鐘響起的時候，我就立即起床了。）

The sports meet was cancelled because the typhoon hit Taiwan this morning.

（運動會取消了，因為颱風今天早上侵襲台灣。）

As long as we have enough money and time, we can achieve our goal.

（只要我們有足夠的金錢和時間，我們就能達成目的。）

Emily decided to go to that private university although her parents did not allow her to do so.

（Emily 決定要上私立大學，雖然她的父母並不同意她這麼做。）

句型解析

A doctor came running towards the surgery room after being called for an urgent surgery.

1. A doctor came running towards... room

   S V Ving Adv. Phr.

   after being called... surgery.

   Participial Construction

2. 在 come, go, sit, stand, run, leave 和 lie 之後常常接 Ving，表示兩個動作同時進行。以本句"A doctor came running towards the surgery room"為例，意為「一位醫生邊跑邊來到手術房」。

   例句：Chuck lay on his bed playing his mobile phones.
   Chuck 躺在床上玩手機。

3. 本句的"... after being called for an urgent surgery"是分詞構句，可還原副詞子句"... after he was called for an urgent surgery"。

The surgery took several hours after which the doctor went out.

1. The surgery took several hours [after which the doctor went out].

   S V O Adj. Cl.

2. take *(v.)* 花費（時間）。其用法為：事物 + take + 時間，需注意主詞不可為人。

   例句：The novel took the writer ten years to complete it.
   這本小說花了作者十年時間才寫完它。

3. 本句的“after which the doctor went out”是形容詞子句，修飾先行詞 several hours。

And now that he saved your son's life, he left running to save his son.

1. And [now that... life], he left running to save his son.

   Adv. Cl. S V Ving Adv. Phr.

2. 本句的 now that 是連接詞，意為「因為……；既然……」(=because=as=since)。

3. 在 come, go, sit, stand, run, leave 和 lie 之後常常接 Ving，表示兩個動作同時進行。以本句“he left running to save his son”為例，意為「他離開手術房跑去救他兒子」。

心情小語

We tend to judge others from our own points of views. For example, we tend to think of a man with a fierce and malicious look as a villain. We are likely to regard a man who does not handle our affairs immediately as a lazy worker. Like the father in the story, he got anxious when he learned that his son would have an operation. However, he got desperate so he started to blame the doctor. In fact, the doctor abandoned his own child and came to rescue his son's life. Although the story ends there, it is easy to figure out the resolution. The father would be much sorry and felt ashamed of his own selfishness and ignorance. If we can be more considerate for others, I believe the society will be much warmer.

我們經常會很自以為是地用自己的觀點去批判別人。例如某個人長得橫眉豎目，就認為他一定是壞蛋、某個人沒有馬上處理我們的事，就一定不認真、打混摸魚去了。像故事中的父親，因為自己的小孩要動手術，心裡頭著急是可想而知的，但卻因為這樣就一直怪罪醫生動作太慢、沒責任感、不管別人小孩死活。事實上，這位醫生卻是丟下自己小孩跑來先救他的兒子；雖然故事只到這邊結束，但可想而知，這位父親此時一定無比後悔，也會因為自己的自私和無知而感到慚愧不已。如果我們每個人能夠有多一點體貼別人的心，在自以為是的責怪別人之前，先想想別人是不是可能有什麼不得已的苦衷，先打從心裡去關心別人，相信會讓這個社會變得溫暖許多。

Jessie was walking down the street when she was approached by a lady beggar asking for money.

Jessie took 20 bucks and asked "If I give you this money, will you spend it on cosmetics?"

"Don't be ridiculous." The beggar replied, "Does it look like I have nothing better to spend money on?"

"Will you spend it on manicure?"

"No." the beggar said, "Don't you understand? I need money to stay alive."

"How about hair? Will you spend it on your hair?" Jessie asked.

The beggar was quite annoyed, "NO! I just need money for food and shelter!"

"In that case, I would like to take you for a dinner with me and my husband tonight.", said Jessie.

"Why?" The beggar asked.

"Well, I think it's important for my husband to see what a lady looks like when she doesn't spend her money on cosmetics, manicure and hair."

潔西在路上走著，突然有個女乞丐過來向她要錢。

潔西拿出 20 塊美金問道：「如果我給妳錢，妳會拿去買化妝品嗎？」

「別胡扯了，」乞丐回答：「我看起來像是有辦法把錢花到其他地方去的樣子嗎？」

「妳會把錢花在指甲美容上嗎？」

「不，」乞丐說道：「難道妳不知道我只是需要錢活下去嗎？」

「那頭髮呢？妳會把錢拿去弄頭髮嗎？」

乞丐已經覺得有點煩了：「不！我只是要錢來買食物並且找個遮風避雨的地方而已！」

「那如果是這樣的話，我想要找妳今晚一起跟我和我丈夫共進晚餐。」潔西說道。

「為什麼？」乞丐問道。

「因為我覺得非常有必要讓我丈夫知道當一個女人如果不把錢花在化妝品、指甲美容和弄頭髮上會是個什麼樣子！」

文法重點

連接詞 (Conjunctions)

> "In that case, I would like to take you for a dinner with me and my husband tonight.", said Jessie.
> （那如果是這樣的話，我想要找妳今晚一起跟我和我丈夫共進晚餐。）

在英文文法中，連接詞是用來連接句子中的字、詞、片語或是子句。連接詞依其功能區分有：對等連接詞、相關連接詞與從屬連接詞。

- 對等連接詞 (Coordinating Conjunctions)：and（和），but（但），or（或者）

對等連接詞是用來連接句子中詞性相對等的字、詞、片語或子句，換句話說，就是「字」對「字」、「片語」對「片語」或「子句」對「子句」。

Jean is beautiful, smart and kind.

（Jean 人長得漂亮、優秀又善良。）

Would you like to have tea, coffee, or water?

（你想要茶、咖啡還是水呢？）

Brad studied hard for the test but failed it in the end.

（Brad 為了這一次的考試用功讀書，但最終還是不及格。）

要注意當對等連接詞連接兩個獨立子句時，連接詞前面須加逗點。

Kim had the breakfast, and Lisa washed the dishes.

（Kim 吃早餐，Lisa 洗碗盤。）

Nina wanted to go to the movies, but Sam would like to go shopping.

（Nina 要去看電影，但是 Sam 想要去逛街。）

We can choose to stand up and fight, or we can stay still and do nothing.

（我們可以選擇挺身而出並且戰鬥，或是按兵不動，什麼都不做。）

- 相關連接詞(Correlative Conjunctions)：either... or （不是……就是……），neither... nor （既不……且不……），not only... but also （不但……而且……），both... and （……和……兩者都）

相關連接詞是需要對等使用的連接詞，此外它們跟對等連接詞一樣，需要連接詞性相對等的字、詞、片語或子句。

Either you or I have to take charge of this shop.

（不是你就是我必須要負責這一間店。）

Brian is neither handsome nor rich.

（Brain 長得不帥也不有錢。）

The accident happened not only because of the poor weather condition but also the driver's carelessness.

（這一個事故的發生，不只是因為天氣狀況惡劣也是因為駕駛的不小心。）

Both Vivian and Catherine will work on this project for you.

（Vivian 和 Catherine 都會幫你來進行這一個項目。）

句型解析

Jessie was walking down the street when she was approached by a lady beggar asking for money.

1. Jessie was walking down the street [when she was... for money].

   S BeV V Progressive Adv. Phr. Adv. Cl.

2. approach *(v.)* 靠近。

   例句：Watch out! There is a car approaching.
   注意一點！有輛車正靠近。

3. 動詞片語 ask for+ N 意為「要求⋯⋯」(=beg for)。

   例句：Ray asked for a new cellphone as his birthday gift.
   Ray 要支新手機當作生日禮物。

If I give you this money, will you spend it on cosmetics?

1. [If I give you this money], will you spend it on cosmetics?

   Adv. Cl. Aux. S V O Adv. Phr.

2. 本句的"If I give you this money"是表示條件的副詞子句。

3. spend *(v.)* 花用。其用法為「人+ spend+金錢/時間+ Ving/on N」。

例句：Pam spent a lot of money collecting silver coins/ on silver coins.
Pam 花了許多錢蒐集銀幣。

Well, I think it's important for my husband to see what a lady looks like when she doesn't spend her money on cosmetics, manicure and hair.

1. Well, I think
S V
[it's important for my husband to... manicure and hair].
N. Cl.→ O

2. 本句的"it's important for my husband to see what a lady looks like when she doesn't spend her money on cosmetics, manicure and hair"是名詞子句作 think 的受詞用。同樣的道理，"what a lady looks like when she doesn't spend her money on cosmetics, manicure and hair"是名詞子句作 see 的受詞。

3. 動詞片語 look like+ N 意為「看起像……」(=resemble)。

例句：Nancy looks like/resembles her mother.
Nancy 看起來跟她媽媽很像。

心情小語

Recently, there has been a TV show in which many celebrities' wives bid their branded bags. In that show, they often took their luxurious bags and told the audience, "They are really cheap; they are so worth your money." Thus, under such influence, many people think that their life will be complete with a branded product even if they have to starve for months. The media should be blamed for conveying this wrong value. Of course, if we can afford to, it is fine to buy expensive and luxurious branded bags. However, how many of us are as rich as those celebrities' wives whose monthly income is up to hundreds of thousands of dollars? In fact, if we are confident, we will be gorgeous with an inexpensive bag from a night market. If we lack confidence, we are nothing more than a copycat which copies how chics and celebrities wear. In short, it is useless to make ourselves someone else. What we should do is to define and refine our own strengths and make them shine!

前陣子電視節目常出現這種單元：叫一堆藝人太太到節目上競標名牌包，然後看她們拿著一個個動輒上萬的名牌包在那邊說「好便宜，好值得」。媒體渲染這種錯誤的價值觀固然該被譴責，但這種單元之所以會一再出現，也表示有很多人愛看。當然如果經濟能力負擔得起，要買多貴的包包都沒人會講話，只是在看這節目的一般大眾，有幾個人是像這些大嫂團這樣，月入數十萬的呢？結果就在這樣的催眠之下，造成許多人有種「就算幾個月不吃不喝，我也要買個名牌包，這輩子才不算白活」的錯誤觀念。其實一個人只要有自信，就算拿的是夜市一個 390 的包包，大家都會覺得很好看；反觀一個人要是缺乏自信，只是照抄一些網路正妹的裝扮、學藝人拿名牌包，這樣你充其量也只是個仿製品而已。所以我們每個人都應該找出自己真正的價值，想辦法讓別人看到自己的優點，從而讓自己有自信；而不是用一些外在的物質來偽裝出一個金玉其外，敗絮其中的自己。

生活篇 對話 1

Situation: Peter and Christie are planning to go trick-or-treating on Halloween night.

情境：Peter 跟 Christie 正在計畫萬聖節要來玩「不給糖，就搗蛋」。

Peter	Wow! Halloween is tomorrow already! Have you decided what you will be dressing up for Halloween yet, Christie?	哇！萬聖節就是明天了耶！妳決定妳萬聖節要裝扮成什麼了嗎，Christie？
Christie	I want to be either a butterfly or a pumpkin. But why do we dress up for Halloween?	我想我不是裝成蝴蝶就是南瓜吧。但是為什麼我們要為了萬聖節盛裝打扮？
Peter	Halloween is a festival for children, and costumes make it more special. I think we have much more fun going from house to house asking for candies in our favorite costumes.	萬聖節是給小孩的節慶，而且奇裝異服使它更具意義。我想我們穿著奇裝異服挨家討糖果會更有趣。
Christie	Yes, I remember having a lot of fun last year when mom took me around in a bunny outfit. Do you know what you want to be yet, Peter?	説的也是，我記得去年我穿著兔子裝跟媽媽四處逛還真好玩。你知道你要打扮成什麼了嗎，Peter？

Peter	I want to be Batman! I like wearing the cape and the mask. I think you should be a butterfly.	我想要裝成蝙蝠俠！我喜歡穿斗篷跟戴面具。我想妳應該扮蝴蝶。
Christie	Well, I will be a butterfly anyway. I can have pretty wings.	好吧，我就扮成蝴蝶，我可以有漂亮的翅膀。
Peter	Great! So you will be a butterfly and I will be Batman. Let's go ask Mom if we can go trick-or-treating tomorrow night by ourselves.	太好了！那麼妳就是蝴蝶而我是蝙蝠俠。我們去問媽媽我們明晚可不可以自己去「不給糖，就搗蛋」吧。

生活篇 對話 2

Situation: Allen is preparing for a party to celebrate New Year's Eve and discussing the party with Meiling, a friend visiting from Taiwan.

情境: Allen 正在準備慶祝新年除夕的宴會，並且跟來自台灣的朋友 Meiling 討論細節。

Allen	This party is going to be the best ever! I am so glad you came to visit in time to celebrate the New Year with me.	這個宴會將會是有史以來最棒的！我很高興你能及時來拜訪並且跟我一起慶祝新年。

Meiling	Thank you for inviting me. Why are you having the party tonight? Why not wait until tomorrow?	謝謝你邀請我。為什麼你今晚辦宴會呢？為什麼不等到明天？
Allen	Well, don't you stay up all night before waiting for New Years to start? We will still be counting down to midnight.	嗯，你們不也是除夕熬夜等待新年降臨？我們到半夜時一樣也會倒數跨年。
Meiling	That's great.	真是好極了。
Allen	I am planning on turning the TV on before the countdown begins. We can count down the last minute of this year and watch the Ball at Times Square drop together.	我計畫在倒數前打開電視。我們可以邊看著時代廣場的球降落然後一起倒數。
Meiling	Awesome! Your New Year customs are so fascinating. I am glad to be here at the right time.	太棒了！你們的跨年習俗真是太迷人。我很高興我來對時間了。

單字與實用例句

- decide *(v.)* 決定

  Miranda decided to quit her job and pursue her dream.
  Miranda 決定辭職去追尋她的夢想。

- dress up *(v. phr.)* (盛裝)打扮

  Many people in the town dressed up to celebrate the carnival.
  鎮上許多人盛裝打扮慶祝嘉年華。

- costume *(n.)* 衣服，戲服

  The stylist carefully arranged the costumes for the show.
  這位造型師仔細地安排表演的服裝。

- fun *(n.)* 樂趣

  Carlie had great fun on her trip to Brazil.
  Carlie 在她的巴西之行中玩得很愉快。

- prepare *(v.)* 準備

  Iris is busy preparing for her wedding ceremony.
  Iris 正忙著準備婚禮。

- celebrate *(v.)* 慶祝

  How do you want to celebrate Mother's birthday?
  你想要怎麼慶祝媽媽的生日？

- stay up *(v. phr.)* 熬夜

  Many students stayed up preparing for the final examination.
  許多學生熬夜準備期末考。

- awesome *(adj.)* 極佳的

  The performance tonight is really awesome.
  今晚的表演真的好棒。

好用主題用語，用法解說

Well, I will be a butterfly anyway. I can have pretty wings.
We can count down the last minute of this year and watch the Ball at Times Square drop together.

情態助動詞：在英文文法中一般助動詞除了可以協助動詞形成疑問句與否定句，情態助動詞（can, could, may, might, must, ought to, should, will, would）還可以表現說話者的語氣。在第 12 章，我們介紹了 would 與 could 除了可以當作是 will 與 can 的過去式，還可以表示「客氣」與「禮貌」的語氣。下列繼續介紹一些常用的情態助動詞用法。

- can/ could 表示能力或請求的語氣

例句：I can sing and dance.
（我能唱能跳。）
Could you help me with my assignments?
（你可以幫我做功課嗎？）

- may/ might 表示可能性與請求的語氣

例句：May I go to the concert with Steve?
（我可以跟Steve去音樂會嗎？）
With abundant rainfall, we may have a good harvest this year.
（由於有充沛的降雨，我們今年可能會豐收。）
The diamond ring might be fake.
（這個鑽戒可能是贗品。）

- must 表示必要性與可能性的語氣

例句：You must pay your entrance fee before entering the museum.

（在進博物館之前你必須先付入門票的費用。）

The party at Linda's must be fun.

（Linda的派對一定很有趣。）

- ought to/ should 表示應該與勸告的語氣

例句：The heavy smoker really ought to quit smoking now.

（煙癮很大的人真的應該要即刻戒煙。）

The doctor suggested that the patient should exercise regularly.

（醫生建議病人應該要規律地運動。）

Unit 17 名詞子句

勵志篇 故事

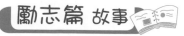

Oliver was walking on a beach one morning when he saw someone walking toward him from a distance. He could tell it was one of the local natives, but he was puzzled when he saw the native kept leaning down, picking something up and throwing it out into the sea.

As their distance got closer, he noticed that the native was picking up the starfish that had been washed upon to the shore and throwing it back into the water. Curiously, Oliver asked the native what he was doing.

"You see, it's low tide right now, and all of these starfish have been washed up to the shore. If I don't throw them back into the sea, they'll just die up here."

"But there must be thousands of starfish on this beach," Oliver replied "You can't possibly save them all. And the same thing is probably happening on hundreds of other beaches. Can't you see it's just not possible to make any difference by yourself?"

The native smiled, picked up another starfish and threw it back into the sea, "It made a difference to that one."

某天早晨奧利佛在海邊走著，他突然注意到遠方有人朝著他走過來。他看出對方是當地的原住民，但他卻對原住民的行為感到不解，因為原住民一直不斷的彎下身子，好像在撿什麼東西，然後又把它丟到海裡。

當兩個人的距離拉近之後，奧利佛發現那位原住民是將被海水沖上岸的海星給丟到海裡頭。奧利佛感到很好奇，便問他到底在做些什麼。

「你看喔，現在是退潮，然後一堆海星就這樣被沖到岸上來；如果我不將它們丟回海裡去的話，它們就會在岸上死掉。」

「但這海灘一定有上千隻的海星，」奧利佛回道：「你不可能救得了每一隻。而且同樣的狀況可能又會在其他幾百個海灘上發生。難道你看不出來光憑你一個人根本就不可能造成什麼差別嗎？」

原住民笑了笑，撿起另一隻海星，並將它丟回海裏：「對這隻來講就有差別了。」

文法重點

名詞子句 (Noun Clause)

As their distance got closer, he noticed that the native was picking up starfish that had been washed upon to the shore and throwing it back into the water.
（當兩個人的距離拉近之後，
奧利佛發現那位原住民是將被海水沖上岸的海星給丟到海裡頭。）

在英文文法中，如果一個句子在另一個句子裡當名詞用，它則稱為名詞子句。在一般英文的句型中，句子分為直述句、Yes/No 問句與 Wh-問句三種。當這三種句子分別要形成名詞子句時，則有不同的變化方式。

- 直述句做名詞子句：that+名詞子句

That water is essential to us is obvious.

（水對我們的必須性是顯而易見的。）

I hope that the rescue team will bring us enough foods.

（我希望救援隊會帶給我們足夠的食物。）

The most important thing is that you have to be honest.

（最重要的是你必須要誠實。）

The fact that the earth is round is well known.

（地球是圓的事實是眾所皆知的。）

- Yes/No 問句做名詞子句：whether / if +還原原時態的 BeV/助動詞

I don't know whether he is a student or not.

（我不知道他是不是學生。）

Whether the typhoon will come or not is still unpredictable.

（颱風到底會不會來還無法預測。）

The problem is whether we have enough money.

（問題是我們會不會有足夠的錢。）

- Wh-問句做名詞子句：將還原原時態的 BeV/助動詞放到主詞後。

The teacher tells us why students should study English.

（老師告訴我們為什麼學生要學英文。）

Jean knows what you have done.

（Jean 知道你做了什麼。）

I don't know what is wrong with you.

（我不知道你到底是怎麼搞的。）

句型解析

He could tell it was one of the local natives, but he was puzzled when he saw the native kept leaning down, picking something up and throwing it out into the sea.

1. He could tell [(that) it was one of the local natives],

   S1 Aux. V N. Cl. → O

   but he was puzzled

   Conj. S2 BeV V Passive

   [when he saw the native kept leaning down, picking... it out into the sea].

   Adv. Cl.

2. 本句的 tell 意為「分別、區別」(=distinguish)。

   例句：Polly is color-blind; she cannot tell green from red.

   Polly 是色盲；她無法區別綠色與紅色。

3. 本句的"when he saw the native kept leaning down, picking something up and throwing it out into the sea"為 V1, V2, and V3 句構，強調先做 V1，再做 V2，然後再做 V3，三個順序的動作。

As their distance got closer, he noticed that the native was picking up starfish that had been washed upon to the shore and throwing it back into the water.

1. [As their distance got closer], he noticed

   Adv. Cl. S V

   [that the native... into the water].

   N. Cl.→ O

2. 本句的 as 是連接詞，意為「隨著……」(=while)。

3. 本句的"that had been washed upon to the shore"是形容詞子句，修飾先行詞 starfish。

Can't you see it's just not possible to make any difference by yourself?

1. Can 't you see [(that) it's just not possible to... by yourself]?

   Aux. Adv. S V N. Cl. → O

2. 本句的"it's just not possible to make any difference by yourself"是名詞子句，作 see 的受詞。

3. 動詞片語 make a difference 意為「做出不同；有影響」。

   例句：What you choose will make a difference to your family.

   你的選擇會對你的家人有所影響。

心情小語

Whenver an election comes, we may feel our own worth, or value, to the society again as candidates start persuading we voters "Your vote counts". Actually, each one of us does have the power to change the world whether it is during an election or in an every single day. Do not think that we are weak and worthless because our every act in fact does influence others. So, if we can stick to what we are doing and make it touching to others, we will gather more power. Just like the native in the story, he obviously knew he could not save all the starfish by himself in one day. However, he did not feel discouraged. He was deeply convinced that he could make a difference even if he just saved one. As for how many starfish he could save, it did not matter. Perhaps Oliver in the story or someone else would be touched by his act and joined him to save starfish together. One after one, he may have hundreds of people to save starfish with him. Therefore, do not underestimate ourselves and refuse to act. Because when we start to make a small step, this world has already been changed.

好像每次只有到了選舉的時候，那些候選人為了要當選，開始猛力宣傳「您的每一票都很重要」，我們才會發現原來自己是有力量對這個社會做出改變的。其實不只是選舉的時候，就算是平常，我們每個人也都具有改變世界的力量；不要一直覺得自己只有一個人，力量很微小，有時我們的行動是可以感染到其他人，讓大家一起來，這樣力量就會越來越大。就像故事中的那位原住民，當然他也知道光靠他一個人是救不了整個海灘上所有的海星，可是他卻沒有因此放棄，因為他知道今天他微小的力量也許一整天下來也只能救個幾隻海星，但是沒關係，只要能造成改變，就算只有一隻也好；因為說不定故事中的主角奧利佛會受到他的感染，加入拯救海星的行列，然後晚一點又有人加入。最後也許就能夠匯集上百人的力量來拯救海星了。所以我們不要覺得自己力量渺小，就想說算了啦，反正只有我這麼做，會有什麼差別；即使再微小，只要我們做了，這個世界就已經被改變了。

幽默篇 故事

Ruby walked into a dentist clinic to make an appointment.

"How much do you charge to pull out a tooth?"

"It's $150", the dentist replied.

"$150!" gasped Ruby, "that's ridiculous! Are there any ways you can go cheaper?"

"Well," The dentist thought for a minute, "If we don't use anesthetic to numb the tooth, we can knock off $50."

"Only $50?" said Ruby, "That's still $100! You've got to make it cheaper!"

"Well," the dentist replied after a long pause, "I suppose if we can take it out with a wrench, we can knock off another $50."

"Perfect!" said Ruby happily, "I'd like to make an appointment for next Tuesday, for my husband, Evan."

露比走進一家牙醫診所想預約看診。

「請問拔一顆牙要多少錢？」

「美金 150 元。」牙醫師說道。

「美金 150 元？！」露比倒抽一口氣：「這實在太扯了，有沒有什麼辦法可以算便宜一點？」

「呃，」牙醫師想了一下：「如果我們不用麻醉藥去麻醉它的話，我想我可以少算妳 50 元。」

「才 50！」露比說道：「這樣還有 100 啊！」

「呃，」在經過一陣很久的沉默之後，牙醫師說道：「我想如果我可以用扳手來拔牙的話，可以再少掉 50 元。」

「太完美了！」露比開心的說道：「我想幫我老公伊凡預約下禮拜二的門診。」

文法重點

名詞子句 (Noun Clause)

I suppose if we can take it out with a wrench, we can knock off another $50.
（我想如果我可以用扳手來拔牙的話，可以再少掉 50 元。）

在英文文法中，如果一個句子當再另一個句子裡當名詞用，它則稱為名詞子句。名詞子句的主要功能為在句子裡作主詞、作受詞、作補語、作同位語用。

- 作主詞用時要注意名詞子句永遠是肯定敘述句的形式，而且為第三人稱單數

例句：How you say matters.
（你怎麼說是有關係的。）
Where Ken left for remains mysterious.
（Ken 去了哪裡一直是個謎。）
What you are talking about seems fishy.
（你所說的聽起來有點可疑。）

- 作受詞時，值得注意的是 that 引導的名詞子句作受詞用，that 常省略

例句：Linda confessed (that) she committed burglary.

（Linda 承認她犯了竊盜罪。）

People wonder if the typhoon will strike the island or not.

（人們在想不知道颱風是不是會侵襲這一個小島。）

Peter did not know what Jessica was talking about.

（Peter 不知道 Jessica 在説些什麼。）

- 作補語用時，值得注意的是 that 引導的名詞子句作受詞用，that 不可省略

例句：The most embarrassing thing is that the boy stepped on a banana peel and fell off.

（最尷尬的是這個男孩採到香蕉皮還摔了一跤。）

The police found it strange that the victim kept silent.

（對於受害人一直保持沈默，警察感到奇怪。）

My mother makes me what I am today.

（我媽媽造就了今日的我。）

- 只有 that 引導的名詞子句可作為同位語用，補充説明前面修飾的名詞

例句：That fact that the sun rises from the east is well accepted now.

（太陽從東方升起的這一個事實現在是被廣泛接受的。）

The idea that there is free lunch in the world is incorrect.

（在這世界上有白吃的午餐這一個想法是不正確的。）

句型解析

Ruby walked into a dentist clinic to make an appointment.

1. Ruby walked into a dentist clinic to make an appointment.

   S V Adv. Phr. Adv. Phr.

2. 本句的"to make an appointment"的 to 是 in order to 或是 so as to，意為「為了……（目的）」。

   例句：Eric took exercise every day in order to keep fit.
   Eric 為了保持身材，每天運動。

How much do you charge to pull out a tooth?

1. How much do you charge to pull out a tooth?

   Adv. Aux. S V Adv. Phr.

2. charge *(v.)* 要價；索價。

   例句：The service will charge you NT100.
   這項服務索價台幣 100 元。

3. pull out a tooth 意為「拔一顆牙」。

   tooth *(n.)* （一顆）牙齒，其複數型為 teeth。

You've got to make it cheaper!

1. You' ve got to make it cheaper!

   S Aux. V Perfect Adv. Phr.

2. 本句的 make it cheaper 用到了 make (v., 使) + O + OC 的句型，cheaper 作為受詞補語修飾受詞 it。

   cheap *(adj.)* 便宜的。

心情小語

Some people like to go after small gains. They may feel great when they take advantage of others. However, what they do not know is "penny wise, pound foolish". Years ago, a friend of mine went to Japan. He saw a cute doll in a small shop in Akihabara, selling 500 yen. Unlike most people, my friend is a very penny-pinching guy. He spent a whole afternoon searching for a cheaper doll in Akihabara. Finally, he found a 450-yen doll and he was extremely happy. When he came back to Taiwan, he took his doll and showed off to others. However, in that afternoon, he did nothing but found a cheaper doll. Was it worth an afternoon? Well, it is good to be frugal in the economic recession. However, being frugal means that we use money wisely and economically instead of saving money on necessities. It is never a wise thing to have instant noodles as meals in order to save money!

有些人喜歡貪小便宜，總是以為我省到那幾塊就賺到了！卻沒想到在省了那幾塊的背後，需要付出多大的代價。多年前有個朋友到日本玩，在秋葉原的一家店裡看到一個可愛的玩偶，售價是 500 日圓。一般人看到可能當場掏錢就買了，但我這位朋友精打細算，覺得貨比三家不吃虧，於是一整個下午，跑遍了整個秋葉原，終於讓他找到一家賣 450 日圓，當場超開心的，回來不斷向大家炫耀自己的成果。但是這一整個下午，他什麼其他的東西都沒逛到、什麼也沒玩到，就為了省這換算成台幣不到 15 塊的錢？這樣真的值得嗎？的確啦，現在經濟不景氣，大家能省一塊算一塊；但「節省」這件事應該是要把我們可能浪費掉的錢省下來，而不是去摳那些應該要花的錢。例如為了省吃飯錢，於是三餐吃泡麵，最後因為營養不良而住院……這樣，真的省到什麼了嗎？

生活篇 對話 1

Situation: Tina is going to visit San Francisco and she is booking a room on phone now.

Situation: Tina 將要去舊金山而她正在電話訂房當中。

Clerk	Hello, this is Holiday Village Hotel. May I help you?	您好，這裡是假日村飯店。有什麼可以為您效勞的嗎？
Tina	I would like a single room this Saturday. Do you have any double rooms available?	我想要訂星期六的單人房。你們還有空房嗎？
Clerk	Yes, we do. Our single rooms are $50 per night. Will you want breakfast?	是的，我們有房間。我們的單人房每晚$50 美金。您需要早餐嗎？
Tina	Yes, please. Oh, do your rooms have the Internet access?	好啊。對了，你們房間可以連接網路嗎？
Clerk	Yes, our rooms have a high-speed DSL Internet connection.	有的，我們房間配有高速 DSL 網路連結。
Tina	Thank you. I will also need a wakeup call tomorrow morning at 7:30.	謝謝你。我還要早上七點半的晨喚服務。
Clerk	I will arrange that for you.	我會為您安排。
Tina	Will you ask the bellboy to take my luggage to the room?	你會叫門僮幫我把行李送到房間嗎？

Clerk	No problem. We will need to see your passport while you check-in. And how would you like to pay for this room?	沒問題。在您登記入住時請出示您的護照。請問您的付款方式是？
Tina	Credit card, please.	刷卡。

生活篇 對話 2

Situation: Tina is visiting San Francisco and she is living at Holiday Village Hotel.

情境：Tina 正拜訪舊金山市，她現在住在假日村飯店。

R/S	Room Service, this is Oliver, how can I help you?	客房服務，我是 Oliver。有什麼可以為您效勞的嗎？
Tina	I'd like to order some food.	我想要點餐。
R/S	What would you like to order?	您想要點些什麼呢？
Tina	I'd like a hamburger with a side order of fries instead of onion rings—no cheese and no onions whatsoever on the burger.	我想要一個漢堡配薯條，不要洋蔥圈。漢堡不要有起司或是洋蔥。
R/S	All right.	好的。
Tina	I'll also have a Caesar salad. What's the difference between traditional and light?	我還要凱薩沙拉。傳統的跟輕食的有什麼不同？

R/S	"Light" means the dressing is non-fat, and "traditional" is regular dressing.	「輕食」是用不含脂肪的醬，然後「傳統」就是一般的凱薩醬。
Tina	I'll take light. OK, that's all.	我要「輕食」的。好了，就這樣。
R/S	Could you tell me your room number and your name, please?	請您告訴我您的房間號碼跟名字。
Tina	Room 1049. I am Tina.	房號 1049，我是 Tina。
R/S	Thank you, ma'am. Your total will be $28. Your order should arrive within the next 20 minutes.	謝謝您，女士。您的費用金額共計為$28 美元。您的餐點在 20 分鐘內會送到您的房間。
Tina	Thank you! Bye-bye.	謝謝，再見。

單字與實用例句

- book *(v.)* 預定

  Many people book their accommodation online before they set out to explore the world.

  許多人在出門探索世界之前會在網路上預訂好他們的住宿。

- single *(adj.)* 單一的

  Now, we only have single rooms available.

  目前，我們只剩下單人房。

- available *(adj.)* 可獲得的

  Daily necessities are readily available in any supermarket.

  在任一間超級市場中都容取得的日常必需用品。

- access *(n.)* 途徑

  The community library is the only access to the literature in this remote village.

  社區圖書館為這個偏鄉提供一個通往文學的途徑。

- order *(v.)* 訂，點(東西、餐)

  The tired and hungry worker ordered many foods.

  這個又累又餓的工人點了許多食物。

- traditional *(adj.)* 傳統的

  The café serves traditional Polish desserts.

  這間咖啡館提供傳統的波蘭點心。

- dressing *(n.)* 醬料

  Mother was mixing the various vegetables with the dressing.

  媽媽把蔬菜跟醬料攪拌在一起。

- total *(n.)* 總額

  The total of this construction is up to 3 million dollars.

  這個建設的總額高達三百萬元。

好用主題用語，用法解說

And how would you like to pay for this room?
Room Service, this is Oliver, how can I help you?

疑問副詞 how：在英文中常見的疑問副詞有 when（問何時）、where（問何地）、why（問何因）與 how（問如何），皆可以與助動詞形成疑問句。其中，how 主要是問做某件事情的「方式」與或是某種狀態的「程度」。以介紹幾個由 how 形成的常用問句：

- How are you?
  （你好嗎?）
  Not too bad, thanks.
  （還過得去啦，謝了。）
- How much is the ticket?
  （票價多少？）
  It's $35.
  （35 元。）
- How often do you exercise?
  （你多常運動？）
  I go jogging twice a week.
  （我每週慢跑兩次。）
- How do you like the cake?
  （你有多喜歡這份蛋糕？）
  I like it very much.
  （我非常喜歡。）
- How does Miranda look?
  （Miranda 看起來如何？）
  She looked bored.
  （她看起來很無聊。）

Unit 18 形容詞子句

勵志篇 故事

Roy lived alone in the suburbs. Every year, he would plant his annual tomato garden, in memory of his wife, who loved tomatoes. But this year it was too difficult for him, as the ground was too hard and he's getting too old. Roy had a son named Randy, who used to help him, was now in prison. Not knowing what to do, Roy wrote a letter to his son:

> Dear Randy,
> I'm feeling sad because it looks like I won't be able to plant my tomato garden this year. I'm getting too old, and digging up the ground is too difficult for me. I really hope you're here to help me, like the old days, but it's just not possible.
> Love,
> Dad

A few days later he received a letter from Randy.

> Dear Dad,
> Don't dig up the garden. That's where the bodies are buried.
> Love,
> Randy.

The next morning, FBI agents and lots of local police arrived and dug up the entire area, but they couldn't find any bodies. They apologized and left. Later that day, Roy received another letter from his son.

Dear Dad,
Go ahead and plant the tomatoes now. This is the best I can do under the circumstances.
Love you,
Randy

羅伊一個人住在郊區。每年，他都會在花園裡種蕃茄，為了紀念他那喜愛蕃茄的太太。但是今年對他來說卻非常困難，因為土壤變得太硬，而他的年紀也太大了。羅伊有個叫做蘭迪的兒子，以往總是有他幫忙，但如今他卻在獄中。不知該如何是好，羅伊寫了封信給蘭迪：

親愛的蘭迪，
我覺得很難過，因為今年我恐怕無法在花園裡種蕃茄了。我已經太老了，要將土壤挖開對我來說太困難了。我真的好希望你可以再身邊幫我，就如以前一樣，但這是不可能的事了。
愛你的爸爸

幾天之後，他收到了蘭迪的回信。

親愛的爸爸，
不要去挖花園，屍體就是被埋在那裡的。
愛你的蘭迪

隔天早上，FBI 探員協同大批地方警察立刻趕到，並將整個花園都挖開了，但卻沒找到任何屍體。他們道歉之後便離開了。那天稍晚，羅伊又收到一封信。

親愛的爸爸，
現在可以去花園裡種蕃茄囉。在這種情況下，我最多也只能做到這樣了。
愛你的蘭迪

文法重點

形容詞子句 (Adjective Clause)

That's where the bodies are buried.
（屍體就是被埋在那裡的。）

在英文文法中，當一個由關係代名詞或關係副詞所引導的子句被當作是形容詞或是補語修飾主要子句中的名詞，代名詞或是主要子句本身，則為「形容詞子句」。

例如：The person who is talking to you is my borther.
（那個跟你說話的人就是我弟弟。）
→ 句子中 who is talking to you 用來修飾名詞 the person。
Michelle lost her purse which her mother bought her in Italy.
（Michelle 弄丟了她媽媽在義大利買給她的錢包。）
→ 句子中 which her mother bought her in Italy 用來修飾名詞 her purse。
Zoe is the best person that I have ever met.
（Zoe 是我遇過最好的人了。）
→ 句子中 that I have ever met 用來修飾名詞 the best person。
Ronald keeps early hours, which makes him healthy and radiant.
（Ronald 早睡早起，讓他身體健康還神采奕奕。）
→ 句子中, which makes him healthy and radiant 用來修飾整個主要子句 Ronarld keeps early hours。

當談到形容詞子句時，我們要先了解：
先行詞：被形容詞子句修飾的名詞
關係代名詞：引導出形容詞子句，兼具連接詞及代名詞的功用。主要的關係代名詞：who(代替人)，which(代替物)，that(代替人或物)

關係代名詞種類

關代格 先行詞	主格	受格	所有格
人	who/that	whom /that/ who / x	whose
物	which/that	which/that / x	whose(of which)
人+物	that	that / x	whose
x ：可省略			

句型解析

But this year it was too difficult for him, as the ground was too hard and he's getting too old.

1. But this year it was too difficult for him,

   Adv. Phr. S BeV Adv. Adj. Prep. N

   [as the ground was too hard and he's getting too old].

   Adv. Cl.

2. too *(adv.)* 太……。用來修飾形容詞或副詞，表示程度(大)。
3. 本句的 as 是連接詞，意為「因為」(=because= since)。

I'm feeling sad because it looks like I won't be able to plant my tomato garden this year.

1. I 'm feeling sad [because it looks like …this year].

   S BeV V Progress Adj. Adv. Cl.

2. look like + N，意為「看起來像」。
3. 本句的"I won't be able to plant my tomato garden this year"用到句型"S + be able to + V"意為「能(做)……」。本句亦可改寫成 "I won't be capable of planting my tomato garden this year."

This is the best I can do under the circumstances.

1. This is the best [I can do] under the circumstances.

   S BeV N.→ S Adj. Cl. Adv. Phr.

2. 本句的“This is the best I can do”可還原成“This is the best thing that I can do”。其中 that I can do 是形容詞子句，修飾先行詞 the best thing。要注意，當先行詞最高級形容詞、序數、all；no；every；any；the only；the same；the very 這些形容詞時，關係代名詞一定要用 that。

3. circumstance *(n.)* 情況。片語“under the circumstances”意思是「在這樣的情況之下」(=in the situation)。

心情小語

Although we know that we have to do good, and help others, we usually have too many excuses not to do so, like inability, tiredness, lack of money and time. However, although Randy was in jail and could not do anything for his father, he reached out to his father in the end even though he may get into trouble since he fooled FBI. Thus, what matters is the willingness to help. If we are willing to help, we can forget our difficulties and limits and then find out ways to give a helping hand. Therefore, from now on, when we see those in needs, just put away our excuses and help out.

大家都知道平常就應該要多做好事、多幫助別人，但我們總是有太多理由；一下覺得自己可能能力不夠、不然就是沒時間、沒體力，也沒錢，好像什麼都做不了；然而，故事中的蘭迪雖然身在獄中，無法在父親身邊幫忙，但最後仍然達成了他幫助父親的目的……雖然事後他很可能因為耍了 FBI 而惹上麻煩。所以其實我們需要的，只是一顆願意幫助別人的心而已！只要有心，我們就能夠忘記自己所處的困境，而找到幫助別人的方法。所以從今天開始，當我們看到需要幫忙的人，就不要再找藉口，勇敢的去做吧！

幽默篇 故事

At the end of a job interview, the Human Resource Officer asked a young engineer who had just graduated from M.I.T "OK, I think we're almost done here. One last question, what starting salary are you looking for?"

The young engineer replied "Well, around $125,000 a year, depending on the benefits package."

The officer said "In that case, what would you say to a package of five weeks vacations, 20 paid holidays a year, full medical and dental, company matching retirement fund to 50% of salary, and a company car issued to you, say, a red convertible?"

The young engineer sat straight up and said "Wow! Are you kidding?"

"Yes," the officer replied, "but you started it."

在一個求職面試即將結束時，人資部的主管問了這個剛從麻省理工學院畢業的年輕工程師問題；「好的，我想我們也面試的差不多了。最後一個問題，你希望起薪大概是多少？」

年輕工程師說道：「嗯，差不多年薪美金 125,000 吧，得看看福利制度怎麼樣。」

主管說道：「這樣的話，那你覺得這樣的福利制度如何：一年有 5 個禮拜的休假、20 天的給薪特休、全額的健保和牙齒給付、公司給付 50%你薪水的的退休金，然後還配給你一輛公司車，比如說……一輛紅色敞篷車？」

年輕工程師立刻坐直身子說道：「哇塞！你是在開玩笑嗎？」

「是啊，」主管回道：「但是你先開始開玩笑的。」

文法重點

形容詞子句(Adjective Clause)

At the end of a job interview, the Human Resource Officer asked a young engineer who had just graduated from M.I.T
（在一個求職面試即將結束時，人資部的主管問了這個剛從麻省理工學院畢業的年輕工程師問題。）

在英文文法中，當一個由關係代名詞或關係副詞所引導的子句被當作是形容詞或是補語修飾主要子句中的名詞，代名詞或是主要子句本身，則為「形容詞子句」。使用形容詞子句除了要注意是否使用正確的關係代名詞，還有下列常見的重點需要注意：

- 形容詞子句限定或非限定用法：

  一般的形容詞子句多為限定的形容詞子句，但是當先行詞為專有名詞或是明確且唯一的人事物，則需用非限定的形容詞子句，之前須加逗號，將形容詞子句跟先行詞分開，表示補充說明，而且此時關係代名詞不可以用 that 替代。

  Lisa is talking to the person <u>who I met early this morning</u>.

  （Lisa 正在跟我早上遇到的人說話。）

  →形容詞子句限定住先行詞用法

  Nadia is yelling at her husband<u>, who came home late last night</u>.

  （Nadia 正在對她丈夫大吼，因為他昨晚晚歸。）

  →丈夫只有一個，需用「非限定」形容詞子句

- 受格的關係代名詞可省略，其餘不可省略。且受格關係代名詞 whom 可用 who 或 that 代替。然而，在介系詞及逗號之後的關代不能省略。

  The boy <u>whom/who/that/ X you met this afternoon</u> is my son.

  （那個你今天下午遇到的男孩是我兒子。）

  The house <u>which/that/X you bought last week</u> is a real bargain.

（你上星期買的那一間房子真的很划算。）

- 關係代名詞 that 的特殊用法：

當先行詞前面是最高級形容詞、序數、all；no；every；any；the only；the same；the very 等這些形容詞時，關係代名詞一定要用 that。此外，先形詞有人跟物，或是先形詞是不定代名詞 someone, something, anyone, anything, no one, nothing 等，關係代名詞一定要用 that。

Teresa is the most charming girl that I have ever seen.

（Teresa 是我見過最迷人的女孩了。）

Betty is the last person that would lie to me.

（Betty 絕不會騙我的。）

Simon is the only student that passes the exam.

（Simon 是唯一一個考試及格的。）

句型解析

At the end of a job interview, the Human Resource Officer asked a young engineer who has just graduated from M.I.T…

1. At the end of a job interview, the Human Resource Officer asked

   Adv. Phr. S V

   a young engineer [who has just graduated from M.I.T.]...

   O Adj. Cl.

2. "at the end of N"意為「在……結束時」。
3. 本句的"who has just graduated from M.I.T."是形容詞子句，修飾先行詞 a young engineer。

…what starting salary are you looking for?

1. ...what starting salary are you looking for?

   Pron. BeV S V Progressive

2. 動詞片語 look for 意為「尋找」(=search for= seek)。

Well, around $125,000 a year, depending on the benefits package.

1. Well, (it is) around $125,000 a year,

   S BeV O Adv. Phr.

   depending on the benefits package.

   Participial Construction

2. depend on (*v. phr.*) 取決於……

   例句：Whether we can go picnicking depends on the weather.

   我們是否能去野餐取決於天氣。

3. 本句的“..., depending on the benefits package”是分詞構句，可以還原為“..., and it depends on the benefits package”。

心情小語

Every time when we are looking for new jobs, we will find that the commonly-seen interview question "what starting salary are you looking for" is a nasty snare. If we answer that we are expecting a high salary, the interviewers may think we are kidding and even too greedy. On the other hand, if we say that we just want a low salary, the interviewers may suppose that we are not confident of ourselves and we are not well-qualified. Therefore, most of us learn to give a safe answer like, "I do not care about how much the salary is. If I can make contribution and learn skills from this position, I am contented." But, in fact, people go to work not only for learning but also for salary to sustain our life. From my perspective, to win a job, in an interview we should try to create a positive and bright image and make interviewers think we are positive and optimistic worker who does not care about the monthly pay. As for the reality, well, that's another story.

每次總覺得在找工作的時候，「希望待遇」這題根本就是陷阱題。報的數字太高，主管覺得你是來亂的；報的太低，主管可能又會認為你是不是對自己沒信心。所以到後來，就衍生出一種標準的公式化回答：「我不在意薪水的多少，只要能夠對公司有所貢獻，並且學到東西，對我來講就足夠了。」。誰工作不是為了賺錢？這種回答也太假了吧？但在求職的時候，需要營造的就是一個「我很正面、我很積極」的「形象」。只要能夠成功的讓面試主管相信你是個充滿幹勁、不在意薪水只想為公司付出、全世界再也找不到像你這樣肯為公司犧牲奉獻的員工、不找你來工作公司可能就倒了……那就等於已經一腳踏入這公司了。至於開始工作之後要不要真的這麼認真，那就再說囉～

生活篇 對話 1

Situation: Gary and Mary are husband and wife. They are visiting Italy. However, they have some quarrels over thier trip.

情境：Gary 跟 Mary 是夫妻。他們正在參觀義大利。但是他們現在對於行程有些爭執。

Mary	You have arranged to visit the Roman ruins tomorrow, but I thought maybe it would be better to cancel that and go shopping instead. I know some good shops.	你已經安排明天要去參觀羅馬遺跡，但我想或許取消這個行程，然後去逛街會比較好。我知道一些不錯的店。
Gary	No, we went shopping all day today. I really do want to see the Roman ruins tomorrow.	不要，我們今天已經逛街一整天了。我真的想要明天去看看羅馬遺跡。
Mary	Well, the show tonight is not very good. Perhaps we should forget that terrible show and go shopping tomorrow instead.	嗯，但是今天晚上的表演真的不好看。或許我們應該去逛逛街忘記這場爛表演。
Gary	No, I think that show tonight is quite interesting. Anyway, most of the shops you go to have been very expensive.	不要，我覺得今晚的表演很有趣啊。無論如何，你今天去的店大多都很貴。

Mary	Oh no, I think the prices are quite reasonable. Do you remember the shopping plaza near the hotel last night? The items there were quite modern and the prices were quite reasonable.	喔，不。我認為價格很合理啊。你還記得昨晚在飯店旁的購物廣場嗎？那裡的物品都很時髦，而且價錢也很合理啊。
Gary	See, you have done enough shopping. It is time for us to visit a real famous tourist spot.	你看，你真的已經逛夠多店了。該是我們去參觀真正知名的觀光景點了。

生活篇 對話 2

Situation: Gary and Mary are husband and wife. They are visiting Italy. However, they have some quarrels over their lunch they just had at a restaurant.

情境：Gary 跟 Mary 是夫妻。他們正在參觀義大利。但是他們現在對於剛剛在餐廳用的午餐有些爭執。

Mary	How do you think of our lunch at that restaurant?	你覺得剛剛在餐廳用的午餐怎麼樣？
Gary	I think the food in the restaurant was pretty excellent.	我覺得剛剛餐廳的午餐很棒啊。

Mary	Really?! To me, the portions were too small, and there was not enough variety.The service was poor as well and the prices were way too expensive. That restaurant really disappointed me!	真的嗎？！對我而言，那份量太小而且又沒多少選擇。服務又糟糕且價錢又昂貴。那間餐廳真是令我失望透了。
Gary	But you are in Europe!	但是你人在歐洲啊！
Mary	Besides, the food was brought out too slowly. I would prefer to begin eating within five minutes of sitting down.	還有，上菜上的都很慢。我比較喜歡坐下來五分鐘就可以開始吃東西了。
Gary	Honey, you are in Europe! The European style is to bring the food out much more slowly. You have to be reasonable!	親愛的，你人在歐洲啊！歐洲風格都是慢慢上菜的。你得要講道理。
Mary	Well, then you have to treat me a nice dessert to make up for the bad lunch.	嗯，那你要請我吃點心來補償剛剛的爛午餐。
Gary	Well, that's Okay.	呃…，好吧。

單字與實用例句

- quarrel *(n.)* 爭吵，爭執

  The newly-wed have a quarrel over small things.
  這對新婚夫妻在小事上爭吵。

- ruins *(n. pl.)* 殘骸，遺址

  The backpacker planned to visit the ruins of the abbey.
  那些背包客計畫去參觀那間修道院的遺址。

- shop *(n.)* 店鋪

  It is not an easy thing to run a shop by your own.
  自己經營一家店鋪並不是一件容易的事。

- terrible *(adj.)* 糟糕的

  Owing the terrible weather condition, the sports event was postponed.
  因為天氣很糟糕，所以運動會延期了。

- pretty *(adv.)* 很，非常

  Kid as Bunnie was, she was pretty courageous.
  雖然 Bunnie 只是個小孩，她很勇敢。

- portion *(n.)* 比例

  Every guest has his or her portion of the soup.
  每一位客人都有自己一份的湯。

- variety *(n.)* 變化，各式各樣

  Sam likes to watch variety shows in his free time.
  Sam 空閒之餘喜歡看綜藝節目。

- disappoint *(v.)* 使…失望

  The poor performance of the basketball team deeply disappointed the coach.
  這支籃球隊不佳表令他們的教練深深失望。

好用主題用語，用法解說

You have arranged to visit the Roman ruins tomorrow, but I thought maybe it would be better to cancel that and go shopping instead.

But you are in Europe!

表示語氣的副詞：在日常英文會話中，適切的語氣的表達十分重要。除了之前介紹的情態助動詞，在英文中也有不少表示語氣的副詞。在這兩篇對話中我們看到表示轉折語氣的副詞 but 與表示對比關係的副詞 instead 用於陳述相反或是不同的意見時。除了轉折語氣，英文會話裡還有一些常見的語氣詞，請見下列介紹。

- 表「因此」語氣：therefore / thus / hence / as a result

例句：Kate got up late this morning; therefore, she missed the train.

（Kate今天睡太晚了，因此她錯過了火車。）

Wendy did not bring an umbrella with her; as a result, she was caught in the heavy rain after work.

（Wendy沒有帶傘，於是她下班後淋了一場大雨。）

- 表「但是」語氣：however / yet / still

例句：Jean worked hard for the final exam. However, she failed in the end.

（Jean為了期末考用功讀書。但是，最後還是不及格。）

- 表「此外」語氣：besides / in addition

例句：Larry works as a programmer. In addition, he takes a part-time job as a taxi driver.

（Larry是個程式設計人員。除此之外，他還兼差做計程車司機。）

- 表「**讓步**」語氣：after all / though

例句：Just accept this job. After all, half a loaf is better than none.

（接受這份工作吧。畢竟，聊勝於無啊。）

- 表「**舉例**」語氣：for example

例句：There are many crisis in the world, for example, food crisis and global warming.

（在這個世界上有著許多的危機，像是糧食危機及全球暖化。）

- 表「**換句話說**」語氣：in other words / that is to say

例句：John hurt his leg badly; that is, he could not run anymore.

（John的腳傷得很嚴重；也就是說，他再也不能跑步了。）

- 表「**加強肯定**」語氣：certainly/ absolutely/ definitely

例句：Tina looked distracted; certainly, she did not like this speech.

（Tina看起來很不專心；一定是，她不喜歡這場演講。）

NOTE

Unit 19

副詞子句

勵志篇 故事

Josh was a 10-year-old boy who wanted to study Judo, but everyone kept telling him it was just not possible, for he had lost his left arm in a car accident.

Finally, he found a Japanese Judo master, Mr. Miyagi, who was willing to train him. Josh was doing quite well, but after three months of training, he found that the master only taught him one move.

"Sensei," Josh asked one day, "Shouldn't I be learning more moves?"

"This is the only move you know, and it is the only move you'll ever need to know." Mr. Miyagi replied.

Not quite understanding, but believing his teacher, Josh kept training.

Several months later, Mr. Miyagi took him to his first tournament. Surprisingly, Josh won all the way to the finals and finally got the championship.

On the way home, he asked Mr. Miyagi, "Sensei, how did I win with only one move?"

"You won for two reasons," said Mr. Miyagi "First, you've almost mastered the most difficult throws in all of Judo. And second, the only known defense for that move is for your opponent to grab your left arm."

賈許是個想學柔道的十歲小男孩，但每個人都跟他說這根本不可能，因為他在一場車禍中失去了他的左手。

最後他終於找到一個願意教他的日本柔道大師，宮城先生。賈許學得很快，但是經過三個月的訓練之後，他發覺師父只教了他一招。

「老師，」賈許說道：「我不是應該多學幾招嗎？」

「這是你唯一會的招式，而你也只要會這招就夠了。」宮城先生回道。

雖然不太懂，但因為相信老師，所以賈許繼續訓練著。

幾個月之後，宮城先生帶他參加了他的第一個比賽。令人驚訝的，賈許竟然一路打到總決賽，最後還贏得冠軍。

在回家的路上，他問了宮城先生：「老師，我是怎麼只用一招就打贏這整場比賽的啊？」

「你會贏是基於兩個原因，」宮城先生說道：「首先，你已經幾乎精通所有柔道招式裏最困難的一個拋技了。再者，對手要對付這招唯一的防守方式，就是抓你的左手臂。」

文法重點

副詞子句 (Adverbial Clause)

Josh was a 10-year-old boy who wanted to study Judo, but everyone kept telling him it was just not possible, for he had lost his left arm in a car accident.
賈許是個想學柔道的十歲小男孩，但每個人都跟他說這根本不可能，因為他在一場車禍中失去了他的左手。

在英文文法中，由從屬連接詞引導的副詞子句在複雜句中當作副詞的功能，修飾主要子句，不能單獨成為一個句子。

例句：Joseph was overjoyed as soon as he heard the good news.

＝As soon as he heard the good news, Joseph was overjoyed

（Joseph 感到欣喜若狂當他一聽到這一個好消息的時候。）

副詞子句與主要子句的關係通常由引導副詞子句的從屬連接詞決定，常見的有表示時間、因果關係、讓步、條件、對比、等子句。

常見引導副詞子句的從屬連接詞：

時間	when, while, as, after, before, as soon as, since, until, by the time, once, as long as, whenever, every time, the moment...
因果	because, since, for, as, now that...
讓步	although, though, even though, even if...
對比對照	while, whereas, but...
條件	If, only if, unless, in case...

表示時間的從屬連接詞：

「當……的時候」：when, while, as...

例句：Orz visited many museums when he was in Spain.

（Orz 在西班牙的時候造訪了許多的博物館。）

Ken was surfing the Internet while his was cooking.

（當 Ken 在煮飯的時候，他還一邊上網。）

As they were talking, the door bell rang.

（當他們聊天的時候，門鈴響了。）

「直到……的時候」：until

例句：The child stayed here until his mother came back.

（這個孩子待在這裡一直到他媽媽回來為止。）

The dog was not fully grown until it was three.

（狗在三歲之前都不算完全長大。）

「在……之後」：after

「在……之前」：before

例句：After I eat breakfast, I go to school.

（我吃過早餐後去上學。）

By the time you get there, it will be dark.

（當你到那裡的時候，天應該就黑了。）

「自從」：since (須注意主要子句需用完成式)

例句：I haven't seen her since she went to the USA.
（她去美國之後我就沒有見過她了。）

「一旦」：once

例句：Once you violate the law, you will be punished.
（你一旦違法，將會被處罰。）

「一……，就……」：as soon as, the moment

例句：As soon as Ethan saw the cockroach, he screamed out.
（Ethan 一看到蟑螂，就會大叫。）

「每一次」：every time, each time, whenever

例句：Whenever it rains, I feel dispirited.
（每當下雨的時候，我就感到沮喪。）

句型解析

Finally, he found a Japanese Judo master, Mr. Miyagi, who was willing to train him.

1. Finally, he found a Japanese Judo master,

   Adv. S V O

   Mr. Miyagi, [who... train him].

   Appositive Phr. ← Adj. Cl.

2. 本句的 Mr. Miyagi 是補充說明受詞 a Japanese Judo master 的同位語。
3. 本句的 who was willing to train him 是形容詞子句，修飾先行詞 a Japanese Judo master。

Not quite understanding, but believing his teacher, Josh kept training.

1. Not quite understanding, but believing his teacher, Josh kept training.

   Participial Construction / S / V / Ving

2. 本句的“Not quite understanding, but believing his teacher, ...” 是分詞構句，可還原為副詞子句“While Josh did not quit understanding, but believed his teacher, ...”。

3. keep *(v.)* 繼續(做)……。其用法為 keep + Ving。

Surprisingly, Josh won all the way to the finals and finally got the championship.

1. Surprisingly, Josh won all the... finals and finally got the championship.

   Surprisingly, = Adv.; Josh = S; won = V1; all the... finals = Adv. Phr.; and = Conj.; finally = Adv.; got = V2; the championship. = O

2. 片語 all the way 意為「一路(到底)」。本句的 Josh won all the way to the finals 意為「Josh 一路得勝到決賽」。

3. championship *(n.)* 冠軍(資格)。champion *(n.)* 冠軍。要注意，我們一般說「贏得冠軍」指的是「贏得冠軍資格(championship)」，而不是「贏得冠軍者(champion)」。

心情小語

One of my friends often posts his complaints about his colleagues, boss, and subordinates on his Facebook wall. At first, everyone and I took pity on him since he seemed to work in an undesirable company. From his words, I originally thought he was cursed since there were only idiots except him in his company. However, as time passes by, now everyone feels weird. Why he complained about this in company A and then he complained the same thing even in company B, C, and D. Is he really cursed? Is he destined to go to bad companies? Or, the real problem is he himself. More often than not, when we meet difficulties, our first response tends to "That is not my fault. It is someone else's." By thinking so, we can easily get rid of the problem and responsibility at the same time. However, as time goes by, we will become those who cannot take any responsibility anymore. If we want our life bright and prosperous, we should get rid of the habit of complaining. Instead, we can try to reflect ourselves at first, take our own defeat well, and never make the same mistake again.

經常會在臉書上看到一個朋友三天兩頭抱怨同事扯後腿、主管不長進、部下沒路用；剛開始大家都很同情他，待到一家爛公司，整間公司除了他以外全都是廢物，真是太辛苦了。可是不久之後就開始覺得怪怪的，為什麼他到A公司抱怨這些事，到了B公司、C公司甚至D公司之後還是一直在抱怨同樣的事？難道說是他真的命運多舛，全台灣所有的爛公司全被他給遇上了？還是說，其實真正的問題，是在其他地方？很多時候當我們遇到問題，第一個反應就是「那不是我的錯，是誰誰誰的責任」。這樣或許可以暫時的將問題從我們肩頭丟開，可是日子一久，養成習慣之後，就會變成那種只會出一張嘴、推諉、卸責、沒擔當的人了。當然這種個性其實很適合當政務官啦。不過如果你希望自己的人生不要朝著腐敗的方向前進的話，就儘早改掉這種惡習，凡事從自己先檢討起，勇敢面對自己的失敗，然後下次絕不再犯同樣的錯誤，這樣我們才能夠走出一個光明的人生。

幽默篇 故事

After graduating from a law school in the big city, Spencer moved back to the small town he has grew up in. He really wanted to impress the town folks, and show them he's an important man from the city. Therefore, he opened a law firm, but the business was very slow.

One day, he saw a man walking towards the front door. He decided to make a big impression on the new client.

As the man came to the door, Spencer picked up the phone. He waved the man in, while he pretended to talk on the phone.

"No, absolutely not! You tell those bozos in New York that I will not settle this case for less than twenty million...Yes, I said that...Oh, by the way, can you tell the DA that I will be free next week... yeah, he's been asking me forever!... yeah, the lake case... I know, right?... "

These sort of things went on for almost 5 minutes. The man just sat there patiently. Finally, Spencer puts down the phone and turned to the man "I'm sorry for the delay, but as you can see, I'm quite busy. What can I do for you?"

"I'm from the phone company... I came to hook up your phone." The man replied.

史賓塞在大都市的法律學校畢業之後，回到他成長的小鄉鎮裡。他真的很想讓這些鄉巴佬開開眼界，知道他是從大都市來的重要人物。所以他便在鎮裡開了個律師事務所，只是生意並不太好。

有一天，他看到有人正朝著門口走來。於是他便決定要讓這個新客戶留下

深刻的印象。

當男子一走進來的時候，他立刻拿起電話。他揮手示意男子進來，並且假裝對著電話說道：

「不，絕對不可能！你去告訴紐約的那些蠢蛋，和解金低於兩千萬根本不用想說要跟我談和解……對，我說的……噢，對了，你可以順便跟檢察官講一下說我下禮拜有空……對啊，他盧我盧超久了啊……對啊，就是那個湖的案子……我知道啊！超扯對吧？」

這樣的「對話」進行了約五分鐘左右。男子只是有耐心地坐在一旁等著。終於，史賓塞掛上電話並轉向男人說道：「我真的非常抱歉讓您等了這麼久，相信您也看得出來，我非常地忙碌。請問您有什麼需要幫忙的嗎？」

「我是電信局的人，今天來幫您接通電話的。」男子回答道。

文法重點

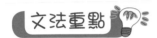

副詞子句 (Adverbial Clause)

As the man came to the door, Spencer picked up the phone. He waved the man in, while he pretended to talk on the phone.
（當男子一走進來的時候，他立刻拿起電話。他揮手示意男子進來，並且假裝對著電話說道）

在英文文法中，由從屬連接詞引導的副詞子句在複雜句中當作副詞的功能，修飾主要子句，不能單獨成為一個句子。以下繼續介紹表示因果關係、讓步、條件、對比、等子句。
表示因果關係的從屬連接詞：
「因為……，所以……」：because, since, as, now that, for, so... (須注意 because 不與連接詞 so 同時出現)

例句：Ray did not go bear hunting with us <u>because</u> he was afraid.

（Ray 因為害怕無法跟我們去獵熊。）

Jamie was sick so she took a sick leave today.

（Jamie 生病了，所以她今天請病假。）

表示讓步的從屬連接詞：although, though, even though, even if...

例句：Although Calvin is poor, he leads a happy life.

（雖然 Calvin 很窮，但他過著快樂的生活。）

The smart kid saved his family from the fire even though he was only five.

（這一個聰明的孩子曾在火災中救了全家人，雖然當時他只有五歲。）

表示對比對照的從屬連接詞：while, whereas, but...

例句：Tina likes to play the flute while her brother likes to play basketball.

（Tina 喜歡吹長笛，而她的哥哥喜歡打籃球。）

表示條件的從屬連接詞：If, only if, unless, in case...

例句：If you tell the truth, I may consider forgiving you.

（如果你說實話的話，我可以考慮原諒你。）

The baby will not stop crying unless her mother feeds her.

（除非她的媽媽餵她，否則這一個寶寶是不會停止哭泣的。）

Please bring an umbrella with you in case it may rain.

（請帶把傘，以防會下雨。）

句型解析

After graduating from a law school in the big city, Spencer moved back to the small town he has grew up in.

1. After graduating... city, Spencer moved back to

Participial Construction S V Phr.→ V

the small town [he has grew up in].

O Adv. Cl.

2. 本句的“After graduating from a law school in the big city,...”是分詞構句，可還原成副詞子句“After Spencer graduated from a law school in the big city,...”。

3. 本句的“he has grew up in”可還原成“which he has grew up in”，為修飾先行詞 the small town 的形容詞子句。

He really wanted to impress the town folks, and show them he's an important man from the city.

1. He really wanted to impress... important man from the city.

   S Adv. V Infinitive Phr.

2. impress *(v.)* 另……印象深刻。本句 He really wanted to impress the town folks...可以改寫成“He really wanted to give the town folks a deep impression...”

3. 本句的“(that)he's an important man from the city”是名詞子句作 show 的受詞。

I'm sorry for the delay, but as you can see, I'm quite busy.

1. I 'm sorry for the delay, but [as you can see],

   S BeV Adj.→SC Prep. N Conj. Adj. Cl. Adj.→SC

   I 'm quite busy.

   S BeV Adv. Adj.

2. sorry *(adj.)* 抱歉。其用法為 S be sorry to someone for something。

3. 本句的 as 為準關係代名詞的用法，意為「如同」。慣用語 as you can see 意為「如同你所見到的，……」。

心情小語

With the prevalence of Facebook, many strange and even weird social phenomena occur. One of them is the booming of "Facebook Showoffs". For example, a person is likely to find a popular restaurant to dine in order to check in on Facebook. Or, one may post her heavy make-up and over photoshopped picture with words "Oh my, I am ugly without any cosmetics" on her Facebook wall. What's more exaggerating, we may read a message like "Just met a normal young office worker. We hit on a conversation and he asked me if we could be friends..." But the truth was that the young man was just asking her for directions.

These "Facebook Showoffs" are actually annoying. Some people may tease or scorn off these ignorant showoffs. However, in my opinion, we don't have to bother teasing or scorning off these people or events. Those who choose to show off on Facebook lay emphasis on showing off because they often have aimless and empty life. If they had happy life in the real world, would they have to show off their status to others in the virtual one? Therefore, we should take pity on those showoffs because vanity is not real happiness, but sadness from the bottom of the heart.

隨著臉書的流行，跟著引發了許多怪現象，其中一個就是炫耀文的大流行：出去吃東西打卡不能隨便找個點，一定要去那種可以引起別人羨慕和討論的點才行；明明妝畫得很濃、修圖軟體修很大，卻硬要在照片上寫說「矮油～人家素顏好醜」；出去逛街遇到路人問路，馬上手機拿出來寫說「剛剛在路上遇到一個看起來很正常，一點都不像是怪叔叔的年輕上班族搭訕，還說要跟我做朋友>////<」。

這種炫耀文很讓人討厭，有些人還會因為看不下去直接去吐槽、酸人家個幾句。不過我倒是覺得大可不必這樣，要知道，這些人之所以會把生活重心全部放在「炫耀給別人看」這件事上，就是因為在現實生活中沒有目標、得不到滿足啊；要是在現實生活中過得很好很幸福，需要這樣不斷 PO 文來靠著別人的認同取暖嗎？所以對這些人我們反而應該同情他們才對。因為過度的虛榮展現出來的並不是幸福，而是一種悲哀。

生活篇 對話 1

Situation: Vicky and Peggy are going to visit Thailand. Now, they are checking tickets, passport, and their baggage at the airline counter.

情境：Vicky 跟 Peggy 將要去泰國旅行。現在她們正在航空公司櫃台登記機票、護照以及行李託運。

Staff	May I have your passports and tickets please?	請出示你們的護照跟機票。
Vicky	Here you are.	在這裡。
Staff	How many pieces of luggage do you have?	你們有多少件行李？
Peggy	ncluding carry-on luggage?	包含手提行李嗎？
Staff	No, just the baggage you want to check in.	不，只是妳要託運的部分。
Vicky	Well, we have 2 pieces of luggage to be checked.	嗯，我們有兩件需要託運。
Staff	Do you have name tags on your luggage?	妳們行李上有掛名牌嗎？
Peggy	Yes, I inspected all of them while we were waiting here in line.	有的，我們剛剛在等待時我已經檢查過了。
Staff	Fine, please put them on the scale here one-by-one. Is Bangkok your final destination today?	好，那請把行李一件一件地放在秤上。妳們的今天的終點站是曼谷嗎？

Vicky	Yes.	是的。
Staff	Okay, here are your passports and boarding passes. Please check the inspector screen and wait until your luggage goes through the X-ray machine before you leave.	好的，這是你們的護照跟登機證。在妳們離開前請先看一下檢查螢幕並確認行李已經通過 X 光機。
Peggy	Thank you.	謝謝你。
Staff	Have a nice flight.	祝您飛航愉快。

生活篇 對話 2

Situation: Vicky and Peggy have checked their tickets, passport, and their baggage at the airline counter. Now they are going to the security check.

情境：Vicky 跟 Peggy 已經在航空公司櫃台登記好機票、護照以及行李托運。現在她們將要去安檢處。

Security	Men this way. Women that way. Please lay your bags flat on the conveyor belt.	男士這邊，女士那邊。請把你們的包包平放在輸送帶上。
Vicky	Will this X-ray machine damage my digital camera.	這台 X 光機會損害我的數位相機嗎？
Security	So far as I know, the chances are slim. You don't have to worry about that.	據我所知，機會很小。妳不必擔心。

Security	Hey, the metal-detector buzzes when you go through. Please stop and come here.	嘿，當妳通過時，金屬探測器響了。請止步並來這裡。
Peggy	Well, I think the problem may be an artificial metal joint in my knee.	嗯，我想可能是因為我膝蓋的人工金屬關節。
	I see. It is OK for you to go. Move along now, please.	嗯，我知道了。妳現在可以走了。請往前行。
Security	Well, we have to check. Please come over here.	嗯，我們得檢查。請到這裡來。
Peggy	The airport security is quite strict.	機場安檢真是嚴格啊。
Vicky	Yes safety is always the best policy in the airport.	對啊，在機場，安全總是上策啊。

單字與實用例句

- baggage *(n.)* 行李(=luggage)

  Make sure your baggage is not overweight; otherwise, you will have to pay extra fee.
  確認你的行李沒有超重。否則，你必須得付額外的費用。

- airline *(n.)* 航線，航空公司

  Jenifer works as a flight attendant in Flying Airline.
  Jenifer 在 Flying Airline 當空服員。

- destination *(n.)* 目的地

  The army rushed to its destination nonstop.
  這支軍隊馬不停蹄地前往目的地。

- security *(n.)* 安全

  Internet security is a very important issue all over the world.
  網路安全是全世界重要的議題。

- digital *(adj.)* 數位的

  The latest digital camera Denial bought yesterday is made in Japan.
  Daniel 昨天買的最新型數位相機是日本製的。

- detector *(n.)* 檢測器

  A lie detector was used when the police officer questioned the suspect.
  當這位警察質問嫌疑犯時，使用了測謊儀。

好用主題用語，用法解說

Yes, I inspected all of them while we were waiting here in line. Hey, the metal-detector buzzes when you go through. Please stop and come here.

表示時間關係的副詞子句：：在英文文法中，當需要表示時間先後關係時，我們會使用 when、while、as（正當……），before（在……之前），after（在……之後）與 as soon as、once（一……，就……）等從屬連接詞來引導副詞子句與主要子句型形成時間先後關係。以下分別介紹常用的表示時間關係的從屬連接詞：

意思	從屬連接詞	例句
正當……	when/while/as	• When Helen visited London last year, she visited 12 museums. （當 Helen 去年去英國的時候，她造訪了 12 個博物館。） • As Irene arrived the airport, the plane left. （當 Irene 抵達機場的時候，飛機已經飛走了。）
在……之前	before	• Wash your hands before you are ready to dine. （在你準備要吃飯之前要先洗手。）
在……之後	after	• Please send the contract back to me after you sign it. （在簽名之後，請將合約寄還給我。）
一……，就……	as soon as/ once	• As soon as the mother learned that her boy was drowned, she burst out crying. （當這位母親一聽到她兒子溺斃時，她就哭出來了。） • Please contact me once you get off the train. （你下火車的時候請馬上聯絡我。）

Unit 20 分詞構句

勵志篇 故事

Percy stumbled across a wooden box on his way down the mountain. Upon opening the box, he found a skull with a necklace inside.

"Young man," the skull suddenly started to talk, "I've been searching for someone like you for a long time! The necklace beside me is the necklace of almighty! It contains power beyond your imagination! I need you to put it on so we can rule the world together!"

Percy looked at the necklace and said, "So what's the catch? Is it going to cost me my soul? Or will I be damned for the eternality once I put it on?"

"No, nothing like that, just put it on and you can have all the powers of the universe!"

"If it's so great and powerful, why don't you wear it yourself?" said Percy.

"Because I lacked something very vital." said the skull.

"Courage?"

"Shoulders", the skull sighed.

波西有天在下山時撿到一個木盒子，打開之後發現裡頭有著一顆骷髏頭和一個項鍊。

「年輕人！」骷髏頭突然開口說話：「我在找像你這樣的人已經很久了！旁邊的項鍊是萬能項鍊，具有超乎你能想像的力量！我要你戴上它，然後和我一起統治世界！」

波西看了一眼那個項鍊，然後說道：「這一定有什麼陰謀吧？是不是需要付出我的靈魂？或是一旦戴上之後就會永生永世受到詛咒？」

「不，完全沒有這些東西，只要你戴上它，就馬上可以享有整個宇宙的力量！」

「那既然那麼強你幹嘛不自己戴就好？」波西說道。

「因為我缺少了一樣非常關鍵的東西。」骷髏頭說道。

「勇氣嗎？」

「肩膀……」骷髏頭嘆了一口氣。

文法重點

分詞構句 (Participial Construction)

Upon opening the box, he found a skull with a necklace inside.
（打開之後發現裡頭有著一顆骷髏頭和一個項鍊。）

在英文文法中，如果一個複雜句前後子句的主詞相同，常常副詞子句的主詞會被省略，其主要動詞改成 Ving，形成分詞構句。分詞構句可以分為兩種：副詞子句的弱化與由對等連接詞(and)轉換的分詞構句。這裡先介紹副詞子句弱化而來的分詞構句。
並非所有的副詞子句都可以弱化為分詞構句，只有與「時間」、「原因」、「條件」、「讓步」有關的連接詞所引導的副詞子句才可以變成分詞構句。

- 表「時間」的分詞構句

例句：After Alan graduated from college, he started his career a tour guide. = After graduating from college, Alan started his career a tour guide.

（Alan 大學畢業之後，他開始作導遊。）

説明：去掉副詞子句的主詞，並且動詞改為 Ving

a. 分詞構句後需有逗點與主要子句隔開，用以修飾整句。

b. 為表達完整語意，可保留副詞子句的連接詞。

- 表「原因」的分詞構句

例句：Because Helen was tired of her dull life, she quit her job to pursue her dream. = (Being) tired of her dull life, Helen quit her job to pursue her dream.

（因為 Helen 厭倦了她無聊的生活，所以她辭職去追求她的夢想。）

說明：去掉副詞子句的主詞，並且動詞改為 Ving

a. 不影響文意理解的情況下，可省略副詞子句的連接詞。

b. 分詞構句中的 being 可省略。

- 表「條件」的分詞構句

例句：If you do not work harder on your work, you will get fired.
= Not working harder on your work, you will get fired.

（如果你不努力工作的話，你將會被開除。）

說明：去掉副詞子句的主詞，並且動詞改為 Ving

a. 不影響文意理解的情況下，可省略副詞子句的連接詞。

b. 若副詞子句有否定詞，分詞構句之後則需置於分詞之前。

- 表「讓步」的分詞構句 (although, though)

例句：Although May loves singing, she does not want to be a singer. = Although loving singing, May does not want to be a singer.

（雖然 May 喜歡唱歌，但她不想當歌手。）

句型解析

Percy stumbled across a wooden box on his way down the mountain.

1. Percy stumbled across a wooden box on his way down the mountain.

   S / V Phr.→ V / O / Adv. Phr.

2. stumble across *(v. phr.)* 被……絆倒

3. 片語 on one way to N/ adv. 意為「去……的路上」。

   例句：Miranda had a fight with her husband on their way home.

   Miranda 在回家的路上跟丈夫吵了一架。

Or will I be damned for the eternality once I put it on?

1. Or will I be damned for the eternality [once I put it on]?

   Aux. / S / BeV / V Passive / Prep. / N / Adv. Cl.

2. eternality *(n.)* 永恆。本句"will I be damned for the eternality" 意為「我會永遠地被詛咒嗎」。

If it's so great and powerful, why don't you wear it yourself?

1. [If it's so great and powerful], why do n't you wear it yourself?

   Adv. Cl. / Adv. / Aux. / Adv. / S / V / O / Pron.

2. 本句的副詞子句"If it's so great and powerful"表示條件，意為「假如真有那麼好跟有力量……」。

3. 句型"why don't you+ Vr" 意為「何不……」，語意上表示建議 (=why not + Vr)。

   例句：Why don't you have a dinner with us?

   你何不跟我一起去吃晚餐？

心情小語

Everyone wants to seize the opportunity whenever it comes. However, sometimes we have to evaluate our own ability first. Otherwise, we will be just like the skull in the story. Although the skull has the most powerful treasure in the world, it could not wear it by itself without a shoulder. If you were the young man, please make yourself a capable and get ready for each coming opportunity. Then, you will never miss any golden opportunity.

當機會來臨時，每個人都想好好把握，但有時候也要衡量一下自己的能力，否則就像故事中的骷髏頭一樣，雖然擁有了全世界力量最強大的的寶物也沒有用，它沒辦法自己戴上它，因為它根本就沒有肩膀。而如果你是那個年輕人，讓自己成為那個有能力的人，隨時都做好準備迎接機會的來臨。那麼，你將不會錯失任何一個千載難逢的好機會。

幽默篇 故事

It's game 7 of the NBA final. Johnny was so excited he got a seat at the baseline section.

He sat down, noticing that the seat next to him was empty. He leaned over and asked the man next to the empty seat if someone was sitting here.

"No," said the man "The seat is empty."

"This is incredible!", said Johnny, "Who in their right mind would have a seat like this and not use it?"

The ma said "Well, actually the seat belongs to my wife, but she passed away. This is the first NBA game we haven't been together since we got married."

"Oh... I'm sorry to hear that." Johnny said, feeling bad for the man, "but couldn't you find someone else? A friend, a relative or even a neighbor to come with you?"

"No," the man said, "they're all at my wife's funeral now."

這是 NBA 總決賽的第七場比賽，強尼很興奮的能夠買到底線區的票。

他坐了下來，注意到旁邊的位子是空的，便側過身問椅子另一邊的男子，這位子有沒有人坐。

「沒有，」男子說道：「這位子是空的。」

「這真是難以置信。」強尼說道：「哪個有正常腦袋的人會買了這樣棒的位子然後不坐？」

男子說道：「呃，其實那原本是我老婆的位子啦，但她已經過世了。這是我們結婚以來第一次沒有一起來看 NBA 的比賽。」

「噢……我真的很抱歉。」強尼說道，突然為男子覺得有點難過：「但你不能找其他人嗎？朋友、親戚，或是鄰居跟你一起來？」

「不行，」男子說道：「他們現在全都在我老婆的葬禮上。」

文法重點

分詞構句 (Participial Construction)

He sat down, noticing that the seat next to him was empty.
（他坐了下來，注意到旁邊的位子是空的。）

在英文文法中，如果一個複雜句前後子句的主詞相同，常常副詞子句的主詞會被省略，其主要動詞改成 Ving，形成分詞構句。分詞構句可以分為兩種：副詞子句的弱化與由對等連接詞(and)轉換的分詞構句。這裡要介紹由對等連接詞(and)轉換的分詞構句。

並非有對等連接詞 and 的句子都可以弱化為分詞構句，只有當對等連接詞 and 連接同主詞且同時發生或進行的兩個動作，才可以轉化為分詞構句。

例句：Jason read this piece of news, and exclaimed out of joy.
= Reading this piece of news, Jason exclaimed out of joy.
（Jason 看了這一則新聞之後，高興地喝采。）
Ben leaned against the wall, and gazed at Iris.
= Leaning against the wall, Ben gazed at Iris.
（Ben 靠著牆，並凝視著 Iris。）
William lay under the tree in the park, and read a novel.
= Lying under the tree in the park, William read a novel.
（William 躺在公園的樹下，讀著小說。）

句型解析

He leaned over and asked the man next to the empty seat if someone was sitting here.

1. He leaned over and asked the man... empty seat
   S V1 Adv. Conj. V2 I.O.
   [if someone... here].
   N. Cl.→D.O.
2. 片語 next to +N 意為「在……的隔壁」(=beside)。本句“the man next to the empty seat”意為「在空座位隔壁的男生」。
3. 本句的“if（是否）someone was sitting here”是名詞片語作為 ask 的受詞用。

Well, actually the seat belongs to my wife, but she passed away.

1. Well, actually the seat belongs to my wife, but she passed away.
   Adv. S1 V. Phr.→ V O Conj. S2 V. Phr.→ V2
2. 動詞片語 belong to +N 意為「(某物)屬於(某人或團體)」，要注意 belong to 只有主動的形式。
   例句：The department store belongs to an old lady.
   這間百貨公司為一位老太太所有。

“Oh... I'm sorry to hear that.” Johnny said, feeling bad for the man...

1. “Oh... I'm sorry to hear that.” Johnny said, feeling bad for the man...
   N. Cl.→ O S V Participial Construction
2. 本句的“feeling bad for the man...”是分詞構句，可還原為“and he felt bad for the man...”。

心情小語

Many people value their interest more than their family since they believe that they should treat themselves better for their endeavor and toil in work. It is indeed wonderful for us to have our own interest and treat ourselves well. However, when we are too involved in our own interest, that is obsession. Like the man in the story, he was going to the extremes. Before her death, his wife accompanied him to go to watch baseball games every year. Was she fond of baseball games? No, that's because she knew her husband loved to. She did so in hope that her husband knew his family supported him.

However, the man was so ignorant that he still went to watch basketball games when his wife passed away. He did not care about her death at all. Of course, this is an exaggerating story. However, we can still see many people obsessed with gambling and playing video games in real life. Those people disregard their friends and family and even kill them when they could not get money from them. Indeed, there are many important things worth our efforts and our interest is just one of them. But bear in mind that interest is the flower of our life rather than the root. If we regard our interest as the center of our life and disregard things around us, we will lose our souls and even the basic dignity as a human being.

很多人把興趣看得比家人還重要，認為自己辛苦的工作那麼久，為什麼不能對自己好一點？有興趣、對自己好一點當然沒有錯，但是當我們過度投入到自己的興趣，到了六親不認的地步，那就叫做「沈迷」了。故事中的男子，他的妻子在過世之前每年都陪他一起去看球賽，這是因為她愛看嗎？不，那是因為她知道她的丈夫愛看，所以才會跟他一起來，希望他知道家人支持自己的興趣。

可是這丈夫是怎麼回報她的？當她過世時丟下所有事情不管，還是看比賽勝過一切，都不怕妻子陰魂不散，晚上回來找他就是了？當然這故事是比較誇大一些，可是在我們生活周遭，的確有許多人是沈迷於賭博、電玩，而棄家人於不顧，甚至還有要不到錢而砍殺家人的都時有所聞。生命中有許多重要的事值得我們去認真地做，興趣當然也是其中之一，但千萬要記得，興趣只是點綴我們生命的花絮，並無法支撐我們所有的生活。如果我們把興趣當成了整個生命的重心而不管身邊的一切，那我們將會變得像行屍走肉一樣，失去靈魂，也失去了身為一個「人」所應具備的基本尊嚴。

生活篇 對話 1

Situation: It is the first time for Vincent to visit Taiwan. Now, he is going to visit National Chiang Kai-shek Memorial Hall.

情境：Vincent 是第一次來台北。現在，他將要去中正紀念堂。

Vincent	Excuse me. I think I am sort of lost. Can you help me?	不好意思。我想我有些迷路了。你能幫忙我嗎？
Passerby	What's wrong?	怎麼了？
Vincent	I would like to visit National Chiang Kai-shek Memorial Hall, but I cannot find the bus stop. Do you know where the bus stop is?	我想要參觀中正紀念堂，但是我找不到公車站牌。你知道公車站牌在哪嗎？
Passerby	Well, it will be more convenient for you to take Taipei Metro. Do you see the sign and metro exit around the corner? Just walk downstairs, and you can take the metro to National Chiang Kai-shek Memorial Hall.	嗯，搭台北捷運會比較方便一點。你有看到街角的指標跟地鐵入口嗎？你只要走下樓，你就可以搭捷運到中正紀念堂。
Vincent	Is it possible for me to go there on foot?	我可以用走的嗎？
Passerby	Well, it is a little bit far from here. It may take you about half an hour.	嗯，這裡離中正紀念堂有點遠。你可能要走半小時。
Vincent	Well, then I will take the metro. Thanks.	啊，那麼我還是搭捷運吧。多謝。

生活篇 對話 2

Situation: Vincent arrives National Chiang Kai-shek Memorial Hall and now he is looking for the National Concert Hall.

情境：Vincent 到了中正紀念堂，現在他正在找國家音樂廳。

Vincent	Excuse me! I am looking for the National Concert Hall. Could you tell me how to get there?	抱歉！我在找國家音樂廳。你能告訴我怎麼去嗎？
Passerby	Go straight along this way. Turn left when you see a huge Chinese-style building. Keep on walking, because the National Concert Hall is just opposite to the huge building.	這條路直直走。當你看到一個巨大的中國式建築時往左轉。繼續走下去，走過廣場，因為國家音樂廳就在巨大的中國式建築的對面。
Vincent	By the way, is the Taipei Botanical Garden far from here?	對了，台北植物園距離這裡遠嗎？
Passerby	No, it is just around, but you have to walk along that street. About two blocks from here you will find the Taipei Botanical Garden on you right. About 10 or 15 minutes.	不遠，就在這附近，但是你要沿著那條街走。走過兩條路口你就會看到台北植物園在你右邊。大概要走 10 或 15 分鐘。
Vincent	Thanks for your help walk	多謝你的幫忙。
Passerby	It is my pleasure. Wish you have a good day.	很樂意協助你。祝你有美好的一天。

單字與實用例句

- passerby *(n.)* 路人

  The old man asked a passerby for help.
  那位老先生向一位路人求助。

- metro *(n.)* 地下鐵

  Can you get there by metro?
  你能乘地鐵到達那裡嗎？

- on foot *(v. phr.)* 步行

  Jessie gets to school on foot every day.
  Jessie 每天走路上學。

- far *(adj.)* 遙遠的

  Where Peter lives is far from his workplace.
  Peter 住的地方離他工作的地點很遠。

- look for *(v. phr.)* 尋找

  Many philosophers have attempted to look for the meaning of life.
  許多哲學家試著找出生命的意義。

- straight *(adv.)* 直接地，一直地

  Keep going straight, and then you will see the library.
  一直直走，你會看到圖書館。

- opposite *(adj.)* 相反的

  The opposite color of green is the color red.
  綠色的相反色是紅色。

- block *(n.)* 街區

  The bookstore is only two blocks away from here.
  書店只離這裡兩個街區。

好用主題用語，用法解說

It may take you about half an hour to get there on foot.
How long does it take to walk there?

take 的用法：除了英文的基礎文法，單字的字意與文義的搭配用法，更是重要。以 take 這個常見的動詞為例，take 有許多意思，像是拿（東西）、花（時間）、搭乘（交通工具）等等意思。要加深單字的搭配用法的王道就是多閱讀、多背單字。以下介紹 take 的常見用法。

意思	例句
拿（東西）	• Would you please take the baggage for me? （你可以幫我拿行李嗎？）
花（時間）	• It took three years for the director to complete making this film. （這位導演花了三年的時間來完成這一部電影。）
搭乘（交通工具）	• Many commuters take the bus to work every day. （許多通勤者每天都搭公車上班。）
接受	• Are you happy to take this offer? （你樂意接受這一個提議嗎？）
洗澡	• Ella took a shower after she went home from work. （Ella 下班回家後淋浴。）
拍照	• Adam took a photo of his child. （Adam 替他的孩子照相。）
吃藥	• Please take the medicine three times a day. （請一天服三次藥。）

Learn Smart! 040

哈英文學文法–文法故事書

Hot English–English Grammar So Easy!

作　　者　Resa Sui
封面構成　高鍾琪
內頁構成　菩薩蠻有限公司

發 行 人　周瑞德
企劃編輯　丁筠馨
執行編輯　陳欣慧
校　　對　徐瑞璞、劉俞青
印　　製　大亞彩色印刷製版股份有限公司
初　　版　2014 年 11 月
定　　價　新台幣 369 元
出　　版　倍斯特出版事業有限公司
電　　話　(02) 2351-2007
傳　　真　(02) 2351-0887
地　　址　100 台北市中正區福州街 1 號 10 樓之 2
E-mail　best.books.service@gmail.com

港澳地區總經銷　泛華發行代理有限公司
地　　　　　址　香港筲箕灣東旺道 3 號星島新聞集團大廈 3 樓
電　　　　　話　(852) 2798-2323
傳　　　　　真　(852) 2796-5471

國家圖書館出版品預行編目(CIP)資料

哈英文學文法 / Resa Sui 著. -- 初版. -- 臺北市 :
倍斯特, 2014.11
面 ;　公分. -- (Learn smart! ; 40)
ISBN 978-986-90883-3-6(平裝)

1.英語 2.語法

805.16　　103020743